evermore

also by alyson noël

Cruel Summer

Saving Zoë

Kiss & Blog

Laguna Cove

Fly Me to the Moon

Art Geeks and Prom Queens

Faking 19

evermore

alyson noël

 st. martin's griffin ☷ new york

This is a work of fiction. All of the characters, organizations, and events portrayed in this novel are either products of the author's imagination or are used fictitiously.

www.stmartins.com

Title page art © Andrzej Tokarski | Dreamstime.com

Library of Congress Cataloging-in-Publication Data

Noël, Alyson.
    Evermore / Alyson Noël.—1st ed.
       p. cm.
    Summary: Since the car accident that claimed the lives of her family, sixteen-year-old Ever can see auras and hear people's thoughts, and she goes out of her way to hide from other people until she meets Damen, another psychic teenager who is hiding even more mysteries.
    ISBN-13: 978-0-312-53275-8
    ISBN-10: 0-312-53275-X
    [1. Psychic ability—Fiction. 2. Immortality—Fiction. 3. Supernatural—Fiction.] I. Title.
PZ7.N67185Ev 2009
    [Fic]—dc22

                                                                    2008033589

For Jolynn "Snarky" Benn—
my friend for many lifetimes.
(Next time we'll be rock stars!)

acknowledgments

I couldn't have written this book without the infinite generosity and wisdom of the following people: Brian L. Weiss, M.D., and Christina Gikas, who showed me a past I never could've imagined; James Van Praagh, who taught me to look at the world in a whole new way; my agent, Kate Schafer, who so deftly guides me along; my editor, Rose Hilliard, who handles my stories with such care; my copy editor for several books now, NaNá V. Stoelzle, who spares me from all manner of grammatical embarrassment; and, as always, Sandy, the last of the Renaissance men!

aura color chart

Red: Energy, strength, anger, sexuality, passion, fear, ego

Orange: Self-control, ambition, courage, thoughtfulness, lack of will, apathetic

Yellow: Optimistic, happy, intellectual, friendly, indecisive, easily led

Green: Peaceful, healing, compassion, deceitful, jealous

Blue: Spiritual, loyal, creative, sensitive, kind, moody

Violet: Highly spiritual, wisdom, intuition

Indigo: Benevolence, highly intuitive, seeker

Pink: Love, sincerity, friendship

Gray: Depression, sadness, exhaustion, low energy, skepticism

Brown: Greed, self-involvement, opinionated

Black: Lacking energy, illness, imminent death

White: Perfect balance

The only secret people keep / Is immortality.

—Emily Dickinson

one

"Guess who?"

Haven's warm, clammy palms press hard against my cheeks as the tarnished edge of her silver skull ring leaves a smudge on my skin. And even though my eyes are covered and closed, I know that her dyed black hair is parted in the middle, her black vinyl corset is worn over a turtleneck (keeping in compliance with our school's dress-code policy), her brand-new, floor-sweeping, black satin skirt already has a hole near the hem where she caught it with the toe of her Doc Martens boots, and her eyes appear gold but that's only because she's wearing yellow contacts.

I also know her dad isn't really away on "business" like he said, her mom's personal trainer is way more "personal" than "trainer," and her little brother broke her Evanescence CD but he's too afraid to tell her.

But I don't know any of this from spying or peeking or even being told. I know because I'm psychic.

"Hurry! Guess! The bell's gonna ring!" she says, her voice hoarse, raspy, like she smokes a pack a day, even though she only tried smoking once.

I stall, thinking of the last person she'd ever want to be mistaken for. "Is it Hilary Duff?"

"Ew. Guess again!" She presses tighter, having no idea that I don't have to *see* to *know*.

"Is it Mrs. Marilyn Manson?"

She laughs and lets go, licking her thumb and aiming for the tarnish tattoo she left on my cheek, but I raise my hand and beat her to it. Not because I'm grossed out by the thought of her saliva (I mean, I *know* she's healthy), but because I don't want her to touch me again. Touch is too revealing, too exhausting, so I try to avoid it at all costs.

She grabs the hood of my sweatshirt and flicks it off my head, then squints at my earbuds and asks, "What're you listening to?"

I reach inside the iPod pocket I've stitched into all of my hoodies, concealing those ubiquitous white cords from faculty view, then I hand it over and watch her eyes bug out when she says, "What *the*? I mean, can it *be* any louder? And who is that?" She dangles the iPod between us so we can both hear Sid Vicious screaming about anarchy in the UK. And the truth is, I don't know if Sid's for it or against it. I just know that he's almost loud enough to dull my overly heightened senses.

"Sex Pistols," I say, clicking it off and returning it to my secret compartment.

"I'm surprised you could even hear me." She smiles at the same time the bell rings.

But I just shrug. I don't need to *listen* to *hear*. Though it's not like I mention that. I just tell her I'll see her at lunch and head toward class, making my way across campus and cringing when I sense these two guys sneaking up behind her, stepping on the hem of her skirt, and almost making her fall. But when she turns and makes the sign of evil (okay, it's not really the sign of evil, it's just something she made up) and glares at them with her yellow eyes, they immediately back off and leave her alone. And I breathe a sigh of relief as I push into class, knowing it won't be long before the lingering energy of Haven's touch fades.

I head toward my seat in the back, avoiding the purse Stacia Miller has purposely placed in my path, while ignoring her daily serenade of *"Looo-ser!"* she croons under her breath. Then I slide onto my chair, retrieve my book, notebook, and pen from my bag, insert my earpiece, pull my hood back over my head, drop my backpack on the empty seat beside me, and wait for Mr. Robins to show.

Mr. Robins is always late. Mostly because he likes to take a few nips from his small silver flask between classes. But that's only because his wife yells at him all the time, his daughter thinks he's a loser, and he pretty much hates his life. I learned all of that on my first day at this school, when my hand accidentally touched his as I gave him my transfer slip. So now, whenever I need to turn something in, I just leave it on the edge of his desk.

I close my eyes and wait, my fingers creeping inside my sweatshirt, switching the song from screaming Sid Vicious to something softer, smoother. All that loud noise is no longer necessary now that I'm in class. I guess the small student/teacher ratio keeps the psychic energy somewhat contained.

I wasn't always a freak. I used to be a normal teen. The kind who went to school dances, had celebrity crushes, and was so vain about my long blond hair I wouldn't dream of scraping it back into a ponytail and hiding beneath a big hooded sweatshirt. I had a mom, a dad, a little sister named Riley, and a sweet yellow Lab named Buttercup. I lived in a nice house, in a good neighborhood, in Eugene, Oregon. I was popular, happy, and could hardly wait for junior year to begin since I'd just made varsity cheerleader. My life was complete, and the sky was the limit. And even though that last part is a total cliché, it's also ironically true.

Yet all of that's just hearsay as far as I'm concerned. Because ever since the accident, the only thing I can clearly remember is dying.

I had what they call an NDE, or "near death experience." Only *they* happen to be wrong. Because believe me, there wasn't anything "near" about it. It's like, one moment my little sister Riley and I were sitting in the back of my dad's SUV, with Buttercup's head resting on Riley's lap, while his tail thumped softly against my leg, and the next thing I knew all the air bags were blown, the car was totaled, and I was observing it all from outside.

I gazed at the wreckage—the shattered glass, the crumbled doors, the front bumper clutching a pine tree in a lethal embrace—wondering what went wrong as I hoped and prayed everyone had gotten out too. Then I heard a familiar bark, and turned to see them all wandering down a path, with Buttercup wagging her tail and leading the way.

I went after them. At first trying to run and catch up, but then slowing and choosing to linger. Wanting to wander through that vast fragrant field of pulsating trees and flowers that shivered, closing my eyes against the dazzling mist that reflected and glowed and made everything shimmer.

I promised myself I'd only be a moment. That soon, I'd go back and find them. But when I did finally look, it was just in time to catch a quick glimpse of them smiling and waving and crossing a bridge, mere seconds before they all vanished.

I panicked. I looked everywhere. Running this way and that,

but it all looked the same—warm, white, glistening, shimmering, beautiful, stupid, eternal mist. And I fell to the ground, my skin pricked with cold, my whole body twitching, crying, screaming, cursing, begging, making promises I knew I could never ever keep.

And then I heard someone say, "Ever? Is that your name? Open your eyes and look at me."

I stumbled back to the surface. Back to where everything was pain, and misery, and stinging wet hurt on my forehead. And I gazed at the guy leaning over me, looked into his dark eyes, and whispered, "I'm Ever," before passing out again.

two

Seconds before Mr. Robins walks in, I lower my hood, click off my iPod, and pretend I'm reading my book, not bothering to look up when he says, "Class, this is Damen Auguste. He just moved here from New Mexico. Okay Damen, you can take that empty seat in the back, right next to Ever. You'll have to share her book until you get your own copy."

Damen is gorgeous. I know this without once looking up. I just focus on my book as he makes his way toward me since I know way too much about my classmates already. So as far as I'm concerned, an extra moment of ignorance really is bliss.

But according to the innermost thoughts of Stacia Miller sitting just two rows before me—*Damen Auguste is totally smoking hot.*

Her best friend, Honor, completely agrees.

So does Honor's boyfriend, Craig, but that's a whole other story.

"Hey." Damen slides onto the seat next to mine, my backpack making a muffled thud as he drops it to the floor.

I nod, refusing to look any further than his sleek, black, motorcycle boots. The kind that are more *GQ* than Hells Angels.

The kind that looks very out of place among the rows of multi-colored flip-flops currently gracing the green-carpeted floor.

Mr. Robins asks us all to turn our books to page 133, prompting Damen to lean in and say, "Mind if I share?"

I hesitate, dreading the proximity, but slide my book all the way over until it's teetering off the edge of my desk. And when he moves his chair closer, bridging the small gap between us, I scoot to the farthest part of my seat and hide beneath my hood.

He laughs under his breath, but since I've yet to look at him, I have no idea what it means. All I know is that it sounded light and amused, but like it held something more.

I sink even lower, cheek on palm, eyes on the clock. Determined to ignore all the withering glances and critical comments directed my way. Stuff like: *Poor hot, sexy, gorgeous new guy, having to sit next to that freak!* That emanates from Stacia, Honor, Craig, and just about everyone else in the room.

Well, all except for Mr. Robins, who wants class to end almost as much as me.

By lunch, everyone's talking about Damen.

Have you seen that new kid Damen? He's so hot—So sexy—I heard he's from Mexico—No I think it's Spain—Whatever, it's some foreign place—I'm totally asking him to Winter Formal—You don't even know him yet—Don't worry I will—

"Omigod. Have you seen that new kid, Damen?" Haven sits beside me, peering through her growing-out bangs, their spiky tips ending just shy of her dark red lips.

"Oh please, not you too." I shake my head and bite into my apple.

"You would so not be saying that if you'd been privileged

enough to actually *see* him," she says, removing her vanilla cup-cake from its pink cardboard box, licking the frosting right off the top in her usual lunchtime routine, even though she dresses more like someone who'd rather drink blood than eat tiny little sweet cakes.

"Are you guys talking about Damen?" Miles whispers, sliding onto the bench and placing his elbows on the table, his brown eyes darting between us, his baby face curving into a grin. "*Gorgeous!* Did you see the boots? So *Vogue.* I think I'll invite him to be my next boyfriend."

Haven gazes at him with narrowed, yellow eyes. "Too late, I called dibs."

"I'm sorry, I didn't realize you were into non-goths." He smirks, rolling his eyes as he unwraps his sandwich.

Haven laughs. "When they look like that I am. I swear he's just so freaking smoldering, you *have* to see him." She shakes her head, annoyed that I can't join in on the fun. "He's like—*combustible!*"

"You haven't seen him?" Miles grips his sandwich and gapes at me.

I gaze down at the table, wondering if I should just lie. They're making such a big deal I'm thinking it's my only way out. Only I can't. Not to them. Haven and Miles are my best friends. My only friends. And I feel like I'm keeping enough secrets already. "I sat next to him in English," I finally say. "We were forced to share a book. But I didn't really get a good look."

"*Forced?*" Haven moves her bangs to the side, allowing for an unobstructed view of the freak who'd dare say such a thing. "Oh that must have been awful for you, that must've really sucked." She rolls her eyes and sighs. "I swear, you have no idea how lucky you are. And you don't even appreciate it."

"Which book?" Miles asks, as though the title will somehow reveal something meaningful.

"*Wuthering Heights.*" I shrug, placing my apple core on the center of my napkin and folding the edges all around.

"And your hood? Up or down?" Haven asks.

I think back, remembering how I raised it right as he moved toward me. "Um, up," I tell her. "Yeah, definitely up." I nod.

"Well thank you for that," she mumbles, breaking her vanilla cupcake in half. "The last thing I need is competition from the blond goddess."

I cringe and gaze down at the table. I get embarrassed when people say things like that. Apparently, I used to live for that kind of thing, but not anymore. "Well, what about Miles? You don't think he's competition?" I ask, diverting the attention away from me and back on someone who can truly appreciate it.

"Yeah." Miles runs his hand through his short brown hair and turns, gracing us with his very best side. "Don't rule it out."

"Totally moot," Haven says, dusting white crumbs from her lap. "Damen and Miles don't play for the same team. Which means his oh-so-devastating, model-quality looks don't count."

"How do you know which team he's on?" Miles asks, twisting the cap off his VitaminWater and narrowing his gaze. "How can you be so sure?"

"Gaydar," she says, tapping her forehead. "And trust me, this guy does not register."

Not only is Damen in my first-period English class, and my sixth-period art class (not that he sat by me, and not that I looked, but the thoughts swirling around the room, even from our teacher,

Ms. Machado, told me everything I needed to know), but now he'd apparently parked next to me too. And even though I'd managed to avoid viewing anything more than his boots, I knew my grace period had just come to an end.

"Omigod, there he is! Right directly next to us!" Miles squeals, in the high-pitched, singsongy whisper he saves for life's most exciting moments. "And check out that ride—shiny black BMW, extra-dark tinted windows. Nice, very nice. Okay, so here's the deal, I'm going to open my door and *accidentally* bump it into his, so then I'll have an excuse to talk to him." He turns, awaiting my consent.

"Do *not* scratch my car. Or his car. Or any other car," I say, shaking my head and retrieving my keys.

"Fine." He pouts. "Shatter my dream, whatever. But just do yourself a favor and *check him out*! And then look me in the eye and tell me he doesn't make you want to freak out and faint."

I roll my eyes and squeeze between my car and the poorly parked VW Bug that's angled so awkwardly it looks like it's trying to mount my Miata. And just as I'm about to unlock the door, Miles yanks down my hood, swipes my sunglasses, and runs to the passenger side where he urges me, via not-so-subtle head tilts and thumb jabs, to look at Damen who's standing behind him.

So I do. I mean, it's not like I can avoid it forever. So I take a deep breath and look.

And what I see leaves me unable to speak, blink, or move.

And even though Miles starts waving at me, glaring at me, and basically giving me every signal he can think of to abort the mission and return to headquarters—I can't. I mean, I'd like to, because I know I'm acting like the freak everyone's already convinced that I am, but it's completely impossible. And it's not just because Damen is undeniably beautiful, with his shiny dark hair that hits just shy of his shoulders and curves around his high-sculpted cheekbones, but when he looks at me, when he lifts his dark sunglasses and meets my gaze, I see that his almond shaped eyes are deep, dark, and strangely familiar, framed by lashes so lush they almost seem fake. And his lips! His lips are ripe and inviting with a perfect Cupid's bow. And the body that holds it all up is long, lean, tight, and clad in all black.

"Um, Ever? Hel-*lo*? You can wake up now. *Please.*" Miles turns to Damen, laughing nervously. "Sorry about my friend here, she usually has her hood on."

It's not like I don't know I have to stop. I need to stop right now. But Damen's eyes are fixed on mine, and their color grows deeper as his mouth begins to curve.

But it's not his complete gorgeousness that has me so transfixed. It has nothing to do with that. It's mainly the way the entire area surrounding his body, starting from his glorious head and going all the way down to the square-cut toes of his black motorcycle boots, consists of nothing but blank empty space.

No color. No aura. No pulsing light show.

Everyone has an aura. Every living being has swirls of color emanating from their body. A rainbow energy field they're not even aware of. And it's not like it's dangerous, or scary, or in any way bad, it's just part of the visible (well, to me anyway) magnetic field.

Before the accident I didn't even know about things like that. And I definitely wasn't able to see it. But from the moment I woke in the hospital, I noticed color everywhere.

"Are you feeling okay?" The red-haired nurse asked, gazing down anxiously.

"Yes, but why are you all pink?" I squinted, confused by the pastel glow that enveloped her.

"Why am I *what*?" She struggled to hide her alarm.

"Pink. You know, it's all around you, especially your head."

"Okay, sweetheart, you just rest and I'll go get the doctor," she'd said, backing out of the room and running down the hall.

It wasn't until after I'd been subjected to a barrage of eye exams, brain scans, and psych evals that I learned to keep the color-wheel sightings to myself. And by the time I started hearing thoughts, getting life stories by touch, and enjoying regular visits with my dead sister, Riley, I knew better than to share.

I guess I'd gotten so used to living like this, I'd forgotten there was another way. But seeing Damen outlined by nothing more than the shiny black paint job on his expensive cool car is a vague reminder of happier, more normal days.

"Ever, right?" Damen says, his face warming into a smile, revealing just another one of his perfections—dazzling white teeth.

I stand there, willing my eyes to leave his, as Miles makes a show of clearing his throat. And remembering how he hates to be ignored, I motion toward him and say, "Oh, sorry. Miles, Damen, Damen, Miles." And the whole time my eyes never once waver.

Damen glances at Miles, nodding briefly before focusing back on me. And even though I know this sounds crazy, for the split second his eyes moved away, I felt strangely cold and weak.

But the moment his gaze returns, it's all warm and good again. "Can I ask a favor?" He smiles. "Would you lend me your copy of *Wuthering Heights*? I need to get caught up and I won't have time to visit the bookstore tonight."

I reach into my backpack, retrieve my dog-eared copy, and dangle it from the tips of my fingers, part of me yearning to brush the tips against his, to make contact with this beautiful stranger, while the other part, the stronger, wiser, psychic part cringes—dreading the awful flash of insight that comes with each touch.

But it's not until he's tossed the book into his car, lowered his sunglasses, and said, "Thanks, see you tomorrow," that I realize that other than a slight tingle in the tips of my fingers, nothing happened. And before I can even respond, he's backing out of the space and driving away.

"Excuse me," Miles says, shaking his head as he climbs in beside me. "But when I said you'd *freak out* when you saw him, it wasn't a *suggestion*, it wasn't supposed to be taken *literally*. Seriously Ever, what *happened* back there? Because that was some mega tense awkwardness, a real *Hello, my name is Ever and I'll be your next stalker* kind of moment. I'm so serious, I thought we were gonna have to *resuscitate* you. And believe me, you are extremely lucky our good friend Haven was not here to see that, because I hate to remind you, but she did call dibs . . ."

Miles continues like that, yammering on and on, the entire way home. But I just let him talk it out as I navigate traffic, my finger absently tracing the thick red scar on my forehead, the one that's hidden under my bangs.

I mean, how can I explain how ever since the accident, the only people whose thoughts I can't hear, whose lives I can't know, and whose auras I can't see, are already dead?

three

I let myself into the house, grab a bottle of water from the fridge, then head upstairs to my room, since I don't have to poke around any further to know Sabine's still at work. Sabine's always at work, which means I get this whole huge house to myself, pretty much all the time, even though I usually just stay in my room.

I feel bad for Sabine. I feel bad that the life she worked so hard for was forever changed the day she got stuck with me. But since my mom was an only child and all of my grandparents had passed by the time I was two, it's not like she had much of a choice. I mean, it was either live with her—my dad's only sibling and twin—or go into foster care until I turned eighteen. And even though she doesn't know anything about raising kids, I wasn't even out of the hospital before she'd sold her condo, bought this big house, and hired one of Orange County's top decorators to trick out my room.

I mean, I have all the usual things like a bed, a dresser, and a desk. But I also have a flat-screen TV, a massive walk-in closet, a huge bathroom with a Jacuzzi tub and separate shower stall, a balcony with an amazing ocean view, and my own private den/game room, with yet another flat-screen TV, a wet bar, microwave, mini fridge, dishwasher, stereo, couches, tables, beanbag chairs, the works.

It's funny how before I would've given anything for a room like this.

But now I'd give anything just to go back to before.

I guess since Sabine spends most of her time around other lawyers and all those VIP executives her firm represents, she actually thought all of this stuff was necessary or something. And I've never been sure if her not having kids is because she works all the time and can't schedule it in, or if she just hasn't met the right guy yet, or if she never wanted any to begin with, or maybe a combination of all three.

It probably seems like I should know all of that, being psychic and all. But I can't necessarily see a person's motivation, mainly what I see are events. Like a whole string of images reflecting someone's life, like flash cards or something, only more in a movie-trailer format. Though sometimes I just see symbols that I have to decode to know what they mean. Kind of like with tarot cards, or when we had to read *Animal Farm* in Honors English last year.

Though it's far from foolproof, and sometimes I get it all wrong. But whenever that happens I can trace it right back to me, and the fact that some pictures have more than one meaning. Like the time I mistook a big heart with a crack down the middle for heartbreak—until the woman dropped to the floor in cardiac arrest. Sometimes it can get a little confusing trying to sort it all out. But the images themselves never lie.

Anyway, I don't think you have to be clairvoyant to know that when people dream of having kids they're usually thinking in terms of a pastel-wrapped, tiny bundle of joy, and *not* some five-foot-four, blue-eyed, blond-haired teenager with psychic powers and a ton of emotional baggage. So because of that, I try to stay quiet, respectful, and out of Sabine's way.

And I definitely don't let on that I talk to my dead little sister almost every day.

The first time Riley appeared, she was standing at the foot of my hospital bed, in the middle of the night, holding a flower in one hand and waving with the other. I'm still not sure what it was that awoke me, since it's not like she spoke or made any kind of sound. I guess I just felt her presence or something, like a change in the room, or a charge in the air.

At first I assumed I was hallucinating—just another side effect of the pain medication I was on. But after blinking a bunch and rubbing my eyes, she was still there, and I guess it never occurred to me to scream or call for help.

I watched as she came around to the side of my bed, pointed at the casts covering my arms and leg, and laughed. I mean, it was silent laughter, but still, it's not like I thought it was funny. But as soon as she noticed my angry expression, she rearranged her face and motioned as though asking if it hurt.

I shrugged, still a little unhappy with her for laughing, and more than a little freaked by her presence. And even though I wasn't entirely convinced it was really her, that didn't stop me from asking, "Where are Mom and Dad and Buttercup?"

She tilted her head to the side, as though they were standing right there beside her, but all I could see was blank space.

"I don't get it."

But she just smiled, placed her palms together, and tilted her head to the side, indicating that I should go back to sleep.

So I closed my eyes, even though I never would've taken orders from her before. Then just as quickly I opened them and said, "Hey, who said you could borrow my sweater?"

And just like that, she was gone.

I admit, I spent the rest of that night angry with myself for asking such a stupid, shallow, selfish question. Here I'd had the opportunity to get answers to some of life's biggest queries, to possibly gain the kind of insight people have been speculating about for ages. But instead, I wasted the moment calling out my dead little sister for raiding my closet. I guess old habits really do die hard.

The second time she appeared, I was just so grateful to see her, I didn't make any mention of the fact that she was wearing not just my favorite sweater, but also my best jeans (that were so long the hems puddled around her ankles), and the charm bracelet I got for my thirteenth birthday that I always knew she coveted.

Instead I just smiled and nodded and acted as though I didn't even notice, as I leaned toward her and squinted. "So where're Mom and Dad?" I asked, thinking they'd appear if I just looked hard enough.

But Riley just smiled and flapped her arms by her sides.

"You mean they're angels?" My eyes went wide.

She rolled her eyes and shook her head, clutching her waist as she bent over in fits of silent laughter.

"Okay, fine, whatever." I threw my body back against the pillows, thinking she was really pushing it, even if she was dead. "So tell me, what's it like over there?" I asked, determined not to fight. "Are you, well, do you like, live in heaven?"

She closed her eyes and raised her palms as though balancing an object, and then right out of nowhere, a painting appeared.

I leaned forward, gazing at a picture of what was surely paradise, matted in off-white and encased in an elaborate gold frame. The ocean was deep blue, the cliffs rugged, the sand golden, the trees flowering, and a shadowy silhouette of a small distant island could be seen in the distance.

"So why aren't you there now?" I asked.

And when she shrugged, the picture disappeared. And so did she.

I'd been in the hospital for more than a month, suffering broken bones, a concussion, internal bleeding, cuts and bruises, and a pretty deep gash on my forehead. So while I was all bandaged and medicated, Sabine was burdened with the thankless task of clearing out the house, making funeral arrangements, and packing my things for the big move south.

She asked me to make a list of all the items I wanted to bring. All the things I might want to drag from my perfect former life in Eugene, Oregon, to my scary new one in Laguna Beach, California. But other than some of my clothes, I didn't want anything. I just couldn't bear a single reminder of everything I'd lost, since it's not like some stupid box full of crap would ever bring my family back.

The whole time I was cooped up in that sterile white room, I received regular visits from a psychologist, some overeager intern with a beige cardigan and clipboard, who always started our sessions with the same lame question about how I was handling my "profound loss" (his words, not mine). After which he'd try to convince me to head up to room 618, where the grief counseling took place.

But no way was I taking part in that. No way would I sit in a circle with a bunch of anguished people, waiting for my turn to share the story of the worst day of my life. I mean, how was that supposed to help? How could it possibly make me feel better to confirm what I already knew—that not only was I solely responsible for what happened to my family, but also that I was stupid enough, selfish enough, and lazy enough to loiter, dawdle, and procrastinate myself right out of eternity?

Sabine and I didn't speak much on the flight from Eugene to John Wayne Airport, and I pretended it was because of my grief and injuries, but really I just needed some distance. I knew all about her conflicting emotions, how on the one hand she wanted so desperately to do the right thing, while on the other she couldn't stop thinking: *Why me?*

I guess I never wonder: *Why me?*

Mostly I think: *Why them and* not *me?*

But I also didn't want to risk hurting her. After all the trouble she'd gone to, taking me in and trying to provide a nice home, I couldn't risk letting her know how all of her hard work and good intentions were completely wasted on me. How she could've just dropped me off at any old dump and it wouldn't have made the least bit of difference.

The drive to the new house was a blur of sun, sea, and sand, and when Sabine opened the door and led me upstairs to my room, I gave it a quick cursory glance then mumbled something sounding vaguely like *thanks.*

"I'm sorry I have to run out on you," she'd said, obviously anxious to get back to her office where everything was organized, consistent, and bore no resemblance to the fragmented world of a traumatized teen.

And the moment the door closed behind her, I threw myself on my bed, buried my face in my hands, and started bawling my eyes out.

Until someone said, "Oh please, would you look at yourself? Have you even seen this place? The flat-screen, the fireplace, the tub that blows bubbles? I mean, Hel-*lo*?"

"I thought you couldn't talk?" I rolled over and glared at my sister, who, by the way, was dressed in a pink Juicy tracksuit, gold Nikes, and a bright fuchsia china doll wig.

"Of course I can talk, don't be ridiculous." She rolled her eyes.

"But the last few times—" I started.

"I was just having a little fun. So shoot me." She stalked around my room, running her hands over my desk, fingering the new laptop and iPod Sabine must have placed there. "I cannot believe you have a setup like this. This is so freaking unfair!" She placed her hands on her hips and scowled. "And you're not even appreciating it! I mean, have you even seen the balcony yet? Have you even bothered to check out the view?"

"I don't care about the view," I said, folding my arms across my chest and glaring. "And I can't believe you tricked me like that, pretending you couldn't speak."

But she just laughed. "You'll get over it."

I watched as she strode across my room, pushed the drapes aside, and struggled to unlock the french doors. "And where are you getting all these clothes?" I asked, scrutinizing her from head to toe, reverting right back to our normal routine of bickering and grudge holding. "Because first you show up in my stuff, and now you're wearing Juicy, and I know for a fact that Mom never bought you those sweats."

She laughed. "Please, like I still need Mom's permission when

I can just head over to the big celestial closet and take whatever I want. *For free,*" she said, turning to smile.

"Serious?" I asked, my eyes going wide, thinking that sounded like a pretty sweet deal.

But she just shook her head and waved me over. "Come on, come check out your cool new view."

So I did. I got up off the bed, wiped my eyes with my sleeve, and headed for my balcony. Brushing right past my little sister as I stepped onto the stone tile floor, my eyes going wide as I took in the scenery before me.

"Is this supposed to be funny?" I asked, gazing out at a view that was an exact replica of the gilt-framed picture of paradise she'd shown me in the hospital.

But when I turned back to face her, she'd already gone.

four

It was Riley who helped me recover my memories. Guiding me through childhood stories and reminding me of the lives we used to live and the friends we used to have, until it all began to resurface. She also helped me appreciate my new Southern California life. Because seeing her get so excited by my cool new room, my shiny red convertible, the amazing beaches, and my new school, made me realize that even though it wasn't the life I preferred, it still had value.

And even though we still fight and argue and get on each other's nerves as much as before, the truth is, I live for her visits. Being able to see her again gives me one less person to miss. And the time we spend together is the best part of each day.

The only problem is, she knows it. So every time I bring up the subjects she's declared strictly off limits, things like: *When do I get to see Mom, Dad, and Buttercup?* And, *where do you go when you're not here?* She punishes me by staying away.

But even though her refusal to share really bugs me, I know better than to push it. It's not like I've confided my new aura-spotting/mind-reading abilities, or how much it's changed me, including the way I dress.

"You're never gonna get a boyfriend dressed like that," she says, lounging on my bed as I rush through my morning routine, trying to get ready for school and out the door—more or less on time.

"Yeah, well, not all of us can just close our eyes and *poof,* have an amazing new wardrobe," I say, shoving my feet into worn-out tennis shoes and tying the frayed laces.

"Please, like Sabine wouldn't hand over her credit card and tell you to have at it. And what's with the hood? You in a gang?"

"I don't have time for this," I say, grabbing my books, iPod, and backpack, then heading for the door. "You coming?" I turn to look at her, my patience running big-time thin as she purses her lip and takes her time to decide.

"Okay," she finally says. "But only if you put the top down. I just love the feel of the wind in my hair."

"Fine." I head for the stairs. "Just make sure you're gone by the time we get to Miles's. It creeps me out to see you sitting in his lap without his permission."

By the time Miles and I get to school, Haven is already waiting by the gate, her eyes darting frantically, scanning the campus as she says, "Okay, the bell's gonna ring in less than five minutes and still no sign of Damen. You think he dropped out?" She looks at us, yellow eyes wide with alarm.

"Why would he drop out? He just started," I say, heading for my locker as she skips alongside me, the thick rubber soles of her boots bouncing off the pavement.

"Uh, because we're not worthy? Because he really is too good to be true?"

"But he has to come back. Ever leant him her copy of

Wuthering Heights, which means he has to return it," Miles says, before I can stop him.

I shake my head, and spin my combination lock, feeling the weight of Haven's glare when she says, "When did this happen?" She puts her hand on her hip and stares at me. "Because you know I called dibs, right? And why didn't I get an update? Why didn't anyone tell me about this? Last I heard you hadn't even seen him yet."

"Oh, she saw him alright. I almost had to dial nine-one-one she freaked out so bad." Miles laughs.

I shake my head, shut my locker, and head down the hall.

"Well, it's true." He shrugs, walking alongside me.

"So let me get this straight; you're more of a liability than a threat?" Haven peers at me through narrowed, heavily lined eyes, her jealousy transforming her aura into a dull puke green.

I take a deep breath and look at them, thinking how if they weren't my friends, I'd tell them how ridiculous this all is. I mean, since when can you call dibs on another person? Besides, it's not like I'm all that datable in my current voice-hearing, aura-seeing, baggy-sweatshirt-wearing condition. But I don't say any of that. Instead I just say, "Yes, I'm a liability. I'm a huge uninsurable disaster waiting to happen. But I'm definitely not a threat. Mainly because I'm not interested. And I know that's probably hard to believe, with him being so gorgeous and sexy and hot and smoldering and combustible or whatever it is that you call him, but the truth is, *I don't like Damen Auguste,* and I don't know how else to say it!"

"Um, I don't think you need to say anything else," Haven mumbles, her face frozen as she stares straight ahead.

I follow her gaze, all the way to where Damen is standing, all shiny dark hair, smoldering eyes, amazing body, and knowing smile, feeling my heart skip two beats as he holds the door open and says, "Hey Ever, after you."

I storm toward my desk, narrowly avoiding the backpack Stacia has placed in my path, as my face burns with shame, knowing Damen's right there behind me, and that he heard every horrifying word I just said.

I toss my bag to the floor, slide onto my seat, lift my hood, and crank my iPod, hoping to drown out the noise and deflect what just happened, assuring myself that a guy like that—a guy so confident, so gorgeous, so completely amazing—is too cool to bother with the careless words of a girl like me.

But just as I start to relax, just as I've convinced myself not to care, I'm jolted by an overwhelming shock—an electric charge infusing my skin, slamming my veins, and making my whole body tingle.

And it's all because Damen placed his hand upon mine.

It's hard to surprise me. Ever since I became psychic, Riley's the only one who can do so, and believe me, she never tires of finding new ways. But when I glance from my hand to Damen's face, he just smiles and says, "I wanted to return this." Then he gives me my copy of *Wuthering Heights*.

And even though I know this sounds weird and more than a little crazy, the moment he spoke, the whole room went silent. Seriously, like one moment it was filled with the sound of random thoughts and voices, and the next:_____.

Yet knowing how ridiculous that is, I shake my head and say, "Are you sure you don't want to keep it? Because I really don't need it, I already know how it ends." And even though he removes his hand from mine, it's a moment before all the tingling dies down.

"I know how it ends too," he says, gazing at me in a way so intense, so insistent, so intimate, I quickly look away.

And just as I'm about to reinsert my earbuds, so I can block out the sound of Stacia and Honor's continuous loop of cruel commentary, Damen places his hand back on mine and says, "What're you listening to?"

And the whole room goes quiet again. Seriously, for those few brief seconds, there were no swirling thoughts, no hushed whispers, nothing but the sound of his soft, lyrical voice. I mean, when it happened before, I figured it was just me. But this time I *know* that it's real. Because even though people are still talking and thinking and engaging in all of the usual things, it's completely blocked by the sound of his words.

I squint, noticing how my body has gone all warm and electric, wondering what could possibly be causing it. I mean, it's not like I haven't had my hand touched before, though I've yet to experience anything remotely like this.

"I asked what you're listening to." He smiles. A smile so private and intimate, I feel my face flush.

"Oh, um, it's just some goth mix my friend Haven made. It's mostly old, eighties stuff, you know like the Cure, Siouxsie and the Banshees, Bauhaus." I shrug, unable to avert my gaze as I stare into his eyes, trying to determine their exact color.

"You're into goth?" he asks, brows raised, eyes skeptical, taking inventory of my long blond ponytail, dark blue sweatshirt, and makeup-free, clean scrubbed skin.

"No, not really. Haven's all into it." I laugh—a nervous, cackling, cringe-worthy sound—that bounces off all four walls and right back at me.

"And you? What are you into?" His eyes still on mine, his face clearly amused.

And just as I'm about to answer, Mr. Robins walks in, his cheeks red and flushed, but not from a brisk walk like everyone thinks. And then Damen leans back in his seat, and I take a deep breath and lower my hood, sinking back into the familiar sounds of adolescent angst, test stress, body image issues, Mr. Robin's failed dreams, and Stacia, Honor, and Craig all wondering what the hot guy could possibly see in me.

five

By the time I make it to our lunch table Haven and Miles are already there. But when I see Damen sitting beside them, I'm tempted to run the other way.

"You're free to join us, but only if you promise *not* to stare at the new kid." Miles laughs. "Staring is very rude. Didn't anyone ever tell you that?"

I roll my eyes and slide onto the bench beside him, determined to show just how blasé I am about Damen's presence. "I was raised by wolves, what can I say?" I shrug, busying myself with the zipper on my lunch pack.

"I was raised by a drag queen and a romance novelist," Miles says, reaching over to steal a candy corn off the top of Haven's pre-Halloween cupcake.

"Sorry, that wasn't you, sweetie, that was Chandler on *Friends*." Haven laughs. "I, on the other hand, was raised in a coven. I was a beautiful vampire princess, loved, worshiped, and admired by all. I lived in a luxurious, gothic castle, and I have no idea how I ended up at this hideous fiberglass table with you losers." She nods at Damen. "And you?"

He takes a sip of his drink, some iridescent red liquid in a glass bottle, then he gazes at all three of us and says, "Italy, France, England, Spain, Belgium, New York, New Orleans, Oregon, India, New Mexico, Egypt, and a few other places in between." He smiles.

"Can you say 'military brat'?" Haven laughs, picking off a candy corn and tossing it to Miles.

"Ever lived in Oregon," Miles says, placing the candy on the center of his tongue before chasing it down with a swig of VitaminWater.

"Portland." Damen nods.

Miles laughs. "Not a question, but okay. What I meant was, our friend Ever here, well, she lived in Oregon," he says, eliciting a sharp look from Haven, who, even after my earlier blunder, still views me as the biggest obstacle in her path to true love, and doesn't appreciate any attention being directed my way.

Damen smiles, his eyes on mine. "Where?"

"Eugene," I mumble, focusing on my sandwich instead of him, because just like in the classroom, every time he speaks it's the only sound I hear.

And every time our eyes meet I grow warm.

And when his foot just bumped against mine, my whole body tingled.

And it's really starting to freak me out.

"How'd you end up here?" He leans toward me, prompting Haven to scoot even closer to him.

I stare at the table, pressing my lips together in my usual nervous habit. I don't want to talk about my old life. I don't see the point in relaying all the gory details. Of having to explain how even though it's completely my fault that my entire family died, I somehow managed to live. So in the end I just tear the crust from my sandwich, and say, "It's a long story."

I can feel Damen's gaze—heavy, warm, and inviting—and it makes me so nervous my palms start to sweat and my water bottle slips from my grip. Falling so fast, I can't even stop it, all I can do is wait for the splash.

But before it can even hit the table, Damen's already caught it and returned it to me. And I sit there, staring at the bottle and avoiding his gaze, wondering if I'm the only one who noticed how he moved so fast he actually blurred.

Then Miles asks about New York, and Haven scoots so close she's practically sitting on Damen's lap, and I take a deep breath, finish my lunch, and convince myself I imagined it.

When the bell finally rings, we all grab our stuff and head toward class, and the second Damen's out of earshot I turn to my friends and say, "How did he end up at our table?" Then I cringe at how my voice sounded so shrill and accusing.

"He wanted to sit in the shade, so we offered him a spot." Miles shrugs, depositing his bottle in the recycling bin and leading us toward the building. "Nothing sinister, no evil plot to embarrass you."

"Well, I could've done without the staring comment," I say, knowing I sound ridiculous and overly sensitive. I'm unwilling to express what I'm really thinking, not wanting to upset my friends with the very valid, yet unkind question: *Why is a guy like Damen hanging with us?*

Seriously. Out of all the kids in this school, out of all the cool cliques he could join, why on earth would he chose to sit with us—the three biggest misfits?

"Relax, he thought it was funny." Miles shrugs. "Besides, he's coming by your house tonight. I told him to stop by around eight."

"You what?" I gape at him, suddenly remembering how all through lunch Haven was thinking about what she was going to wear, while Miles wondered if he had time for a spray tan, and now it all makes sense.

"Well, apparently Damen hates football as much as we do, which we happened to learn during Haven's little Q and A that took place just moments before you arrived." Haven smiles and curtseys, her fishnet-covered knees bowing out to either side. "And since he's new, and doesn't really know anyone else, we figured we'd hog him all to ourselves and not give him the chance to make other friends."

"But—" I stop, unsure how to continue. All I know is that I don't want Damen coming over, not tonight, not ever.

"I'll swing by sometime after eight," Haven says. "My meeting's over by seven, which gives me just enough time to go home and change. *And,* by the way, I call dibs on sitting next to Damen in the Jacuzzi!"

"You can't do that!" Miles says, shaking his head in outrage. "I won't allow it!"

But she just waves over her shoulder as she skips toward class, and I turn to Miles and ask, "Which meeting is it today?"

He opens the classroom door and smiles. "Friday is for overeaters."

Haven is what you'd call an anonymous-group addict. In the short time I've known her, she's attended twelve-step meetings for alcoholics, narcotics, codependents, debtors, gamblers, cyber addicts, nicotine junkies, social phobics, pack rats, and vulgarity lovers. Though as far as I know, today is her first one for overeaters. But then again, at five foot one with the slim, lithe body of a music box ballerina, Haven is definitely not an overeater. She's also not an alcoholic, a debtor, a gambler, or any of those other things. She's just terminally ignored by her self-involved parents, which makes her seek love and approval from just about anywhere she can get it.

Like with the whole goth thing. It's not that she's really all that into it, which is pretty obvious by the way she always skips instead of skulks, and how her Joy Division posters hang on the pastel pink walls of her not-so-long-ago ballerina phase (that came shortly after her J. Crew catalog preppy phase).

Haven's just learned that the quickest way to stand out in a town full of Juicy-clad blondes is to dress like the Princess of Darkness.

Only it's not really working as well as she hoped. The first time her mom saw her dressed like that, she just sighed, grabbed her keys, and headed off to Pilates. And her dad hasn't been home long enough to really get a good look. Her little brother, Austin, was freaked, but he adjusted pretty quickly. And since most of the kids at school have grown so used to the outrageous displays of behavior brought on by the presence of last year's MTV cameras, they usually ignore her.

But I happen to know that beneath all the skulls, and spikes, and death-rocker makeup is a girl who just wants to be seen, heard, loved, and paid attention to—something her earlier incarnations have failed to produce. So if standing before a room full of people, creating some sob story about her tormented struggle with that day's fill-in-the-blank addiction makes her feel important, well, who am I to judge?

In my old life I didn't hang with people like Miles and Haven. I wasn't connected with the troubled kids, or the weird kids, or the kids everyone picked on. I was part of the popular crowd, where most of us were cute, athletic, talented, smart, wealthy, well liked, or all of the above. I went to school dances, had a best friend named Rachel (who was also a cheerleader like me), and I even had a boyfriend, Brandon, who happened to be the sixth boy I'd ever kissed (the first was Lucas, but that was only because of a dare back in sixth grade, and trust me, the ones in between are hardly worth mentioning). And even though I was never mean to anyone who wasn't part of our group, it's not like I really noticed them either. Those kids just didn't have anything to do with me. And so I acted like they were invisible.

But now, I'm one of the unseen too. I knew it the day Rachel and Brandon visited me in the hospital. They acted so nice and supportive on the outside, while inside, their thoughts told a whole other story. They were freaked by the little plastic bags dripping liquids into my veins, my cuts and bruises, my cast-covered limbs. They felt bad for what happened, for all that I'd lost, but as they tried not to gape at the jagged red scar on my forehead, what they really wanted to do was run away.

And I watched as their auras swirled together, blending into the same dull brown, knowing they were withdrawing from me, and moving closer to each other.

So on my first day at Bay View, instead of wasting my time with the usual hazing rituals of the Stacia and Honor crowd, I headed straight for Miles and Haven, the two outcasts who accepted my friendship with no questions asked. And even though we probably look pretty strange on the outside, the truth is, I don't know what I'd do without them. Having their friendship is one of the few good things in my life. Having their friendship makes me feel almost normal again.

And that's exactly why I need to stay away from Damen. Because his ability to charge my skin with his touch, and silence the world with his voice is a dangerous temptation I cannot indulge.

I won't risk hurting my friendship with Haven.

And I can't risk getting too close.

six

Even though Damen and I share two classes, the only one where we sit next to each other is English. So it's not until I've already put away my materials and am heading out of sixth-period art that he approaches.

He runs up beside me, holding the door as I slink past, eyes glued to the ground, wondering how I can possibly uninvite him.

"Your friends asked me to stop by tonight," he says, his stride matching mine. "But I won't be able to make it."

"Oh!" I say, caught completely off guard, regretting the way my voice just betrayed me by sounding so happy. "I mean, are you sure?" I try to sound softer, more accommodating, like I really do want him to visit, even though it's too late.

He gazes at me, eyes shiny and amused. "Yah, I'm sure. See you Monday," he says, picking up his pace and heading for his car, the one that's parked in the red zone, its engine inexplicably humming.

When I reach my Miata, Miles is waiting, arms crossed, eyes narrowed, his annoyance clearly displayed in his signature smirk. "You better tell me what just happened back there, because that did not look good," he says, sliding in as I open my side.

"He cancelled. Said he couldn't make it." I shrug, glancing over my shoulder as I shift in reverse.

"But what did *you* say that made him cancel?" He glares at me.

"Nothing."

The smirk deepens.

"Seriously, I'm not responsible for wrecking your night." I pull out of the parking lot and onto the street, but when I feel Miles still staring I go, "What?"

"Nothing." He lifts his brows and stares out the window, and even though I know what he's thinking, I focus on driving instead. So then of course he turns to me and says, "Okay, promise you won't get mad."

I close my eyes and sigh. *Here we go.*

"It's just that—I so don't get you. It's like, nothing about you makes any sense."

I take a deep breath and refuse to react. Mostly because it's about to get worse.

"For one thing, you're completely knock-down, drag-out gorgeous—at least I think you might be, because it's really hard to tell when you're always hiding under those ugly stretched-out hoodies. I mean, sorry to be the one to say it, Ever, but the whole ensemble is completely tragic, like camouflage for the homeless, and I don't think we should have to pretend otherwise. Also, I hate to be the one to break it to you, but making a point to avoid the completely hot new guy, who is so obviously into you, is just weird."

He stops long enough to give me an encouraging look, as I brace for what's next.

"Unless—of course—you're gay."

I make a right turn and exhale, grateful for my psychic abilities for probably the first time ever, since it definitely helped lessen the blow.

"Because it's totally cool if you are," he continues. "I mean, obviously, since I'm gay, and it's not like I'm gonna discriminate against you, *right*?" He laughs, a sort of nervous, we're-in-virgin-territory-now kind of laugh.

But I just shake my head and hit the brake. "Just because I'm not interested in Damen doesn't mean I'm gay," I say, realizing I sounded far more defensive than I intended. "There's a lot more to attraction than just looks, you know."

Like warm tingling touch, deep smoldering eyes, and the seductive sound of a voice that can silence the world—

"Is it because of Haven?" he asks, not buying my story.

"No." I grip the steering wheel and glare at the light, willing it to change from red to green so I can drop Miles off and be done with all this.

But I know I answered too quickly when he goes, "Ha! I *knew* it! It *is* because of Haven—because she called dibs. I can't believe you're actually honoring dibs! I mean, do you even realize you're giving up a chance to lose your virginity to the hottest guy in school, maybe even the *planet*, all because Haven called dibs?"

"This is ridiculous," I mumble, shaking my head as I turn onto his street, pull into his driveway, and park.

"What? You're not a virgin?" He smiles, obviously having a wonderful time with all this. "You been holding out on me?"

I roll my eyes and laugh in spite of myself.

He looks at me for a moment, then grabs his books and heads for his house, turning back long enough to say, "I hope Haven appreciates what a good friend you are."

———

As it turns out, Friday night was cancelled. Well, not the night, just our plans. Partly because Haven's little brother, Austin, got sick and she was the only one around to take care of him, and partly because Miles's sports-loving dad dragged him to a football game and forced him to wear the team colors and act like he cared. And as soon as Sabine learned I'd be home by myself, she left work early and offered to take me to dinner.

Knowing she doesn't approve of my fondness for hoodies and jeans, and wanting to please her after everything she's done, I slip on this pretty blue dress she recently bought me, slide my feet into the heels she got to go with it, slick on some lip gloss (a relic from my old life, when I cared about things like that), transfer my essentials from my backpack to the little metallic clutch that goes with the dress, and trade my usual ponytail for loose waves.

And just as I'm about to walk out the door, Riley pops up behind me and says, "It's about time you started dressing like a girl."

And I nearly jump out of my skin.

"Omigod, you scared the heck out of me!" I whisper, shutting the door so Sabine can't hear.

"I know." She laughs. "So where you going?"

"Some restaurant called Stonehill Tavern. It's in the St. Regis hotel," I say, my heart still racing from the ambush.

She raises her brows and nods. "Chichi."

"How would you know?" I peer at her, wondering if she's been. I mean, it's not like she ever tells me where she spends her free time.

"I know lots of things." She laughs. "Way more than you." She jumps onto my bed and rearranges the pillows before she leans back.

"Yeah, well, not much I can do about that, huh?" I say, annoyed to see how she's wearing the exact same dress and shoes as I am. Only since she's four years younger and quite a bit shorter, she looks like she's playing dress-up.

"Seriously though, you should dress like that more often. Because I hate to say it, but your usual look is *so* not working for you. I mean, you think Brandon ever would've gone for you if you'd dressed like that?" She crosses her ankles and gazes at me, her posture as relaxed as a person, living or dead, could ever be. "Speaking of, did you know he's dating Rachel now? Yep, they've been together five months. That's like, even longer than you guys, huh?"

I press my lips and tap my foot against the floor, repeating my usual mantra: *Don't let her get to you. Don't let her—*

"And omigod, you're never gonna believe this but they almost went all the way! Seriously, they left the homecoming dance early, they had it all planned out, but then—well . . ." She pauses long enough to laugh. "I know I probably shouldn't repeat this, but let's just say that Brandon did something very regrettable and extremely embarrassing that turned out to be a major mood breaker. You probably had to be there, but I'm telling you, it was *hilarious*. I mean, don't get me wrong, he misses you and all, even accidentally called her by your name once or twice, but as they say, life goes on, right?"

I take a deep breath and narrow my eyes, watching as she lounges on my bed like Cleopatra on her litter, critiquing my life, my look, virtually everything about me, giving me updates on former friends I never even asked for, like some kind of prepubescent authority.

Must be nice to just drop in whenever you feel like it, to not have to get down here in the trenches and do all the dirty work like the rest of us!

And suddenly I feel so annoyed with her little pop-in visits that are really just glorified sneak attacks, wishing she'd just leave me in peace and let me live whatever's left of my crummy life without her constant stream of bratty commentary, that I look her right in the eye and say, "So when are you scheduled for angel school? Or have they banned you because you're so evil?"

She glares at me, her eyes squeezing into angry little slits as Sabine taps on my door and calls, "Ready?"

I stare at Riley, daring her with my eyes to do something stupid, something that will alert Sabine to all the truly strange goings on around here.

But she just smiles sweetly and says, "Mom and Dad send their love," seconds before disappearing.

seven

On the ride to the restaurant all I can think about is Riley, her snide remark, and how completely rude it was to just let it slip and then disappear. I mean, I've been begging her to tell me about our parents, pleading for just one smidgen of info this whole entire time. But instead of filling me in and telling me what I need to know, she gets all fidgety, acts all cagey, and refuses to explain why they've yet to appear.

You'd think being dead would make a person act a little nicer, a little kinder. But not Riley. She's just as bratty, spoiled, and awful as she was when she was alive.

Sabine leaves the car with the valet and we head inside. And the moment I see the huge marble foyer, the outsized flower arrangements, and the amazing ocean view, I regret everything I just thought. Riley *was* right. This place really is chichi. Big-time, major chichi. Like the kind of place you bring a date—and *not* your sullen niece.

The hostess leads us to a cloth-covered table adorned with flickering candles and salt and pepper shakers that resemble small silver stones, and when I take my seat and gaze around the room,

I can hardy believe how glamorous it is. Especially compared to the kind of restaurants I'm used to.

But just as soon as I think it, I make myself stop. There's no use examining the before and after photos, of reviewing the *how things used to be* clip stored in my brain. Though sometimes being around Sabine makes it hard not to compare. Her being my dad's twin is like a constant reminder.

She orders red wine for herself and a soda for me, then we look over our menus and decide on our meals. And the moment our waitress is gone, Sabine tucks her chin-length blond hair back behind her ear, smiles politely, and says, "So, how's everything? School? Your friends? All good?"

I love my aunt, don't get me wrong, and I'm grateful for everything that she's done. But just because she can handle a twelve-man jury doesn't mean she's any good at the small talk. Still, I just look at her and say, "Yep, it's all good." Okay, maybe I suck at the small talk too.

She places her hand on my arm to say something more, but before she can even get to the words, I'm already up and out of my seat.

"I'll be right back," I mumble, nearly knocking over my chair as I dart back the way we came, not bothering to stop for directions since the waitress I just brushed against took one look at me and doubted I'd make it out the door and down the long hallway in time.

I head in the direction she unknowingly sent me, passing through a hall of mirrors—gigantic gilt-framed mirrors, all lined up in a row. And since it's Friday, the hotel is filled with guests for a wedding that, from what I can *see,* should never take place.

A group of people brush past me, their auras swirling with alcohol-fueled energy that's so out of whack it's affecting me too, leaving me dizzy, nauseous, and so light-headed that when I glance in the mirrors, I see a long chain of Damens staring right back.

I stumble into the bathroom, grip the marble counter, and fight to catch my breath. Forcing myself to focus on the potted orchids, the scented lotions, and the stack of plush towels resting on a large porcelain tray, I begin to feel calmer, more centered, contained.

I guess I've grown so used to all of the random energy I encounter wherever I go, I've forgotten how overwhelming it can be when my defenses are down and my iPod's at home. But the jolt I received when Sabine placed her hand on mine was filled with such overwhelming loneliness, such quiet sadness, it felt like a punch in the gut.

Especially when I realized I was to blame.

Sabine is lonely in a way I've tried to ignore. Because even though we live together it's not like we see each other all that often. She's usually at work, I'm usually at school, and nights and weekends I spend holed up in my room, or out with my friends. I guess I sometimes forget that I'm not the only one with people to miss, that even though she's taken me in and tried to help, she still feels just as alone and empty as the day it all happened.

But as much as I'd like to reach out, as much as I'd like to ease her pain, I just can't. I'm too damaged, too weird. I'm a freak who hears thoughts and talks to the dead. And I can't risk getting found out, can't risk getting too close, to anyone, not even her. The best I can do is just get through high school, so I can go away to college, and she can get back to her life. Maybe then she can get together with that guy who works in her building. The one she doesn't even know yet. The one whose face I saw the moment her hand touched mine.

I run my hands through my hair, reapply some lip gloss, and
head back to the table, determined to try a little harder and make
her feel better, all without risking my secrets. And as I slip back
onto my seat, I sip from my drink, and smile when I say, "I'm fine.
Really." Nodding so that she'll believe it, before adding, "So tell
me, any interesting cases at work? Any cute guys in the building?"

After dinner, I wait outside while Sabine gets in line to pay the
valet. And I'm so caught up in the drama unfolding before me, between tomorrow's bride-to-be and her so-called maid of "honor,"
that I actually jump when I feel a hand on my sleeve.

"Oh, hey," I say, my body flooding with heat and tingling the
second my eyes meet his.

"You look amazing," Damen says, his gaze traveling all the
way down my dress to my shoes, before working their way back
to mine. "I almost didn't recognize you without the hood." He
smiles. "Did you enjoy your dinner?"

I nod, feeling so on edge I'm amazed I could even do that.

"I saw you in the hall. I would've said hello, but you seemed
in such a rush."

I gaze at him, wondering what he's doing here, all alone, at
this swanky hotel on a Friday night. Dressed in a dark wool
blazer, a black open-neck shirt, designer jeans, and those boots—
an outfit that seems far too slick for a guy his age, yet somehow
looks just right.

"Out-of-town visitor," he says, answering the question I hadn't
yet asked.

And just as I'm wondering what to say next, Sabine appears.
And while they're shaking hands I say, "Um, Damen and I go to
school together."

*Damen's the one who makes my palms sweat, my stomach spin,
and he's pretty much all I can think about!*

"He just moved here from New Mexico," I add, hoping that'll
suffice until the car arrives.

"Where in New Mexico?" Sabine asks. And when she smiles I
can't help but wonder if she's flooded with that same wonderful
feeling as me.

"Santa Fe." He smiles.

"Oh, I hear it's lovely. I've always wanted to go there."

"Sabine's an attorney, she works a lot," I mumble, focusing in
the direction that the car will be coming from in just ten, nine,
eight, sev—

"We're headed back home, but you're more than welcome to
join us," she offers.

I gape at her, panicked, wondering how I failed to see that
coming. Then I glance at Damen, praying he'll decline as he says,
"Thanks, but I have to head back."

He hooks his thumb over his shoulder, and my eyes follow in
that direction, stopping on an incredibly gorgeous redhead,
dressed in the slinkiest black dress and strappy high heels.

She smiles at me, but it's not at all kind. Just pink glossy lips
slightly lifting and curving, while her eyes are too far, too distant
to read. Though there's something about her expression, the tilt
of her chin, that's so visibly mocking, as though the sight of us
standing together could be nothing short of amusing.

I turn back to face him, startled to find him looming so close,
his lips moist and parted, mere inches from mine. Then he brushes
his fingers along the side of my cheek, and retrieves a red tulip
from behind my ear.

Then the next thing I know, I'm standing alone as he heads
back inside with his date.

And I gaze at the tulip, touching its waxy red petals, wondering where it could've possibly come from—especially two seasons past spring.

Though it's not until later, when I'm alone in my room, that I realize the redhead was auraless too.

I must've been in a really deep sleep because the moment I hear someone moving around in my room, my head feels so groggy and murky I don't even open my eyes.

"Riley?" I mumble. "Is that you?" But when she doesn't answer, I know she's up to her usual pranks. And since I'm too tired to play, I grab my other pillow and plop it over my head.

But when I hear her again, I say, "Listen Riley, I'm exhausted, okay? I'm sorry if I was mean to you, and I'm sorry if I upset you, but I really don't feel like doing this now at—" I lift the pillow and open one eye to peer at my alarm clock. "At three forty-five in the morning. So why don't you just go back to wherever it is that you go and save it for a normal hour, okay? You can even show up in that dress I wore to the eighth grade graduation and I won't say a word, scout's honor."

Only, the thing is, now that I've said all of that, I'm awake. So I toss the pillow aside and glare at her shadowy form lounging on the chair by my desk, wondering what could possibly be so important it can't keep until morning.

"I said I'm sorry, okay? What more do you want?"

"You can see me?" she asks, pushing away from the desk.

"Of course I can see—" Then I stop in midsentence when I realize the voice isn't hers.

eight

I see dead people. All the time. On the street, at the beach, in the malls, in restaurants, wandering the hallways at school, standing in line at the post office, waiting in the doctor's office, though never at the dentist. But unlike the ghosts you see on TV and in movies, they don't bother me, they don't want my help, they don't stop and chat. The most they ever do is smile and wave when they realize they've been seen. Like most people, they like being seen.

But the voice in my room definitely wasn't a ghost. It also wasn't Riley. The voice in my room belonged to Damen.

And that's how I know I was dreaming.

"Hey." He smiles, slipping into his seat seconds after the bell rings, but since this is Mr. Robins's class it's the same as being early.

I nod, hoping to appear casual, neutral, not the least bit interested. Hoping to hide the fact that I'm so far gone I'm now dreaming of him.

"Your aunt seems nice." He looks at me, tapping the end of his pen on his desk, making this continuous *click click click* sound that really sets me on edge.

"Yeah, she's great," I mumble, mentally cursing Mr. Robins for lingering in the faculty bathroom, wishing he'd just stow the flask and come do his job already.

"I don't live with my family either," Damen says, his voice quieting the room, quieting my thoughts, as he spins the pen on the tip of his finger, twirling it around and around without faltering.

I press my lips together and fumble with the iPod in my secret compartment, wondering how rude it would seem if I turned it on and blocked him out too.

"I'm emancipated," he adds.

"Seriously?" I ask, even though I was firmly committed to keeping our conversations to an absolute minimum. It's just, I've never met anyone who was emancipated, and I always thought it sounded so lonely and sad. Though from the looks of his car, his clothes, and his glamorous Friday nights at the St. Regis hotel, he doesn't seem to be doing so badly.

"Seriously." He nods. And the moment he stops talking I hear the heightened whispers of Stacia and Honor, calling me a freak, and a few other things much worse than that. Then I watch as he tosses his pen in the air, smiling as it forms a series of slow lazy eights before landing right back on his finger. "So where's your family?" he asks.

And it's so weird how all the noise just stops and starts, starts and stops, like some messed up game of musical chairs. One where I'm always left standing. One where I'm always it.

"What?" I squint, distracted by the sight of Damen's magic pen now hovering between us, as Honor makes fun of my clothes, and her boyfriend pretends to agree even though he's secretly wondering why she never dresses like me. And it makes me want to lift my hood, crank my iPod, and drown it all out. Everything. Including Damen.

Especially Damen.

"Where does your family live?" he asks.

I close my eyes when he speaks—silence, sweet silence, for those fleeting few seconds. Then I open them again and gaze right into his. "They're dead," I say, as Mr. Robins walks in.

"I'm sorry."

Damen gazes at me from across the lunch table as I scan the area, eager for Haven and Miles to show. I just opened my lunch pack to find a single red tulip lying smack between my sandwich and chips—*a tulip!* Just like the one from Friday night. And even though I've no idea how he did it, I'm sure Damen's responsible. But it's not so much the strange magic tricks that bother me, it's more the way he looks at me, the way he speaks to me, the way he makes me feel—

"About your family. I didn't realize . . ."

I gaze down at my juice, twisting the cap back and forth, forth and back, wishing he'd just let it go. "I don't like to talk about it." I shrug.

"I know what it's like to lose the people you love," he whispers, reaching across the table and placing his hand over mine, infusing me with a feeling so good, so warm, so calm, and so safe—I close my eyes and allow it. Allow myself to enjoy the peace of it. Grateful to hear what he says and not what he thinks. Like an average girl—with a much better than average boy.

"Um, excuse me."

I open my eyes to find Haven leaning against the edge of the table, her yellow eyes narrowed and fixed on our hands. "So sorry to interrupt."

I pull away, shoving my hand in my pocket like it's something shameful, something no one should have to see. Wanting to explain how what she saw was nothing, how it meant nothing, even though I know better. "Where's Miles?" I finally say, not knowing what else to say.

She rolls her eyes and sits beside Damen, her hostile thoughts transforming her aura from bright yellow to a very dark red. "Miles is texting his latest Internet crush, hornyyoungdingdong307," she says, avoiding my eyes as she as she busies herself with her cupcake. Then gazing at Damen, she adds, "So, how was everyone's weekend?"

I shrug, knowing she wasn't really addressing me, watching as she taps the frosting with the tip of her tongue, performing her usual test lick, even though I've yet to see her reject one. And when I glance at Damen, I'm shocked to see him shrug too, because from what I saw, he was poised for a much better weekend than me.

"Well, as you can probably guess, my Friday night sucked. Big-time. I spent most of it cleaning up Austin's vomit, since the housekeeper was in Vegas and my parents couldn't be bothered to come home from wherever the hell they were. But Saturday totally made up for it. I mean, it *rocked*! Like, seriously, it was probably the best night of my entire life. And I totally would've invited you guys if it hadn't been so last minute." She nods, deigning to look at me again.

"Where'd you go?" I ask, trying to sound casual even though I just envisioned a dark scary place.

"This totally awesome club that some girl from my group took me to."

"Which group?" I sip from my water.

"Saturday is for codependents." She smiles. "Anyway, this girl, Evangeline? She's like a hardcore case. She's what they call a donor."

"What who calls a donor?" Miles asks, placing his Sidekick on the table and sitting down beside me.

"The codependents," I say, bringing him up to speed.

Haven rolls her eyes. "No, not them, the *vampires*. A donor is a person who allows other vamps to feed off them. You know, like suck their blood and stuff, whereas I'm what they call a *puppy,* because I just like to follow them around. I don't let anyone feed. Well, not yet." She laughs.

"Follow who around?" Miles asks, lifting his Sidekick and flipping through his messages.

"Vampires! Jeez, try to keep up. Anyway, what I was saying is this codependent donor chick, Evangeline, which, by the way, is her vampire name, not her real name—"

"People have vampire names?" Miles asks, setting his phone on the table where he can still peek at it.

"Totally." She nods, poking her finger deep into the frosting, then licking the tip.

"Is that like a stripper name? You know, like your first childhood pet plus your mom's maiden name? Because that makes me Princess Slavin, thank you very much." He smiles.

Haven sighs, striving for patience. "Uh, no. It's nothing like that. You see, a vampire name is serious. And unlike most people, I don't even have to change mine, because Haven is like an *organic* vamp name, one hundred percent natural, no additives or preservatives." She laughs. "I told you I'm a dark princess! Anyway, we went to this really cool club somewhere up in L.A. called Nocturnal, or something like that."

"Nocturne," Damen says, gripping his drink as his eyes focus on hers.

Haven sets down her cupcake and claps. "Yay! Finally, some-one cool at this table," she says.

"And did you run into any *immortals*?" he asks, still gazing at her.

"Tons! The place was packed. There was even a VIP coven room, which I totally snuck into and hung out at the blood bar."

"Did they card you?" Miles asks, his fingers racing over his Sidekick as he partakes in two conversations at once.

"Laugh all you want, but I'm telling you it was way cool. Even after Evangeline sort of ditched me for some guy she met, I ended up meeting this other girl, who was even cooler, and who also, by the way, just moved here. So we'll probably start hanging out and stuff."

"Are you breaking up with us?" Miles gapes at her in mock alarm.

Haven rolls her eyes. "Whatever. All I know is that it was bet-ter than your guys' Saturday night—well, maybe not yours, Damen, since you seem to be up on these things, but definitely those two," she says, pointing at Miles and me.

"So how was the game?" I elbow Miles, trying to get his at-tention back on us and away from his electronic boyfriend.

"All I know is there was *way* too much team spirit, somebody won, somebody lost, and I spent most of it in the bathroom text-messaging this guy who's apparently a *big fat liar!*" He shakes his head and shows us the screen. "Look, right there!" He stabs it with his finger. "I've been asking for a picture all weekend because no way am I meeting up without getting a solid visual. And *this* is what he sends. Stupid phony poseur!"

I squint at the thumbnail, not quite getting what he's so angry about. "How do you know it's not him?" I ask, glancing at Miles.

And then Damen says, "Because it's me."

nine

Apparently Damen modeled for a short time, back when he lived in New York, which is why his image is out there, floating around cyberspace, just waiting for someone to download and claim that it's them.

And even though we passed it around and had a good solid laugh at the whole weird coincidence, there's still one thing I can't quite get past: If Damen just moved here from New Mexico and *not* New York, well, doesn't it seem like he should've looked a little bit younger in that picture? Because I can't think of anyone who looks exactly the same at seventeen as they did at fourteen, or even fifteen, and yet, that thumbnail on Miles's Sidekick showed Damen looking exactly the same as he does right now.

And it just doesn't make any sense.

When I get to art, I beeline for the supply closet, grab all my stuff, and head for my easel, refusing to react when I notice how Damen is set up right next to mine. I just take a deep breath and go about the business of buttoning my smock and selecting a brush, stealing the occasional glance at his canvas and trying not to gawk at his masterpiece in the making—a seriously perfect rendition of Picasso's *Woman with Yellow Hair*.

Our assignment is to emulate one of the great masters, to choose one of those iconic paintings and attempt to re-create it. And somehow I got the idea that those simple Van Gogh swirls would be a sure thing, a cinch to reproduce, an easy A. But from the looks of my chaotic, hectic strokes, I completely misjudged it. And now it's so far gone, I can't possibly save it. And I've no idea what to do.

Ever since I became psychic, I'm no longer required to study. I'm not even required to read. All I have to do is place my hands on a book, and the story appears in my head. And as far as tests go? Well, let's just say there's no more "pop" in the quiz. I just brush my fingers over the questions and the answers are instantly revealed.

But art is totally different.

Because talent cannot be faked.

Which is why my painting is pretty much the exact opposite of Damen's.

"*Starry Night?*" Damen asks, nodding at my drippy, pathetic, blue mottled canvas, as I cringe in embarrassment, wondering how he could've made such an accurate guess from such a poorly realized mess.

Then just to torture myself even further, I take another glance at his effortless, curving brushstrokes, and add it to the never-ending list of things he's amazingly good at.

Seriously, like in English, he can answer all of Mr. Robins's questions, which is kind of weird since he only had one night to skim all three hundred and some odd pages of *Wuthering Heights*. Not to mention how he usually goes on to include all manner of random historical facts, talking about those long-ago days as though he was actually there. He's ambidextrous too, which might not sound like all that big a deal, until you watch him write with one hand and paint with the other, with neither project seeming to suffer. And don't even get me started on the spontaneous tulips and magic pen.

"Just like Pablo himself. Wonderful!" Ms. Machado says, smoothing her long glossy braid as she stares at his canvas, her aura vibrating a beautiful cobalt blue, as her mind performs cartwheels and somersaults, jumping in glee, racing through her mental roster of talented former students, realizing she's never had one with such innate, natural ability—until now.

"And Ever?" On the outside she's still smiling, but inside she's thinking: *What on earth could it possibly be?*

"Oh, um, it's supposed to be Van Gogh. You know, *Starry Night?*" I cringe in shame, my worst suspicions confirmed by her thoughts.

"Well—it's an honorable start." She nods, struggling to keep her face neutral, relaxed. "Van Gogh's style is much more difficult than it seems. Just don't forget the golds, and the yellows! It is a starry, starry night after all!"

I watch her walk away, her aura expanding and glowing, knowing she dislikes my painting, but appreciating her effort to hide it. Then without even thinking I dip my brush in yellow, before wiping off the blue, and when I press it to my canvas it leaves a big blob of green.

"*How* do you do it?" I ask, shaking my head in frustration, gazing from Damen's amazingly good painting to my amazingly bad one, comparing, contrasting, and feeling my confidence plummet.

He smiles, his eyes finding mine. "Who do you think taught Picasso?" he says.

I drop my brush to the floor, sending mushy globs of green paint splattering across my shoes, my smock, and my face, holding my breath as he leans down to retrieve it, before placing it back in my hand.

"Everyone has to start somewhere," he says, his eyes dark and smoldering, his fingers seeking the scar on my face.

The one on my forehead.

The one that's hidden under my bangs.

The one he has no way of knowing about.

"Even Picasso had a teacher." He smiles, withdrawing his hand and the warmth that came with it, returning to his painting, as I remind myself to breathe.

ten

The next morning as I'm getting ready for school, I make the mistake of asking Riley's help in choosing a sweatshirt.

"What do you think?" I hold up a blue one, before replacing it with a green.

"Do the pink one again," she says, perched on my dresser, head cocked to the side as she considers the options.

"There is no pink one." I scowl, wishing she could just be serious for a change, stop making everything into such a big game. "Come on, help me out, clock's ticking."

She rubs her chin and squints. "Would you say that's more of a *cerulean* blue or a *cornflower* blue?"

"That's it." I toss the blue one and start yanking the green over my head.

"Go with the blue."

I stop, eyes visible, nose, mouth, and chin sheltered in fleece.

"Seriously. It brings out your eyes." I squint at her for a moment, then I toss the green one and do as she says. Rummaging for lip gloss and stopping just short of applying it when she goes,

"Okay, what gives? I mean, the sweatshirt crises, the sweaty palms, the makeup, what's going on?"

"I'm not wearing makeup," I say, cringing as my voice nears a shout.

"Not to fault you on a technicality, Ever, but lip gloss counts. It definitely qualifies as makeup. And you, dear sister, were just about to apply it."

I drop it back in the drawer and reach for my usual ChapStick instead, smearing it across my lips in a waxy dull line.

"Um, hello? Still waiting for an answer over here!"

I press my lips, heading out the door and down the stairs.

"Fine, play that way. But don't think you can stop me from guessing," she says, trailing behind me.

"Whatever," I mumble, going into the garage.

"Well, we know it's not Miles, since you're not really *his* type, and we know it's not Haven since she's not really *your* type, which leaves me with—" She slips right through the closed and locked car door and onto the front seat while I try not to cringe. "Well, I guess that's pretty much it for your circle of friends, so tell me, I give up."

I open the garage door and climb in my car the old-fashioned way, then rev up the engine to drown out her voice.

"I know you're up to something," she says, talking over the roar. "Because excuse me for saying so, but you're acting just like you did right before you hooked up with Brandon. Remember how nervous and paranoid you were? Wondering if he liked you back, and bippidy-blah-blah. So come on, tell me. Who's the unlucky guy? Who's your next victim?"

And the second she says that, an image of Damen flashes before me, looking so gorgeous, so sexy, so smoldering, so palpable, I'm tempted to reach out and claim it. But instead I just clear my throat, shift into reverse, and say, "No one. I don't like anyone. But trust me, that's the last time I'll ever ask you to help."

By the time I get to English, I'm as giddy, nervous, sweaty palmed, and anxious as Riley accused me of being. But when I see Damen talking to Stacia, I add *paranoid* to the already long list.

"Um, excuse me," I say, blocked by Damen's gloriously long legs, which are taking the place of her usual booby trap.

But he just ignores me and remains perched on her desk, and I watch as he reaches behind her ear, and comes away with a rosebud.

A single white rosebud.

A fresh, pure, glistening, dewy, white rosebud.

And when he hands it to her, she squeals so loud you'd think he just gave her a diamond.

"Oh-my-*gawd*! No *way*! *How'd* you do that?" She shrieks, waving it around so everyone can see.

I press my lips and gaze down at the ground, fiddling with my iPod and cranking the sound until I can no longer hear her.

"I need to get by," I mumble, my eyes meeting Damen's, catching the briefest flash of warmth before his gaze turns to ice and he moves out of my way.

I storm toward my desk, my feet moving like they're supposed to, one in front of the other, like a zombie, a robot, some dense numb thing just going through its preprogrammed motions, unable to think on its own. Then I settle onto my chair and continue the routine, retrieving paper, books, and a pen, pretending I don't notice how reluctant Damen is, how he drags his feet when Mr. Robins makes him return to his seat.

"What the *fug*?" Haven says, moving her bangs to the side and staring straight ahead, her profanity ban the only New Year's resolution she's ever been able to keep, but only because she thinks *fug* is funny.

"I knew it wouldn't last." Miles shakes his head and gazes at Damen, watching him wow the A-list with his natural charm, magic pen, and stupid fugging rosebuds. "I knew it was too good to be true. In fact, I said exactly that the very first day. Remember when I said that?"

"No," Haven mumbles, still staring at Damen. "I don't remember that at all."

"Well, I did." Miles swigs his VitaminWater, and nods. "I said it. You just didn't hear me."

I gaze down at my sandwich and shrug, not wanting to get into the whole "who said what when" debate, and definitely not willing to look anywhere near Damen, Stacia, or anyone else at that table. I'm still reeling from English, when Damen leaned toward me, right in the middle of roll call, so he could pass me a note.

But only so I could pass it to Stacia.

"Pass it yourself," I'd said, refusing to touch it. Wondering how a single piece of notebook paper, folded into a triangle, could possibly cause so much pain.

"Come on," he said, flicking it toward me so it landed just shy of my fingers. "I promise you won't get caught."

"It's not about getting caught." I glared at him.

"Then what is it about?" he asked, dark eyes on mine.

It's about not wanting to touch it! Not wanting to know what it says! Because the moment my fingers make contact, I'll see the words in my head—the whole, sexy, adorable, flirty, unfiltered message. And even though it'll be bad enough to hear it in her thoughts, at least then I can pretend that it's compromised, diluted by her dimwitted brain. But if I touch that piece of paper, then I'll know the words are true— and I just can't bear to see them—

"Pass it yourself," I finally said, tapping it with the tip of my pencil and sending it off the edge of my desk. Hating the way my heart slammed against my chest as he laughed and bent down to retrieve it.

Hating myself for the flood of relief when he slid it into his pocket instead of passing it to *her.*

"Um, hel-*lo*, earth to Ever!"

I shake my head and squint at Miles.

"I asked what happened? I mean, not to point fingers or any-thing, but you *are* the last one who saw him today . . ."

I gaze at Miles, wishing I knew. Remembering yesterday in art, the way Damen's eyes sought mine, the way his touch warmed my skin, so sure we'd shared something personal—*magical* even. But then I remember the girl before Stacia, the gorgeous haughty redhead at the St. Regis, the one I conveniently managed to for-get. And I feel like a fool, for being so naïve, for thinking he just might've liked me. Because the truth is, that's just Damen. He's a player. And he does this all the time.

I gaze across the lunch tables, just in time to see Damen com-pile an entire bouquet of white rosebuds from Stacia's ear, sleeve, cleavage, and purse. Then I press my lips and avert my gaze, sparing myself the gratuitous hug that soon follows.

"I didn't *do* anything," I finally say, as confused by Damen's er-ratic behavior as Miles and Haven, only far less willing to admit it.

I can hear Miles's thoughts, weighing my words, trying to decide if he should believe me. Then he sighs and says, "Do you feel as dejected, jilted, and heartbroken as me?"

I look at him, wanting to confide, wishing I could tell him *everything,* the whole sordid jumble of feelings. How just yesterday I was sure something significant had passed between us, only to wake up today and be presented with *this.* But instead I just shake my head, gather my things, and head off to class, long before the bell even rings.

All through fifth-period French, I think of ways to get out of art. Seriously. Even as I'm participating in the usual drills, lips moving, foreign words forming, my mind is completely obsessed with faking a stomachache, nausea, fever, a dizzy spell, the flu, whatever. Any excuse will do.

And it's not just because of Damen. Because the truth is, I don't even know why I signed up for that class in the first place. I have no artistic ability, my project's a mess, and it's not like I'm going to be an artist anyway. And yeah, I guess if you throw Damen into that already full mix, you end up not only with a seriously compromised GPA, but fifty-seven minutes of awkwardness.

But in the end, I go. Mostly because it's the right thing to do. And I'm so focused on gathering my supplies and donning my smock, that at first I don't realize he's not even there. And as the minutes tick by with still no sign of him, I grab my paints and head for my easel.

Only to find that stupid triangle note balanced on the edge.

I stare at it, focusing so intensely that everything around me grows dark and out of focus. The entire classroom reduced to one single point. My entire world consisting of a triangle-shaped letter resting on a thin wooden ledge, the name *Stacia* scrawled on its front. And even though I've no idea how it got there, even though a quick survey of the room reaffirms Damen's not there, I don't want it anywhere near me. I refuse to participate in this sick little game.

I grab a paintbrush and flick it as hard as I can, watching as it soars through the air before tumbling to the ground, knowing I'm acting childish, ridiculous, especially when Ms. Machado comes by and swoops it up in her hand.

"Looks like you dropped something!" she sings, her smile bright and expectant, having no idea that I put it there on purpose.

"It's not mine," I mumble, rearranging my paints, figuring she can get it to Stacia herself, or better yet, throw it away.

"So there's another *Ever* I'm not aware of?" She smiles.

What?

I take the note she dangles before me, *Ever* clearly scrawled across its front, and written in Damen's unmistakable hand. Having no idea how this happened, no logical explanation. Because I know what I saw.

My fingers tremble as I begin to unfold it, opening all three corners and smoothing the crease, gasping when a small detailed sketch is unveiled—a small detailed sketch of one beautiful red tulip.

eleven

Halloween is just a few days away and I'm still working on the final touches for my costume. Haven's going as a vampire (duh), Miles is going as a pirate—but that's only after I talked him out of going as Madonna in her cone-breast phase, and I'm not telling what I'm going as. But only because my once great idea has morphed into an overly ambitious project I'm quickly losing faith in.

Though I have to admit I was pretty surprised Sabine even wanted to throw a party to begin with. Partly because she never really seems interested in stuff like that, but mostly because I figured that between the two of us we'd be lucky to come up with five guests max. But apparently Sabine's a lot more popular than I realized, as she quickly filled two and a half columns, while my list was pathetically shorter—consisting of my only two friends and their possible plus ones.

So while Sabine hired a caterer to handle the food and drink, I put Miles in charge of audio/visual (which means he'll dock his iPod and rent some scary movies), and asked Haven to provide the cupcakes. Which pretty much left Riley and me as the sole members of the decorations committee. And since Sabine handed me a catalog and a credit card with specific instructions to "don't hold back," we've spent the last two afternoons transforming the house from its usual look of semicustom Tuscan track home to spooky, scary, crypt-keeper's castle. And it's been so much fun, reminding me of when we used to decorate our old house for Easter, Thanksgiving, and Christmas. Not to mention how staying busy and focused has really helped curb some of our bickering.

"You should go as a mermaid," Riley says. "Or as one of those kids from those OC reality shows."

"Oh jeez, don't tell me you still watch that stuff?" I say, balancing precariously on the second to last rung, so I can string up yet another faux spiderweb.

"Don't blame me, Tivo's got a mind of its own." She shrugs.

"You have Tivo?" I turn, desperate for any information I can get since she's always so stingy with the afterlife details.

But she just laughs. "I swear, you are so gullible—the things you believe!" She shakes her head and rolls her eyes, reaching into a cardboard box and retrieving a string of fairy lights. "Wanna trade?" she offers, unraveling the cord. "I mean, it's ridiculous the way you insist on climbing up and down that ladder when I can just levitate and get the job done."

I shake my head and frown. Even though it might be easier, I still like to pretend my life is somewhat normal.

"So what are you going as?"

"Forget it," I say, attaching the web to the corner, before climbing down the ladder to get a good look. "If you can have secrets, then I can too."

"No fair." She crosses her arms and pouts in the way that always worked on Dad, but never on Mom.

"Relax, you'll see it at the party," I tell her, picking up a glow-in-the-dark skeleton and untangling the limbs.

"You mean, I'm invited?" she asks, her voice squeaky, eyes wide with excitement.

"Like I could stop you?" I laugh, propping Mr. Skeleton near the entryway so he can greet all our guests.

"Is your boyfriend coming too?"

I roll my eyes and sigh. "You know I don't have a boyfriend," I say, bored with this game before it's even begun.

"Please. I'm not an idiot." She scowls. "It's not like I've forgotten the great sweatshirt debate. Besides, I can't wait to meet him, or I guess I should say, *see* him, since it's not like you'd ever introduce me. Which is really pretty rude if you think about it. I mean just because he can't see me doesn't mean—"

"Jeez, he's not invited, okay?" I shout, not realizing I've stumbled into her trap until it's too late.

"Ha!" She looks at me, eyes wide, brows raised, lips curving with delight. "I *knew* it!" She laughs, tossing the fairy lights and jumping in glee, spinning and thrusting and pointing at me. "I *knew* it, I *knew* it, I *knew* it!" she sings, punching her fists in the air. "Ha! I *knew* it!" She twirls.

I close my eyes and sigh, chiding myself for falling into her poorly concealed trap. "You don't *know* anything." I glare at her and shake my head. "He was never my boyfriend, okay? He—he was just some new kid, who at first I thought was kind of cute, but then, when I realized what a total player he is, well, let's just say that I'm over it. In fact, I don't even think he's cute anymore. Seriously, it lasted like ten seconds, but only because I didn't know any better. And it's not like I'm the only one who fell for his game, because Miles and Haven were practically fighting over him. So why don't you just stop with all the air punching and hip thrusts, and get back to work, okay?"

And the moment I stop, I know I sounded way too defensive

to ever be believed. But now that it's out there I can't take it back, so I just try to ignore her as she hovers around the room singing, "Yup! I *so so* knew it!"

By Halloween night the house looks amazing. Riley and I taped webs in all of the windows and corners, and stuck huge black widow spiders in their middles. We hung black rubber bats from the ceiling, scattered bloodied, severed (fake) body parts all around, and set up a crystal ball next to a plug-in raven whose eyes light up and roll around when he says, "You'll be sorry! Squawk! You'll be sorry!" We dressed zombies in "blood" covered rags and placed them where you'd least expect to find them. We put steaming cauldrons of witches' brew (really just dry ice and water) in the entry, and scattered skeletons, mummies, black cats and rats (well, fake ones, but still creepy), gargoyles, coffins, black candles, and skulls pretty much everywhere. We even decorated the backyard with jack-o'-lanterns, floating pool globes, and blinking fairy lights. And oh yeah, we placed a life-sized grim reaper out on the front lawn.

"How do I look?" Riley asks, gazing down at her purple shell-covered chest and red hair as she swishes her sparkly, metallic, green fish tail around.

"Like your favorite Disney character," I say, powdering my face until it's very pale, trying to think of a way to get rid of her so I can change into my costume and maybe surprise her for a change.

"I'll take that as a compliment." She smiles.

"As you should." I brush my hair back and pin it close to my head, preparing for the big, blond, towering wig I'll wear.

"So who are you going as?" She gazes at me. "I mean, would

you just tell me already, because the suspense is really killing me!" She clutches her stomach in a fit of laughter, rocking back and forth, and nearly falling off the bed. She loves making death puns. Thinks they're hysterical. But mostly they just make me cringe.

Ignoring the joke, I turn to her and say, "Do me a favor? Sneak down the hall and check out Sabine's costume, and let me know if she tries to wear that big rubber nose with the hairy wart on the end. I told her it's a really great witch's costume, but she needs to ditch the nose. Guys don't usually go for that sort of thing."

"She's got a guy?" Riley asks, clearly surprised.

"Not if she wears the nose," I say, watching as she slips off the bed and heads across the room, mermaid tail dragging behind her. "But don't make any noise, or do anything to scare her, okay?" I add, cringing as she slinks through my closed bedroom door, not even bothering to open it. I mean, just because I've witnessed that like a gazillion times doesn't mean I've gotten used to it.

I head into my closet and unzip the bag I've hidden in the back, removing the beautiful black gown with the low square neckline, the sheer three-quarter-length sleeves, and the super tight bodice that swells into shiny, loose folds—just like the one Marie Antoinette wore to the masked ball (well, as portrayed by Kirsten Dunst in the movie). And after struggling with the zipper in the back, I slip on my very tall platinum blond wig (because even though I'm already blond, I could never get my hair to go that high), apply some red lipstick, fasten a filmy black mask over my eyes, and insert some long, dangly, rhinestone earrings. And when my costume's complete I stand before my mirror twirling and spinning and smiling as my shiny black dress sways all around, and I'm thrilled with how good it turned out.

The second Riley pops back in she shakes her head and says,

"All clear—*finally!* I mean, first she put the nose on, then she took it off, then she put it back on and turned to check out her profile, only to take it back off again. I swear it took all of my will not to just snatch it off her face and chuck it out the window."

I freeze, holding my breath, hoping she didn't do any such thing, because with Riley you just never know.

She plops herself onto my desk chair and uses the tip of her sparkly green fin to propel herself around. "Relax," she says. "Last I saw, she left it in the bathroom, next to the sink. And then some guy called needing directions, and she went on and on about what a great job you did on the house, and how she can hardly believe you handled it all by yourself, and bippidy-blah-blah." She shakes her head and frowns. "You must really love that, huh? Taking all the credit for *our* hard work." She stops spinning and gives me a long, appraising look. "So, Marie Antoinette," she finally says, her eyes taking a tour of my costume. "I never would've guessed. I mean, it's not like you're all that big on cake."

I roll my eyes. "For your information, she never said that about the cake. It was a vicious tabloid rumor, so don't you believe it," I tell her, unable to stop mirror gazing, as I recheck my makeup and pat my wig, hoping it will all stay where it's supposed to. But when I catch Riley's reflection, something about the way she looks makes me stop and move toward her. "Hey, you okay?"

She closes her eyes and bites her lip. Then she shakes her head and says, "Jeez, would you look at us? You're dressed as a tragic teen queen, and I'd do anything just to *be* a teen."

I start to reach for her, but my hands fumble at my sides. I guess I'm so used to having her around that I sometimes forget how she's not *really* here, how she's no longer part of this world, and how she'll never grow any older, never get the chance to be thirteen. And then I remember how it's all my fault to begin with, and I feel a million times worse. "Riley, I—"

But she just shakes her head and waves her tail around. "No worries." She smiles, floating up from the chair. "Time to greet the guests!"

Haven came with Evangeline, her codependent donor friend, who, big surprise, is dressed like a vampire too, and Miles brought Eric, some guy he knows from his acting class who looks like he might actually be pretty cute beneath that black satin Zorro mask and cape.

"I can't believe you didn't invite Damen," Haven says, shaking her head and skipping right past *hello*. She's been mad at me all week, ever since she learned he didn't make the list.

I roll my eyes and take a deep breath, tired of defending the obvious, of having to point out yet again how he's clearly ditched us, becoming a permanent fixture not just at Stacia's lunch table but also her desk. Procuring rosebuds from all manner of places, and how his art project, *Woman with Yellow Hair* is beginning to look suspiciously like her.

I mean, excuse me for not wanting to dwell on the fact of how despite the red tulips, the mysterious note, and the intimate gaze we once shared, he hasn't spoken to me in almost two weeks.

"It's not like he would've come anyway," I finally say, hoping she won't notice how my voice just cracked in betrayal. "I'm sure he's out somewhere with Stacia, or the redhead, or—" I shake my head, refusing to continue.

"Wait—*redhead?* There's a redhead too?" She squints at me.

I shrug. Because the truth is, he could be with just about anyone. All I know is that he isn't here with me.

"You should see him." She turns to Evangeline. "He's *amazing*. Gorgeous like a movie star—sexy like a rock star—he even does illusions." She sighs.

Evangeline raises her brows. "Sounds like he *is* an illusion. No one's that perfect."

"Damen is. Too bad you can't see for yourself." Haven frowns at me again, her fingers fiddling with the black velvet choker she wears around her neck. "But if you do happen to meet him, don't forget that he's mine. I called it way before I knew you."

I gaze at Evangeline, taking in her dark murky aura, fishnet stockings, tiny black boy shorts, and mesh T-shirt, knowing she has no intention of keeping any such promise.

"You know I could lend you some fangs and fake blood for your neck and you could be a vampire too," Haven offers, looking at me, her mind flip-flopping back and forth, wanting to be my friend, convinced I'm her foe.

But I just shake my head and steer them to the other side of the room, hoping she'll move on to something else and soon forget about Damen.

Sabine's talking to her friends, Haven and Evangeline are spiking their drinks, Miles and Eric are dancing, while Riley plays with the tail of Eric's whip, swinging the fringe up and down and back and forth, then looking around to see if anyone notices. And just as I'm about to give her the signal, the one that means she better cut it out if she wants to stick around, the doorbell rings, and we race each other to get it.

And even though I beat her to it, when I open the door I forget to gloat, because Damen is there. Flowers in one hand, gold-tipped hat in the other, with his hair gathered into a low ponytail, his usual sleek black clothes replaced with a frilly white shirt, a coat with gold buttons, and what can only be described as breeches, tights, and pointy black shoes. And just as I'm thinking how Miles is going to be completely envious of that costume, I realize who he's dressed as, and my heart skips two beats.

"Count Fersen," I mumble, barely managing the words.

"Marie." He smiles, offering a deep, gallant bow.

"But . . . it was a secret . . . and you weren't even invited," I whisper, peering past his shoulder, searching for Stacia, the red-head, anyone at all, knowing he couldn't possibly be here for me.

But he just smiles and hands me the flowers. "Then it must be a lucky coincidence."

I swallow hard and turn on my heel, leading him through the entry, past the living and dining rooms, and into the den, my cheeks burning as my heart beats so hard and so fast I fear it might burst through my chest. Wondering how this possibly could've happened, searching for some logical explanation for Damen's showing up at my party dressed as my perfect other half.

"Omigod, Damen's here!" Haven squeals, arms waving, face all lit up—well, as much as a heavily powdered, fang-wearing, blood-dripping, vampire face can light up. But the moment she sees his costume, realizing he came as Count Axel Fersen, the not-so-secret lover of Marie Antoinette, her entire face dims, and her eyes turn to me, glaring accusingly.

"So, when'd you two arrange it?" she asks, advancing on us, trying to keep her voice light, neutral, but more for Damen's benefit than mine.

"We didn't," I say, hoping she'll believe it, yet knowing she won't. I mean, it's such a bizarre coincidence I'm beginning to doubt it myself, wondering if I somehow let it slip, even though I know that I didn't.

"Complete fluke," Damen says, hooking his arm around my waist. And even though he only keeps it there for a moment, it's still long enough to leave my whole body tingling.

"You've *got* to be Damen," Evangeline says, slinking up beside him, fingers plucking at the ruffles on his shirt. "I thought for sure Haven was exaggerating, though apparently not!" She laughs. "And who're you dressed as?"

"Count Fersen," Haven says, voice hard and brittle, eyes narrowed on mine.

"Whoever." Evangeline shrugs, stealing his hat and perching it on top of her head, smiling seductively from under the brim before grabbing his hand and leading him away.

The moment they're gone, Haven turns to me and says, "I can't *believe* you!" Her face is angry, fists clenched, but that's nothing compared to the horrible thoughts that swirl through her head. "You know how much I like him. I *confided* in you, I *trusted* you!"

"Haven, I swear, it wasn't planned. It's just some freaky coincidence. I don't even know what he's doing here, and you know I didn't invite him," I say, wanting to convince her, yet knowing it's useless, she's already made up her mind. "And I don't know if you noticed, but your good friend Evangeline is practically humping his leg over there."

Haven glances across the room then turns back to me, shrugging when she says, "She does that with everyone, she's hardly a threat. Unlike you."

I take a deep breath, striving for patience and trying not to laugh as Riley stands beside her, mimicking every word, reenacting every move, mocking her in a way that's definitely funny though not at all kind. "Listen," I finally say. "I *don't* like him! I mean, how can I convince you of that? Just tell me and I'll do it!"

She shakes her head and looks away, shoulders sinking, thoughts turning dark, redirecting all of that anger back on herself. "Don't." She sighs, blinking rapidly, staving off tears. "Don't say a word. If he likes you then he likes you, and there's nothing I can do. I mean, it's not your fault you're smart and pretty and guys are always going to like you better than me. Especially once they see you without your hood." She tries to laugh, but doesn't quite make it.

"You're making something out of nothing," I say, hoping to convince her, hoping to convince myself. "The only thing Damen and I have in common is our taste in movies and costumes. That's it, I swear." And when I smile, I'm hoping it plays more real than it feels.

She gazes across the room at Evangeline who's taken hold of Zorro's whip and is demonstrating the proper way to use it, then she turns back to me and says, "Just do me a favor."

I nod, willing to do just about anything to put an end to all this.

"Stop lying. You really suck at it."

I watch as she walks away, then I turn to Riley who's jumping up and down, shouting, "Omigod, this has *got* to be your best party ever! Drama! Intrigue! Jealousy! An almost–cat fight! I am *so* glad I didn't miss this!"

And I'm just about to tell her to *shush* when I remember how I'm the only one who can actually hear her and how it might look a little strange for me to do that. And when the doorbell rings again, despite the fish tail flopping behind her, this time, she beats me to it.

"Oh my," says the woman standing on the porch gazing between Riley and me.

"Can I help you?" I ask, noticing how she's not dressed up, unless California casual counts as a costume.

She looks at me, her brown eyes meeting mine when she says, "Sorry I'm late, traffic was a bitc—well you know." She nods at Riley as though she can actually see her.

"Are you a friend of Sabine's?" I ask, thinking maybe it's some weird nervous tic that keeps her eyes darting to where Riley is standing, because even though she has a nice purple aura, for some reason, I can't read her.

"I'm Ava. Sabine hired me."

"Are you one of the caterers?" I ask, wondering why she's wearing a black off-the-shoulder top, skinny jeans, and ballet flats instead of a white shirt and black pants like the rest of the team.

But she just laughs and waves at Riley, who's hiding behind the folds of my dress, like she used to do with our mom whenever she felt shy. "I'm the psychic," she says, brushing her long auburn hair off her face, and kneeling down beside Riley. "And I see you have a little friend with you."

twelve

Apparently Ava the psychic was supposed to be this fun surprise for everyone. But trust me, no one was more surprised than me. I mean, how did I not see it coming? Was I so wrapped up in my own world that I forgot to poke around in Sabine's?

And it's not like I could just send her away, even though I was tempted. But before I could even react to the shock of her seeing Riley, Sabine was at the door, inviting her in.

"Oh good, you made it. And I see you've met my niece," she says, ushering her into the den where a table is set up and waiting.

I hover close by, wondering if Ava the Psychic will try to mention my dead little sister. But then Sabine asks me to fetch Ava a drink, and by the time I return she's giving a reading.

"You should get in line before it gets any longer," Sabine says, her shoulder pressed against Frankenstein, who, with or without the creepy mask, is *not* the cute guy who works in her building. He's also not the big, successful investment banker he pretends to be. In fact, he still lives with his mother.

But I don't want to tell her any of that and destroy her good mood, so I just shake my head and say, "Maybe later."

———

It's nice to see Sabine enjoying herself for a change, good to know she has a whole network of friends, and from what I can see, a renewed interest in dating. And even though it's fun watching Riley dance with unsuspecting people and eavesdrop on conversations she probably shouldn't hear, I need a break from all of the random thoughts, vibrating auras, swirling energy, but most of all—Damen.

So far I've done my best to keep my distance, to act cool and ignore him when I see him at school, but seeing him tonight, dressed in what is clearly the other half of a couple's costume—well, I'm not sure what to think. I mean, last I saw, he was into the redhead, Stacia, anyone but me. Enchanting them with his charm, good looks, charisma, and inexplicable magic tricks.

I bury my nose in the flowers he brought me, twenty-four tulips, all of them red. And even though tulips aren't exactly known for their scent, somehow these are heady, intoxicating, and sweet. I inhale deeply, losing myself in their fragrant bouquet and secretly admitting I like him. I mean, I *really* like him. I can't help it. I just do. And no matter how hard I try to pretend otherwise, it doesn't make it any less true.

Before Damen came along, I'd resigned myself to a solitary fate. Not that I was thrilled with the idea of never having another boyfriend, of never getting close to another person again. But how can I date when touch feels so overbearing? How can I be in a relationship when I'll always know what my partner is thinking? Never getting the chance to obsess, dissect, and guess at the secret meaning of everything he says and does?

And even though it probably seems cool to read minds and

energy and auras, trust me, it so isn't. I would give anything to get my old life back, to be as normal and clueless as every other girl. Because sometimes even your best friends can think some pretty unflattering things, and not having an *off* switch requires a heck of a lot of forgiveness.

But that's what's so great about Damen. He's like an *off* switch. He's the only one I can't read, the only one who can silence the sound of everyone else. And even though he makes me feel wonderful and warm and as close to normal as I'll ever get to be, I can't help but think that there's nothing normal about it.

I sit on one of the lounge chairs and arrange my full skirt all around, watching the water globes bob and change color as they glide across the pool's shiny surface. And I'm so lost in my thoughts and the amazing view before me, that at first I don't notice when Damen appears.

"Hey." He smiles.

And when I glance at him, my whole body heats.

"It's a good party. I'm glad I crashed." He sits down beside me, as I stare straight ahead, aware that he's teasing but too nervous to respond. "You make a good Marie," he says, his finger tapping the long black feather I stuck in my wig at the very last moment.

I press my lips together, feeling anxious, nervous, tempted to flee. Then I take a deep breath and relax and go with it. Allow myself to live a little—if just for one night. "And you make a good Count Fersen," I finally say.

"Please, call me Axel." He laughs.

"Did they charge extra for the moth hole?" I ask, nodding at the frayed spot near his shoulder, though choosing not to mention its musty scent.

He looks at me, his eyes right on mine when he says, "That's no moth hole. That's the by-product of artillery fire, a real *near miss* as they say."

"Well, if I remember right, in this particular scene you were pursuing a dark-haired girl." I glance at him, remembering a time when flirting came easy, summoning the girl I used to be.

"There's been a last-minute rewrite." He smiles. "Didn't you get the new script?"

I kick my feet up and smile, thinking how nice it feels to finally let go, to act like a normal girl, with a normal crush, just like anyone else.

"And in this new version it's just us. And you, Marie, get to keep your pretty head." He takes his finger, the very tip of his index finger, and slides it across the width of my neck, leaving a trail of warm wonderful sizzle as he lingers just under my ear. "Why didn't you get in line for a reading?" he whispers, his fingers traveling along my jaw, my cheek, tracing the curve of my ear, as his lips loom so close our breaths meet and mingle.

I shrug and press my lips, wishing he'd just shut up and kiss me already.

"Are you a skeptic?"

"No—I just—I don't know," I mumble, so frustrated I'm tempted to scream.

Why does he insist on talking? Doesn't he realize this may be my last remaining shot at a normal boy-girl experience? That an opportunity like this may never present itself again?

"How come you're not in line?" I ask, no longer trying to hide my frustration.

"Waste of time." He laughs. "It's not possible to read minds, or tell the future—*right?*"

I shift my gaze to the pool, blinking at the water globes that have not only turned pink but are forming a heart.

"Have I angered you?" he asks, his fingers cupping my chin, bringing my face back to his.

And that's another thing. Sometimes he uses California surf speak as well as anyone else around here, and other times, he sounds like he just walked straight out of the pages of *Wuthering Heights.* "No. You have not *angered* me," I say, laughing in spite of myself.

"What's so funny?" he asks, his fingers sliding under my bangs, seeking the scar on my forehead and causing me to pull away. "How'd you get that?" he asks, hand back to his side, gazing at me with such warmth and sincerity I almost confide.

But I don't. Because this is the one night of the year when I get to be someone else. When I get to pretend that I'm not responsible for the end of everything I held dear. Tonight I get to flirt, and play, and make reckless decisions I'll probably live to regret. Because tonight I'm no longer Ever, I'm Marie. And if he's any kind of a Count Fersen he'll shut up and kiss me already.

"I don't want to talk about it," I say, blinking at the water globes that are now red and forming into a tulip.

"What do you want to talk about?" he whispers, gazing at me with those eyes, two infinite pools luring me in.

"I don't want to talk," I whisper, holding my breath as his lips meet mine.

thirteen

If I thought his voice was amazing with the way it envelopes me in silence, if I thought his touch was incredible with the way it awakens my skin, well, the way he kisses is *otherworldly*. And even though I'm no expert, having only kissed a few guys before, I'm still willing to bet that a kiss like this, a kiss this complete and transcendent, is a once-in-a-lifetime thing.

And when he pulls away and gazes into my eyes, I close mine again, grab his lapels, and bring him back to me.

Until Haven says, "Jeez, I've been looking all over for you. I should've known you'd be hiding out here."

I pull away, horrified to be caught in the act, not long after swearing that I don't even like him.

"We were just—"

She raises her hand to stop me. "Please. Spare me the details. I just wanted you to know that Evangeline and I are taking off."

"Already?" I ask, wondering how long we've been out here.

"Yeah, my friend Drina stopped by, she's taking us to another party. You guys are welcome to tag along too—though you seem pretty busy." She smirks.

"Drina?" Damen says, standing so fast his whole body blurs.

"You know her?" Haven asks, but Damen's already gone, moving so fast we scramble to follow.

I rush behind Haven, anxious to catch up, desperate to explain, but when we reach the french doors and I grab onto her shoulder I'm filled with such darkness, such overwhelming anger and despair, the words freeze on my tongue.

Then she pulls away and glares over her shoulder, saying, "I told you you suck at lying," before continuing on.

I take a deep breath and follow behind, trailing them through the kitchen, the den, making my way to the door, my eyes fixed on the back of Damen's head, noticing how he moves so fast and sure, it's as though he knows just where to find her. And by the time I step into the foyer, I freeze when I see them together—he in his eighteenth-century splendor—and she dressed as a Marie Antoinette so rich, so lovely, so exquisite, she puts me to shame.

"And you must be . . ." She lifts her chin as her eyes land on mine, two glowing spheres of deep emerald green.

"Ever," I mumble, taking in the pale blond wig, the creamy flawless skin, the tangle of pearls at her throat, watching as her perfect pink lips display teeth so white they hardly seem real.

I turn to Damen, hoping he can explain, provide some logical explanation for how the redhead from the St. Regis ended up in my foyer. But he's too busy gazing at her to even notice my existence.

"What are you doing here?" he asks, his voice nearly a whisper.

"Haven invited me." She smiles.

And as I glance from her to him, my body fills with a cold hard dread. "How do you know each other?" I ask, noting how Damen's entire demeanor has changed, suddenly growing chilly, cold, and distant—a dark cloud where the sun used to be.

"I met her at Nocturne," Drina says, gazing right at me.

"We're headed there now. I hope you don't mind my stealing her away?"

I narrow my eyes, ignoring the twitch in my heart, the pang in my gut, as I struggle to get some kind of read. But her thoughts are inaccessible, sealed off completely, and her aura nonexistent.

"Oh, silly me, you were referring to Damen and I, weren't you?" She laughs, her eyes traveling slowly over my costume, until coming back to meet mine. And when I don't respond she nods when she says, "We knew each other back in New Mexico."

Only, when she says, "New Mexico," Damen says, "New Orleans." Causing Drina to laugh in a way that never quite reaches her eyes.

"Let's just say we go way back." She nods, extending a hand to my sleeve, her fingers trailing its beaded edge, before sliding down to my wrist. "Lovely dress," she says, clasping me tightly. "Did you make it yourself?"

I wrench my arm free, less from the shock of being mocked and more from the chill of her fingers, the frigid scratch of her cold sharp nails freezing my skin and shooting ice through my veins.

"Isn't she the coolest?" Haven says, gazing at Drina with the sort of awe she usually reserves for vampires, goth rockers, and Damen. While Evangeline stands beside her, rolling her eyes and checking her watch.

"We really need to go if we're going to make it to Nocturne by midnight," Evangeline says.

"You're welcome to join us." Drina smiles. "Fully stocked limo."

And when I glance at Haven, I can hear her thinking: *Say no, say no, please say no!*

Drina glances between Damen and me. "Driver's waiting," she sings.

I turn to him, my heart caving when I see how conflicted he is. Then I clear my throat and force myself to say, "You can go if you want. But I need to stay. I can't exactly leave my own party." Then I laugh, attempting to sound light and breezy, when the truth is, I can barely breathe.

Drina glances between us, brows arched, face haughty, betraying just the briefest glimmer of shock when Damen shakes his head and takes my hand instead of hers.

"So wonderful to meet you Ever," Drina says, pausing before climbing into the limo. "Though I'm sure we'll meet again."

I watch as they disappear from the driveway and onto the street, then I turn to Damen and say, "So, who should I expect next, Stacia, Honor, and Craig?"

And the second it's out, I'm ashamed for having said it, for revealing what a petty, jealous, pathetic person I am. It's not like I didn't know better. So I shouldn't feel so surprised.

Damen's a player. Pure and simple.

Tonight just happened to be my turn.

"Ever," he says, smoothing his thumb over my cheek.

And just as I start to pull away, unwilling to hear his excuses, he looks at me and whispers, "I should probably go too."

I search his eyes, my mind accepting a truth my heart would rather refuse, knowing there's more to the statement, words he failed to include—*I should go—so I can catch up with her.*

"Okay, well thanks for coming," I finally say, sounding less like a prospective girlfriend and more like a waitress after a particularly long shift.

But he just smiles, removes the feather from the back of my

wig, and guides it down the length of my neck, tapping the very tip to my nose as he says, "Souvenir?"

And I've barely had a chance to respond before he's in his car and driving away.

I sink down onto the stairs, my head in my hands, wig teetering precariously, wishing I could just disappear, go back in time, and start over. Knowing I never should've allowed him to kiss me, never should've invited him in—

"There you are!" Sabine says, grabbing hold of my arm and pulling me to my feet. "I've been looking all over for you. Ava agreed to stay just long enough to give you a reading."

"But I don't want a reading," I tell her, not wanting to offend, but not wanting to go through with it either. I just want to go to my room, ditch this wig, and fall into a long, dreamless sleep.

But Sabine's been hitting the party punch, which means she's too tipsy to listen. So she grabs my hand and leads me into the den where Ava is waiting.

"Hello, Ever." Ava smiles as I sink onto the seat, grip the table, and wait for Sabine's inebriated energy to fade.

"Take all the time you need." She smiles.

I gaze at the tarot cards laid out before me. "Um, nothing personal, but I don't want a reading," I say, meeting her eyes before averting my gaze.

"Then I won't give you a reading." She shrugs, gathering the cards and beginning to shuffle. "What do you say we just go through the motions so we can make your aunt happy? She worries about you. Wonders if she's doing the right thing—providing enough freedom, providing too much freedom." She looks at me. "What do you think?"

I shrug and roll my eyes. That hardly qualifies as a revelation.

"She's getting married, you know."

I look up, startled, my eyes meeting hers.

"But not today." She laughs. "Not tomorrow either. So don't worry."

"Why would I worry?" I shift in my seat, watching as she cuts the deck in half before spreading the cards into a crescent. "I want Sabine to be happy, and if that's what it takes—"

"True. But you've experienced so many changes this past year already, haven't you? Changes you're still trying to adjust to. It's not easy, is it?" She gazes at me.

But I don't respond. And why should I? She's yet to say anything remotely earth shattering or insightful. Life is full of change, big deal. I mean, isn't that pretty much the point? To grow, and change, and move along? Besides, it's not like Sabine's an enigma. It's not like she's all that complex, or hard to figure out.

"So how are you handling your gift?" Ava asks, turning some cards, while leaving others face down.

"My *what?*" I peer at her, wondering where she could possibly be going with this.

"Your psychic gift." She smiles, nodding as though it's a fact.

"I don't know what you're talking about." I press my lips together and glance around the room, seeing Miles and Eric dance with Sabine and her date, and unbeknownst to them, Riley.

"It's hard at first." She nods. "Believe me, I know. I was the first to know about my grandmother's passing. She came right into my room, stood at the foot of my bed, and waved good-bye. I was only four at the time, so you can imagine how my parents reacted when I ran into the kitchen to tell them." She shakes her head and laughs. "But you understand, because you see them too, right?"

I stare at the cards, my hands clasped together, not saying a word.

"It can feel so overwhelming, so isolating. But it doesn't have to. You don't have to hide under a hood, killing your eardrums with music you don't even like. There are ways to handle it, and I'd be happy to show you because, Ever, you don't have to live like that."

I grip the edge of the table and rise from my seat, my legs feeling shaky, unsure, my stomach unstable. This lady is crazy if she thinks what I have is a *gift*. Because I know better. I know it's just one more punishment for everything that I did, everything that I caused. It's my own personal burden, and I just have to deal with it. "I have no idea what you're talking about," I finally say.

But she just nods, and slides her card toward me. "When you're ready, you can reach me here."

I take her card, but only because Sabine's watching from across the room and I don't want to seem rude. Then I fold it in the palm of my hand, squishing it into a hard, angry ball, as I ask, "Are we done?" anxious to get away.

"One last thing." She slides the deck into a brown leather case. "I'm worried about your little sister. I think it's time she moves on, don't you?"

I look at her, sitting there so smug and knowing, judging my life when she doesn't even know me. "For your information Riley *has* moved on! She's dead!" I whisper, dropping her crumbled-up card on the table, no longer caring who sees.

But she just smiles and says, "I think you know what I mean."

fourteen

That night, long after the party had ended and all of our guests were gone, I was lying in bed, thinking about Ava, what she said about Riley being stuck, and how I was to blame. I guess I'd always assumed Riley *had* moved on and was choosing to visit on her own free will. Since it's not like I *ask* her to drop by all the time, it's just something she chooses to do. And the times she's not with me, well, I figure she's kicking it somewhere in Heaven. And even though I know Ava's only trying to help, offering to stand in as some sort of psychic big sister, what she doesn't realize is that I don't want any help. That even though I yearn to be normal again, go back to the way things were before, I also know that this is my punishment. This horrible *gift* is what I deserve for all the harm that I've caused, for the lives I cut short. And now I just have to live with it—and try not to harm anyone else.

When I finally did fall asleep, I dreamt of Damen. And everything about it felt so powerful, so intense, so urgent, I thought it was real. But by morning, all I had left were fragmented pieces, shifting images with no beginning or end. The only thing I could clearly remember was the two of us running through a cold windswept canyon—rushing toward something I couldn't quite see.

"What's your problem? Why so grumpy?" Riley asks, perched on the edge of my bed, dressed in a Zorro costume identical to the one Eric wore to the party.

"Halloween's over," I say, staring pointedly at the black leather whip she slaps against the floor.

"Duh." She makes a face and continues to punish the carpet. "So I like the costume, big deal. I'm thinking about dressing up every day."

I lean toward the mirror, insert my tiny diamond-chip studs, and scrape my hair into a ponytail.

"I can't believe you're still dressing like that," she says, her nose crinkling in disgust. "I thought you bagged yourself a boyfriend?" She drops the whip and grabs my iPod, her fingers sliding around the wheel as she scrolls through my playlist.

I turn, wondering what exactly she saw.

"Hel-*lo*? At the party? By the pool? Or was that just a hookup?"

I stare at her, my face flushing crimson. "What do you know about hookups? You're only twelve! And why the heck are you spying on me?"

She rolls her eyes. "Please, like I'd waste my time spying on you when there's way better stuff I can see. For your information, I just so happened to go outside at the exact same moment you shoved your tongue down that Damen guy's throat. And trust me, I wish I *hadn't* seen it."

I shake my head and ransack my drawer, transferring my annoyance at Riley onto my sweatshirts. "Yeah, well, I hate to break it to you, but he's hardly my boyfriend. I haven't talked to him since," I say, hating the way my stomach just curled in on itself when I said that. Then I grab a clean gray sweatshirt and yank it over my head, completely destroying the ponytail I just made.

"I can spy on him if you want. Or haunt him." She smiles.

I look at her and sigh. Part of me wanting to take her up on it, the other part knowing it's time to move on, cut my losses, and forget it ever happened. "Just stay out of it, okay?" I finally say. "I'd like just one normal high school experience, if you don't mind."

"Up to you." She shrugs, tossing me the iPod. "But just so you know, Brandon's back on the market."

I grab a stack of books and stuff them into my backpack, amazed at how that bit of news doesn't make me feel any better.

"Yup, Rachel dumped him on Halloween when she caught him making out with a *Playboy* bunny. Only it wasn't really a *Playboy* bunny, it was Heather Watson dressed as one."

"Seriously?" I gape. "Heather Watson? You're joking." I try to picture it in my mind, but it doesn't add up.

"Scouts honor. You should see her, she lost twenty pounds, ditched the headgear, got her hair straightened, and she looks like a totally different person. Unfortunately, she also acts like a totally different person. She's kind of a, well, you know, a *B* with an itch," she whispers, going back to whipping the floor, as I let that bizarre piece of news sink in.

"You know, you really shouldn't be spying on people," I say, more concerned with her spying on me than any of my old friends. "It's kind of rude, don't you think?" I heave my bag onto my shoulder and head for the door.

Riley laughs. "Don't be ridiculous. It's good to keep up with people from the old neighborhood."

"Are you coming?" I ask, turning impatiently.

"Yup, and I call shotgun!" she says, slipping right past me and hopping onto the banister, her black Zorro cape floating on air as she slides all the way down.

By the time I get to Miles's, he's waiting outside, thumbs tapping his Sidekick. "Just—one—second—okay, done!" He slips onto the passenger seat and peers closely at me. "Now—tell me *everything*! Start to finish. I want all the dirty details, leave nothing out!"

"What're you talking about?" I back out of his driveway and onto the street, shooting a warning glance at Riley who's perched on his knee, blowing on his face and laughing when he tries to adjust the air vent.

Miles looks at me and shakes his head. "Hel-*lo*? Damen? I heard you guys were macking in the moonlight, making out by the pool, hooking up under the moon's silvery—"

"Where are you going with this?" I ask, even though I already know, but hoping there's some way to stop him.

"Listen, word's out so don't even try to deny it. And I would've called you yesterday but my dad confiscated my phone and dragged me to the batting cages, so he could watch me swing like a girl." He laughs. "You should've seen me, I totally camped it up and he was *horror-fied*! That'll teach him. But anyway, back to you. Come on, the divulging starts now. Tell me everything," he says, turning toward me and nodding impatiently. "Was it as awesome as we all dreamed it would be?"

I shrug, glancing at Riley and warning her with my eyes to either cease and desist or disappear. "Sorry to disappoint you," I finally say. "But there's nothing to tell."

"That's not what I heard. Haven said—"

I press my lips and shake my head. Just because I already

know what Haven said doesn't mean I want to hear it spoken out loud. So I cut him off when I say, "Okay fine, we kissed. But just once." I can feel him looking at me, brows raised, lips smirked in suspicion. "Maybe twice. I don't know, it's not like I counted," I mumble, lying like a red-faced, sweaty-palmed, shifty-eyed amateur, and hoping he doesn't notice. Because the truth is I've replayed that kiss so many times it's tattooed on my brain.

"And?" he says, impatient for more.

"And—nothing," I say, relieved when I glance at him and see Riley's gone.

"He didn't call? Or text? Or e-mail? Or drop by?" Miles gasps, visibly upset, wondering what it means not only for me, but the future of our group.

I shake my head and stare straight ahead, angry with myself for not dealing with it better, hating the way my throat's gone all tight as my eyes start to sting.

"But what did he *say*? When he left the party, I mean? What were his very last words?" Miles asks, determined to find some ray of hope in this bleak and bitter landscape.

I turn at the light, remembering our strange and sudden good-bye at the door. Then I face Miles, swallow hard, and say, "He said, 'souvenir?'"

And the moment it's out, I know it's a really bad sign.

Nobody takes a souvenir from a place they plan to frequent.

Miles looks at me, his eyes expressing the words his lips have refused.

"Tell me about it," I say, shaking my head as I pull into the lot.

Even though I'm fully committed to not thinking about Damen, I can't help but feel disappointed when I get to English and see he's not there. Which, of course, makes me think about him even that much more, until I'm teetering on the edge of obsession.

I mean, just because our kiss seemed like something more than just a random hookup doesn't mean he felt the same way. And just because it felt solid and true and transcendent to me doesn't mean he was in on it too. Because no matter how hard I try, I can't shake the image of him and Drina standing together, a perfect Count Fersen with an idyllic Marie. While I stood on the sidelines all shiny and pouffy like the world's biggest wannabe.

I'm just about to click on my iPod when Stacia and Damen burst through the door. Laughing and smiling, shoulders nearly touching, two single white rosebuds clutched in her hand.

And when he leaves her at her desk and heads toward me, I fumble with some papers and pretend I didn't see.

"Hey," he says, sliding onto his seat. Acting like everything's perfectly normal. Like he didn't pull a grope-and-run less than forty-eight hours before.

I place my cheek on my palm and force my face into a yawn, hoping to come off as bored, tired, worn out from activities he couldn't begin to imagine, doodling on a piece of notebook paper with fingers so shaky my pen slips right out of my hand.

I bend down to retrieve it, and when I come back up I find a single red tulip on top of my desk.

"What happened? You run out of white rosebuds?" I ask, flipping through books and papers, as though I've something important to do.

"I would never give you a rosebud," he says, his eyes searching for mine.

But I refuse to meet his gaze, refuse to get sucked into his sadistic little game. I just grab my bag and pretend to search for something inside, cursing under my breath when I find it stuffed full of tulips.

"You're strictly a tulip girl—a red tulip girl." He smiles.

"How exciting for me," I mumble, dropping my bag to the ground and scooting to the farthest part of my seat, having no idea what any of it could possibly mean.

By the time I get to our lunch table, I'm a sweaty mess. Wondering if Damen will be there, if Haven will be there—because even though I haven't seen or spoken to her since Saturday night, I'm willing to bet she still hates me. But despite spending all of third-period chemistry practicing an entire speech in my head, the second I see her, I've lost all the words.

"Well, look who's here," Haven says, gazing at me.

I slide onto the bench beside Miles who's far too busy texting to even notice my existence, and I can't help but wonder if I should try to find some new friends—not that anyone would have me.

"I was just telling Miles how he totally missed out on Nocturne, only he's determined to ignore me." She scowls.

"Only because I was forced to listen to it all through history, and then you still weren't finished and you made me late to Spanish." He shakes his head and continues thumb thumping.

Haven shrugs. "You're just jealous you missed out." Then looking at me, she tries to retreat. "Not that your party wasn't cool or anything, because it was, *totally cool*. It's just—this was more my scene, you know? I mean, you understand, right?"

I polish my apple against my sleeve and shrug, reluctant to hear any more than I already have about Nocturne, *her scene*, or Drina. But when I finally do look at her, I'm startled to see how her usual yellow contacts have been swapped for a brand-new green.

A green so familiar it robs me of breath.

A green that can only be described as—*Drina green*.

"You should've seen it, there was this huge long line out front, but the second they saw Drina, they let us right in. We didn't even have to pay! Not for *anything,* the whole night was comped! I even crashed in her room. She's staying in this amazing suite at the St. Regis until she finds a more permanent place. You should see it: ocean view, Jacuzzi tub, rockin' minibar, the works!" She looks at me, emerald eyes wide with excitement, waiting for an enthusiastic response I just can't provide.

I press my lips together and take in the rest of her appearance, noticing how her eyeliner is softer, smokier, more like Drina's, and how her bloodred lipstick has been swapped for a lighter, rosier, Drina-like shade. Even her hair, which she's ironed straight for as long as I've known her, is now soft and wavy and styled like Drina's. And her dress is fitted, silky, and vintage, like something Drina might wear.

"So where's Damen?" Haven looks at me as though I should know.

I take a bite of my apple and shrug.

"What happened? I thought you guys hooked up?" she asks, refusing to let it go.

And before I can answer, Miles looks up from his Sidekick and shoots her *the look*—the one with the direct translation of: *Caution all ye who enter.*

She glances from Miles to me, then shakes her head and sighs. "Whatever. I just want you to know that I'm totally cool with it, so no worries, okay? And I'm sorry if I got a little weird on you." She shrugs. "But I'm totally over it now. Seriously. Pinky-swear."

I reluctantly curl my pinky around hers and tune into her energy. And I'm completely amazed to *see* that she really does mean it. I mean, just this weekend she'd pegged me as Public Enemy #1, but now she's clearly not bothered, though I can't really see why.

"Haven—" I start, wondering if I should really do this, but then figuring, *oh, what the hell, I have nothing to lose.*

She looks at me, smiling, waiting.

"Um, when you guys went to—Nocturne, did you maybe—by chance—happen to run into Damen?" I press my lips and wait, feeling Miles give me a sharp look, while Haven just stares at me, clearly confused. "Because the thing is, he left shortly after you guys—so I thought maybe—"

She shakes her head and shrugs. "Nope, never saw him," she says, removing a dab of frosting from her lip with the tip of her tongue.

And even though I know better, I choose that moment to take a visual journey through the lunch table caste system, the alphabetical hierarchy, starting with our lowly table Z and working toward A. Wondering if I'll find Damen and Stacia frolicking in a field of rosebuds, or engaging in some other sordid act I'd rather not see.

But even though it's business as usual over there, with everyone up to the same old antics, for today at least, it's flower free.

I guess because Damen's not there.

fifteen

I'd just fallen asleep when Damen calls. And even though I'd spent the last two days convincing myself not to like him, the second I hear his voice, I surrender.

"Is it too late?"

I squint at the glowing green numbers on my alarm clock, confirming it is, but answering, "No, it's okay."

"Were you asleep?"

"Almost." I prop my pillows against my cloth-covered headboard, then lean back against them.

"I was wondering if I could come over?"

I gaze at the clock again, but only to prove his question is crazy. "Probably not such a good idea," I tell him, which is followed by such a prolonged silence I'm sure he's hung up.

"I'm sorry I missed you at lunch," he finally says. "Art too. I left right after English."

"Um, okay," I mumble, unsure how to respond, since it's not like we're a couple, it's not like he's accountable to me.

"Are you sure it's too late?" he asks, his tone deep and persuasive. "I'd really like to see you. I won't stay long."

I smile, thrilled with this tiny shift in power, to be calling the shots for a change, and allowing myself a mental high-five when I say, "Tomorrow in English works for me."

"How about I drive you to school?" he asks, his voice nearly convincing me to forget about Stacia, Drina, his hasty retreat, everything—just clean the slate, let bygones be bygones, start all over again.

But I haven't come this far to give up so easily. So I force the words from my lips when I say, "Miles and I carpool. So I'll just see you in English." And knowing better than to risk his changing my mind, I snap my phone shut and toss it across the room.

The next morning when Riley pops in, she stands before me and says, "Still cranky?"

I roll my eyes.

"I'll take that as a *yes*." She laughs, hopping on top of my dresser and kicking her heels against the drawers.

"So, who are you dressed as today?" I toss a pile of books into my bag and glance at her tight bodice, full skirt, and cascading brown hair.

"Elizabeth Swann." She smiles.

I squint, trying to remember that name. *"Pirates?"*

"Duh." She crosses her eyes and sticks out her tongue. "So what's up with you and Count Fersen?"

I sling my bag over my shoulder and head for the door, determined to ignore the question when I call, "Coming?"

She shakes her head. "Not today. I have an appointment."

I lean against the doorjamb and squint. "What do you mean by 'appointment'?"

But she just shakes her head and hops off the dresser. "None of your beeswax." She laughs, walking straight through the wall and disappearing.

Since Miles was running late, I end up running late too, and by the time we make it to school, the parking lot is completely full. All except for the very best, most sought-after space.

The one on the very end.

The one closest to the gate.

The one that just happens to be right next to Damen's.

"*How* did you do it?" Miles asks, grabbing his books and climbing out of my tiny red car, gazing at Damen like he's the world's sexiest magic act.

"Do what?" Damen asks, gazing at me.

"Save the spot. You have to get here like, way before the school year even begins to snatch this one."

Damen laughs, his eyes searching mine. But I just nod like he's my pharmacist or mailman, *not* the guy I've been obsessing over since the moment I saw him.

"Bell's gonna ring," I say, rushing past the gate and heading toward class, noticing how he moves so quickly he beats me to the door with no visible effort.

I storm toward Honor and Stacia, purposely kicking Stacia's bag when she gazes at Damen and says, "Hey, where's my rosebud?"

Then regretting it the second he answers, "Sorry, not today."

He slides onto his seat and gives me an amused look. "Someone's in a foul mood." He laughs.

But I just shrug and drop my bag to the floor.

"What's the rush?" He leans toward me. "Mr. Robins stayed home."

I turn. "How'd you—" but then I stop before I can finish. I mean, how can Damen possibly know what I know—that Mr. Robins is still at home, still hungover, still grieving the wife and daughter who recently left him?

"I saw the substitute while I was waiting for you." He smiles. "She looked a little lost, so I escorted her to the teachers' lounge, but she seemed so confused she'll probably end up in the science lab instead."

And the second he says it I know that it's true, having just *seen* her entering the wrong class, having mistaken it for our room.

"So tell me. What have I done to anger you so?"

I glance up as Stacia whispers in Honor's ear, watching as they shake their heads and glare at me.

"Ignore them, they're idiots," Damen whispers, leaning toward me and placing his hand over mine. "I'm sorry I haven't been around much. I had a visitor; I couldn't get away."

"You mean Drina?" And the moment it's out, I cringe at how awful and jealous I sound. Wishing I could be cool, calm, and collected, act as though I didn't even notice how everything changed the moment she appeared. But the truth is, that's pretty much impossible for me, since I'm much closer to paranoid than naïve.

"Ever—" he starts.

But since I've already started, I may as well continue. "Have you seen Haven lately? She's like a Drina Mini-Me. She dresses like her, acts like her, even has the same eye color. Seriously, stop by the lunch table sometime, you'll see." I glare at him, as though he's responsible, as though it's his fault. But the moment our eyes meet, I'm right back under his spell, a helpless hunk of steel to his irresistible magnet.

He takes a deep breath then shakes his head as he says, "Ever, it's not what you think."

I pull away and press my lips together. *You have no idea what I think.*

"Let me make it up to you. Let me take you out, somewhere special, please?"

I can feel the warmth of his gaze on my skin, but I won't risk trying to meet it. I want him to wonder, to doubt. I want to drag it out for as long as I possibly can.

So I shift in my seat, glance at him briefly, and say, "We'll see."

When I exit fourth-period history, Damen is waiting outside the door. And assuming he just wants to walk me to the lunch table, I say, "Let me just drop my bag in my locker before we head over."

"No need." He smiles, securing his arm around my waist. "The surprise starts now."

"Surprise?" And when I look into his eyes, the whole world shrinks, until it's just me and him, surrounded by static.

He smiles. "You know, I take you somewhere special—so special you forgive my transgressions."

"And what about our classes? We just blow off the rest of the day?" I fold my arms across my chest, though it's mostly for show.

He laughs and leans toward me, his lips grazing the side of my neck as they form the word—*Yes.*

And as I pull away I'm amazed to hear myself answer with *how* instead of *no.*

"No worries." He smiles, squeezing my hand as he leads me through the gate. "You'll always be safe with me."

sixteen

"Disneyland?" I climb out of my car and gaze at him in shock. Out of all the places I thought we'd end up, this never cracked the list.

"I hear it's the happiest place on earth." He laughs. "Have you been?"

I shake my head.

"Good, then I'll be your guide." He slips his arm through mine and leads me through the gates, and as we wander down Main Street I try to imagine him coming here before. He's so sleek, so sophisticated, so sexy, so smooth—it's hard to imagine him trolling a place where Mickey Mouse rules. "It's always better during the week when it's not so crowded," he says, crossing the street. "Come on, I'll show you New Orleans, it's my favorite part."

"You come here enough to have favorites?" I stop in the middle of the street and stare at him. "I thought you just moved here?"

He laughs. "I did just move here. But that doesn't mean I haven't been," he says, pulling me toward the Haunted Mansion.

After the Haunted Mansion we head for the *Pirates* ride, and when that's over, he looks at me and says, "So which one's your favorite?"

"Um, *Pirates*." I nod. "I think."

He looks at me.

"Well, they're both pretty cool." I shrug. "But *Pirates* has Johnny Depp, so that kind of gives it an unfair advantage, don't you think?"

"Johnny Depp? So that's what I'm up against?" He raises a brow.

I shrug, taking in Damen's dark jeans, black long-sleeved T-shirt, and those boots, his easy good looks dwarfing every Hollywood actor I can think of, though it's not like I'll admit that.

"Wanna go again?" he asks, dark eyes flashing.

So we do. And then we head back to the Haunted Mansion. And when we reach the part at the end, where the ghosts hitch a ride in your car, I half expect to see Riley scrunched in between us, laughing and waving and clowning around. But instead, it's just one of those cartoon Disney ghosts, and I remember Riley's appointment and figure she must be too busy.

After yet another go on those rides, we end up at a waterfront table in the Blue Bayou, the restaurant inside the *Pirates* ride. And as I sip my iced tea I look at him and say, "Okay, I happen to know this is a really big park with more than two rides. Rides that have nothing to do with pirates or ghosts."

"I heard that too." He smiles, spearing calamari with his fork and offering it to me. "They used to have this one called Mission to Mars. It was known as the make-out ride, mostly because it was very dark inside."

"Is it still here?" I ask, my face turning every shade of crimson when I realize how eager I sound. "Not that I want to ride it or anything. I was just curious."

He looks at me, his face clearly amused. Then he shakes his head and says, "No, it closed a long time ago."

"So you were going on the make-out ride when you were what—two?" I ask, reaching for a sausage-stuffed mushroom and hoping I'll like it.

"Not me." He smiles. "That was way before my time."

Normally I'd do anything to avoid a place like this. A place so congested with the random energy of people, their bright swirling auras, their odd collection of thoughts. But it's different with Damen, effortless, pleasant. Because whenever we touch, whenever he speaks, it's like we're the only ones here.

After lunch, we stroll around the park, going on all the fast rides and avoiding the water rides, or at least the ones where you get soaked. And when it gets dark, he leads me over to Sleeping Beauty Castle, where we stop near the moat and wait for the fireworks show to begin.

"So, am I forgiven?" he asks, arms snaking around my waist, teeth nipping at my neck, my jaw, my ear. The sudden burst of fireworks, their booming crackle and snap, seem faint and far away, as our bodies press together and his lips move against mine.

"Look," he whispers, pulling away and pointing toward the expanse of night sky, a profusion of purple color wheels, golden waterfalls, silver fountains, pink chrysanthemums, and for the grand finale—a dozen red tulips. All of it flaring and blasting, in such quick succession it vibrates the concrete under our feet.

Wait—red tulips?

I glance at Damen, eyes full of questions, but he just smiles and nods toward the sky, and even though the edges are sparking and fading, the memory is solid, imprinted on my mind.

Then he pulls me close, lips to my ear when he says, "Show's over, fat lady sang."

"You calling Tinkerbell fat?" I laugh as he takes my hand and leads me through the gates and back to our cars.

I climb into my Miata and get settled in, smiling as he leans through my window and says, "Don't worry, there'll be more days like this. Next time I'll take you to California Adventure."

"I thought we just had a California adventure." I laugh, amazed by the way he always seems to know just what I'm thinking before I've even had a chance to utter the words. "Should I follow you again?" I slip my key in the ignition and start the engine.

He shakes his head. "I'll follow *you*." He smiles. "Got to see you home safely."

I pull out of the lot, merge onto the southbound freeway, and head home. And when I check the rearview mirror, I can't help but smile when I see Damen right there behind me.

I have a boyfriend!

A gorgeous, sexy, smart, charming boyfriend!

One who makes me feel normal again.

One who makes me forget that I'm not.

I reach over to the passenger seat and pluck my new sweat-shirt from its bag, running my fingers over the Mickey Mouse appliqué on the front, remembering the moment Damen chose it for me.

"Notice how this one doesn't have a hood," he'd said, holding it against me, and estimating the fit.

"What are you trying to say?" I squinted into the mirror, wondering if he hates my look as much as Riley thinks.

But he just shrugged. "What can I say? I prefer you hoodless."

I smile at the memory, the way he kissed me as we stood in line to pay, the warm, sweet feel of his lips on mine—

And when my cell phone rings, I glance in my rearview mirror to see Damen holding his.

"Hey," I say, lowering my voice so that it's husky and deep.

"Save it," Haven says. "Sorry to disappoint you, but it's just little ole me."

"Oh, so what's up?" I ask, signaling my intended lane change so that Damen can follow.

Only he's no longer there.

I glance between my side and rearview mirrors, frantically scanning all four lanes, but still, no Damen.

"Are you even listening to me?" Haven asks, clearly annoyed.

"Sorry, what?" I ease up on the gas and look over my shoulder, searching for Damen's black BMW, as someone in a monster truck passes, honks, and flips me the bird.

"I said Evangeline is missing!"

"What do you mean 'missing'?" I ask, hesitating for as long as I can before merging onto the 133, with Damen still nowhere in sight, even though I'm sure he didn't pass me.

"I called her cell a bunch of times and she didn't pick up."

"*And,*" I say, anxious to get through this call-screening story so I can get back to my own missing person's case.

"*And,* not only does she not answer, not only is she not in her apartment, but nobody's seen her since *Halloween.*"

"What do you mean?" I check my side mirrors, my rearview mirrors, and glance over each shoulder, but still come up empty. "Didn't she go home with you guys?"

"Not exactly," Haven says, her voice small, contrite.

And after two more cars honk and give me the finger, I give up. Promising myself that as soon as I'm done with Haven I'll call Damen on his cell and sort it all out.

"Hel-*lo*?" she says, practically shouting. "I mean, jeez, if you're too busy for me, then just say so. I can always call Miles, you know."

I take a deep breath, striving for patience. "Haven, I'm sorry, okay? I'm trying to drive and I'm a little distracted. Besides, you and I both know Miles is still at acting class, which is why you called me." I merge over to the far left lane, determined to punch it and get home as quickly as I can.

"Whatever," she mumbles. "Anyway, I haven't exactly told you this yet, but, well, Drina and I kind of left without her."

"You *what?*"

"You know, at Nocturne. She just sort of—disappeared. I mean, we looked everywhere, but we just couldn't find her. So we figured she met someone, which believe me, is not out of character, and then—well, we sort of—*left.*"

"You left her in L.A.? *On Halloween night?* When every freak in the city is on the loose?" And the second it's out of my mouth, I *see* it—the three of them in some dark, seamy club, Drina leading Haven to the VIP room for a drink, purposely eluding Evangeline. And even though it goes blank after that, I definitely didn't see any guy.

"What were we supposed to do? I mean, I don't know if you know this, but she's eighteen, which means she can pretty much do what she wants. Besides, Drina said she'd keep an eye on her, but then she lost track of her too. I just got off the phone with her, she feels awful."

"Drina feels awful?" I roll my eyes, finding that hard to believe. Drina doesn't seem like the type to feel much of anything, much less remorse.

"What's that supposed to mean? You don't even know her."

I press my lips and accelerate hard, partly because I *know* this strip of road is currently cop-free, and partly because I want to outrun Haven, Drina, Evangeline, and Damen's strange disappearance, everything, all of it—even though I know that I can't.

"Sorry," I finally mumble, lifting my foot and easing into a regular speed.

"Whatever. I just—I feel so awful, and I don't know what to do."

"Did you call her parents?" I ask, even though I just sensed the answer.

"Her mom's a drunk, lives in Arizona somewhere, and her dad skipped out when she was still in the womb. And trust me, her landlord just wants her stuff cleared out so he can turn the apartment. We even filed a police report, but they didn't seem overly concerned."

"I know," I say, adjusting my lights for the dark, canyon route.

"What do you mean *you know?*"

"I mean I *know* how you must feel." I scramble to cover.

She sighs. "So where are you? Why weren't you at lunch?"

"I'm in Laguna Canyon, on my way home from Disneyland. Damen took me." I smile at the memory, though it turns pretty quick.

"Omigod that's *so* bizarre," Haven says.

"Tell me," I agree, still not used to the idea of him kicking it in the Magic Kingdom even after seeing it with my own eyes.

"No, I mean Drina went too. Said she hasn't been in years and wanted to see how it's changed. Isn't that wild? Did you guys run into her?"

"Um, no," I say, trying to sound matter of fact despite my churning stomach, sweaty palms, and overwhelming feeling of dread.

"Huh. Weird. But then again, it is pretty huge and crowded." She laughs.

"Yeah, yeah it is," I say. "Listen, I gotta go, see you tomorrow?" And before she can even respond, I pull to the side of the road and park by the curb, searching my call list for Damen's number, and pounding hard on the wheel when I see it's marked *private*.

Some boyfriend. I don't even have his phone number, much less know where he lives.

seventeen

Last night, when Damen finally called (at least I assumed it was him since the display read *private*), I let it go straight into voice mail. And this morning, while I'm getting ready for school, I delete it without even listening.

"Aren't you at least curious?" Riley asks, spinning around in my desk chair, her slicked-back hair and *Matrix* costume a shiny black blur.

"No." I glare at the Mickey Mouse sweatshirt still in its bag, then reach for one that he *didn't* buy me.

"Well, you could've let me listen, so I could give you the gist."

"Double no." I twist my hair into a bun, then stab it with a pencil to hold it in place.

"Well, don't take it out on your hair. I mean, jeez, what'd it ever do to you?" She laughs. But when I don't respond she looks at me and says, "I don't get you. Why are you always so angry? So you lost him on the freeway, and he forgot to give you his number. Big deal. I mean, when did you get so dang paranoid?"

I shake my head and turn away, knowing she's right. I am angry. And paranoid. And things far worse than that. Just your everyday, garden-variety, easily annoyed, thought-hearing, aura-seeing, spirit-sensing freak. But what she doesn't know is that there's more to the story than I'm willing to share.

Like Drina trailing us to Disneyland.

And how Damen always disappears whenever she's near.

I turn back to Riley, shaking my head as I take in her sleek shiny costume. "How long are you going to play Halloween?"

She folds her arms and pouts. "For as long as I want."

And when I see her bottom lip quiver, I feel like the world's biggest grouch.

"Look, I'm sorry," I say, grabbing my bag and slinging it over my shoulder, wishing my life would just stabilize, find some kind of balance.

"No you're not." She glares at me. "It's so obvious you're not."

"Riley, I am, really. And believe me, I don't want to fight."

She shakes her head and gazes up at the ceiling, tapping her foot against the carpeted floor.

"Are you coming?" I head for the door, but she refuses to answer. So I take a deep breath, and say, "Come on, Riley. You know I can't afford to be late. Please make up your mind."

She closes her eyes and shakes her head and when she looks at me again, her eyes have gone red. "I don't have to be here, you know!"

I grip the door handle, needing to leave yet knowing I can't, not after she's said that. "What're you talking about?"

"I mean, *here*! All of *this*! You and me. Our little visits. I don't have to *do* this."

I stare at her, my stomach curling, willing her to stop, not wanting to hear any more. I've gotten so used to her presence I never considered the alternative, that there might be someplace else she'd rather be.

"But—but I thought you liked being here?" I say, my throat tight and sore, my voice betraying my panic.

"I *do* like being here. But, well, maybe it's not the right thing. Maybe I should be somewhere *else*! Did you ever think of that?" She's looking at me, her eyes full of anguish and confusion, and even though I'm now officially late for school, there's no way I can leave.

"Riley—I—what exactly do you mean?" I ask, wishing I could rewind this whole morning and start over again.

"Well, Ava says—"

"*Ava?*" My eyes practically bug out of my head.

"Yeah, you know, the psychic, from the Halloween party? The one who could see me?"

I shake my head and open the door, looking over my shoulder to say, "I hate to break it to you, but Ava's a quack. A phony. A charlatan. A con artist! You shouldn't listen to a word she says. She's *crazy!*"

But Riley just shrugs, her eyes on mine. "She said some really interesting things."

And her voice bears so much pain and worry, I'll say anything to make it go away. "Listen." I peer down the hall, even though I know Sabine's no longer here. "I don't want to hear about Ava. I mean, if you want to visit her, even after everything I just told you, then fine, it's not like I can stop you. Just remember that Ava doesn't know us. And she has absolutely no right to judge us or the fact that we like to hang together. It's none of her business. It's *our* business." And when I look at her, I see that her eyes are still wide, her lip still quivering, and my heart sinks right to the floor.

"I really need to leave, so are you coming or not?" I whisper.

"Not." She glares.

So I take a deep breath, shake my head, and slam the door behind me.

Since Miles was smart enough not to hang out and wait, I drive to school alone. And even though the bell already rang, Damen is there, waiting next to his car, in the second best spot next to mine.

"Hey," he says, coming around to my side and leaning in for a kiss.

But I just grab my bag and race for the gate.

"I'm sorry I lost you yesterday. I called your cell but you didn't answer." He trails alongside me.

I grab hold of the cold iron bars and shake them as hard as I can. But when they don't even budge, I close my eyes and press my forehead against them, knowing I'm too late, it's useless.

"Did you get my message?"

I let go of the gate and head for the office, envisioning the awful moment when I'll step inside and get nailed for yesterday's ditching and today's tardy.

"What's wrong?" he asks, grabbing hold of my hand and turning my insides to warm molten liquid. "I thought we had fun. I thought you enjoyed it?"

I lean against the low brick wall and sigh. Feeling rubbery, weak, completely defenseless.

"Or were you just humoring me?" He squeezes my hand, his eyes begging me not to be mad.

And just as I start to fold, just when I've almost swallowed his bait, I drop his hand and move away. Wincing as memories of Haven, our phone call, and his strange disappearance on the freeway rush over me like a tidal wave. "Did you know Drina went to Disneyland too?" I say, and the second I say it, I realize how petty I sound. Yet now that it's out there, I may as well continue. "Is there something I should know? Something you need to tell me?" I press my lips together and brace for the worst.

But he just looks at me, gazing into my eyes as he says, "I'm not interested in Drina. I'm only interested in *you*."

I stare at the ground, wanting to believe, wishing it were only that easy. But when he takes my hand again, I realize it *is* that easy, because all of my doubts just slip right away.

"So now's the part when you tell me you feel the same way," he says, gazing at me.

I hesitate, my heartbeat so severe I'm sure he can hear it. But when I pause for too long, the moment flees, and he slips his arm around my waist and leads me back to the gate.

"That's okay." He smiles. "Take your time. There's no rush, no expiration date." He laughs. "But for now, let's get you to class."

"But we have to go through the office." I stop in my tracks and squint at him. "The gate's locked, remember?"

He shakes his head. "Ever, the gate's not locked."

"Uh, sorry, but I just tried to open it. It's locked," I remind him.

He smiles. "Will you trust me?"

I look at him.

"What's it going to cost you? A few steps? Some additional tardy minutes?"

I glance between the office and him, then I shake my head and follow, all the way back to the gate that is somehow, inexplicably open.

"But I saw it! And you saw it too!" I face him, not understanding how any of this could have happened. "I even shook them, as hard as I could, and they wouldn't budge an inch."

But he just kisses my cheek and ushers me through, laughing as he says, "Go on. And don't worry, Mr. Robins is incapacitated and the sub's in a daze. You'll be fine."

"You're not coming?" I ask, that needy, panicky feeling building inside me again.

But he just shrugs. "I'm emancipated. I do what I want."

"Yeah, but—" I stop, realizing his phone number's not the only thing missing. I barely even know this guy. And I can't help but wonder how he can possibly make me feel so good, so normal, when everything about him is so *abnormal.* Though it's not until I've turned away that I realize he's yet to explain what happened on the freeway last night.

But before I can ask he's right there beside me, taking my hand as he says, "My neighbor called. My sprinklers failed and my yard was flooding. I tried to get your attention but you were on the phone, and I didn't want to bother you."

I gaze down at our hands, bronze and pale, strong and frail, such an unlikely pair.

"Now go. I'll see you after school, I promise." He smiles, plucking a single red tulip from the back of my ear.

Usually, I try not to dwell on my old life. I try not to think about my old house, my old friends, my old family, my old self. And even though I've gotten pretty good at heading off that particular storm, recognizing the signs—the stinging eyes, the shortness of breath, the overwhelming feeling of hollowness and despair—before they can take hold, sometimes it just hits, without warning, without time to prepare. And all I can do when that happens is curl up in a ball and wait for it to pass.

Which is pretty hard to do in the middle of history class.

So while Mr. Munoz is going on and on about Napoleon, my throat closes, my stomach clenches, and my eyes start to sear so abruptly, I bolt from my seat and race for the door, oblivious to the sound of my teacher calling me back, immune to my classmates' derisive laugh.

I turn the corner, blinded by tears, gasping for air, my insides feeling empty, cleaned out, a hollow shell folding in on itself. And by the time I see Stacia it's way too late, and I knock her with such speed and force she crashes to the ground and rips a hole in her dress.

"What *the*—" She gapes at her splayed limbs and torn dress, before leveling her gaze right on me. "You *fucking* ripped it, you *freak!*" She pokes her fist through the tear, displaying the damage.

And even though I feel bad for what happened, there's no time to help. The grief is about to consume me and I can't let her see.

I start to brush past her just as she grabs hold of my arm and struggles to stand, the touch of her skin infusing me with such dark dismal energy it robs me of breath.

"For your information, this dress is *designer*. Which means *you* are going to replace it," she says, fingers squeezing so tight, I fear I might faint. "And trust me, it doesn't stop there." She shakes her head and glares. "You are gonna be so fucking sorry you ran into me, you're gonna wish you *never* came to this school."

"Like Kendra?" I say, my stance suddenly steady, my stomach settling into a much calmer state.

She loosens her grip but doesn't let go.

"You planted those drugs in her locker. You got her expelled, destroyed her credibility so they'd believe you and not her," I say, transcribing the scene in my head.

She drops my arm and takes a step back, the color draining from her face as she says, "Who told you that? You didn't even go here when that happened."

I shrug, knowing that's true, though it's hardly the point. "Oh, and there's more," I say, advancing on her, my own personal storm having passed, my overwhelming grief miraculously cured by the fear in her eyes. "I know you cheat on tests, steal from your parents, clothing stores, your friends—it's all fair game as far as you're concerned. I know you record Honor's phone calls and keep a file of her e-mails and text messages in case she ever decides to turn on you. I know that you flirt with her stepdad, which, by the way, is totally disgusting, but unfortunately it gets much worse than that. I know all about Mr. Barnes—Barnum? Whatever, you know who I mean, your ninth-grade history teacher? The one you tried to seduce? And when he wouldn't bite you tried to blackmail him instead, threatening to tell the school principal and his poor pregnant wife . . ." I shake my head in disgust, her behavior so squalid, so self-serving, it hardly seems real.

And yet, there she is, standing before me, eyes wide, lips trembling, stunned to have all of her dirty little secrets revealed. And instead of feeling bad or guilty for exposing her, for using my *gift* in this way, seeing this despicable person, this awful selfish bully who's taunted me since my very first day, reduced to a shaky, sweaty mess, is more gratifying than I ever would've imagined. And with my nausea and grief now merely a memory, I figure, *what the heck,* I may as well continue.

"Should I go on?" I ask. "Because believe me, I can. There's plenty more, but you already know that, don't you?"

I go after her, me walking forward, her stumbling backward, eager to put as much distance between us as she possibly can.

"What are you? Some kind of witch?" she whispers, eyes scanning the corridor, looking for help, an exit, anything to get away from me.

I laugh. Not admitting, not denying, just wanting her to think twice before she messes with me again.

But just as quickly she stops, finds her footing, and looks me in the eye when she says, "Then again, it's your word against mine." Her lips curve into a grin. "And who do you think people will believe? *Me,* the most popular girl in the junior class? Or *you,* the biggest fucking freak that ever came to this school?"

She has a point.

She fingers the hole in her dress, then shakes her head, and says, "Stay away from me, *freak*. Because if you don't, I swear to God you'll regret it."

And when she steps forward, she slams into my shoulder so hard, I've no doubt she means it.

When I get to the lunch table I try not to gawk, but Haven's hair is purple and I'm not sure if I should mention it.

"Don't even try to pretend you don't see it. It's awful, I know." She laughs. "Right after I hung up with you last night I tried to dye it red, you know, that gorgeous coppery shade like Drina's? Only this is what I ended up with." She grabs a chunk of it and scowls. "I look like an eggplant on a stick. But only for a few more hours, 'cuz after school, Drina's taking me to some big celebrity salon up in L.A. You know, one of those A-list hot spots booked a full year in advance? Only she was totally able to sneak me in last minute. I swear, she is *so* connected, she's amazing."

"Where's Miles?" I ask, cutting her off, not wanting to hear another word about the *amazing* Drina and her velvet rope–crashing abilities.

"Memorizing his lines. Community theater's doing a production of *Hairspray,* and he's hoping for the lead."

"Isn't the lead a girl?" I open my lunch pack, finding half a sandwich, a cluster of grapes, a bag of chips, and more tulips.

She shrugs. "He tried to convince me to try out too, but it's so not my thing. So, where's tall, dark, and hot, a.k.a. your boyfriend?" she asks, unfolding her napkin, and using it as a placemat for her strawberry-sprinkle cupcake.

I shrug, remembering how, yet again, I forgot to secure his number, or find out where he lives. "Enjoying the perks of emancipation I guess," I finally say, unwrapping my sandwich and taking a bite. "Any news on Evangeline?"

She shakes her head. "None. But check this out." She raises her sleeve, showing me the underside of her wrist.

I squint at the beginnings of a small circular tattoo, a rough sketch of a snake eating its tail. And even though it's far from complete, for the briefest moment, I actually see it slither and move. But as soon as I blink, it's stagnant again.

"What is that?" I whisper, noticing how the energy it emanates fills me with dread, though I can't fathom why.

"It's supposed to be a surprise. I'll show you when it's finished." She smiles. "In fact, I shouldn't have even told you." She adjusts her sleeve and glances around. "I mean, I promised I wouldn't. I guess I'm just too excited, and sometimes I suck at keeping secrets. Especially my own."

I look at her, trying to tune into her energy, find some logical reason for why my stomach should feel as awful as it does, but I come up empty. "Promised who? What's going on?" I ask, noticing how her aura is a dull charcoal gray, its edges loose and frayed all around.

But she just laughs and pretends to zip her lips shut. "Forget it," she says. "You'll just have to wait."

eighteen

When I get home from school, Damen is waiting on the front steps, smiling in a way that clears the sky of clouds and erases all doubts.

"How'd you get past the gate guard?" I ask, knowing for a fact that I didn't call him in.

"Charm and an expensive car works every time." He laughs, brushing the seat of his dark designer jeans and following me inside. "So, how was your day?"

I shrug, knowing I'm breaking the most fundamental rule of all—never invite a stranger inside—even if this stranger is supposedly my boyfriend. "You know, the usual routine," I finally say. "The substitute vowed to never return, Ms. Machado asked *me* to never return—" I glance at him, tempted to keep making stuff up since it's clear he's not listening. Because even though he nods like he is, his gaze is preoccupied, distant.

I head for the kitchen, poke my head in the fridge, and ask, "What about you? What'd you do?" Then I hold up a bottle of water in offering, but he shakes his head and sips his red drink.

"Went for a drive, surfed, waited for the bell to ring so I could see you again." He smiles.

"You know you could've just gone to school and then you wouldn't have had to wait for anything," I say.

"I'll try to remember that tomorrow." He laughs.

I lean against the counter, twisting the cap on my bottle around and around, nervous about being alone with him in this big empty house, with so many unanswered questions and no idea where to begin.

"You wanna go outside and hang by the pool?" I finally say, thinking the fresh air and open space might calm my nerves.

But he shakes his head and takes my hand. "I'd rather go upstairs, and check out your room."

"How do you know it's upstairs?" I ask, squinting at him.

But he just laughs. "Aren't they always?"

I hesitate, wavering between allowing this to happen and finding a polite way to evict him.

But when he squeezes my hand and says, "Come on, I promise not to bite," his smile is so irresistible, his touch so warm and inviting, that my only hope as I lead him upstairs is that Riley won't be there.

The moment we reach the top of the stairs, she runs from the den and calls, "Omigod, I am *so* sorry! I so don't want to fight with—*oops!*" She stops short and gapes, her eyes wide as Frisbees, darting between us.

But I just continue toward my room as though I didn't even see her, hoping she'll have the good sense to disappear until later. Much later.

"Looks like you left your TV on," Damen says, going into the den, while I glare at Riley who's skipping alongside him, looking him up and down, and giving him two very enthusiastic thumbs up.

And even though I beg her with my eyes to leave, she

plops right down on the couch and places her feet on his knees.

I storm into the bathroom, furious with her for not taking the hint, for overstaying her visit and refusing to split, knowing it's just a matter of time before she does something crazy, something I can never explain. So I yank off my sweatshirt and race through my routine, brushing my teeth with one hand, rolling deodorant with the other, spitting into the sink just seconds before pulling on a clean white tee. Then I ditch the ponytail, smear on some lip balm, spritz some perfume, and rush out the door, only to find Riley still there, peering into his ears.

"Let me show you the balcony, the view's amazing," I say, anxious to remove him from Riley.

But he just shakes his head and says, "Later." Patting the cushion beside him as Riley jumps up and cheers.

I watch as he sits there, innocent, unaware, trusting he's got the couch to himself, when the truth is, that prick in his ear, that itch on his knee, that chill on his neck, is courtesy of my dead little sister.

"Um, I left my water in the bathroom," I say, looking pointedly at Riley and turning to leave, thinking she'll follow if she knows what's good for her.

But Damen stands up and says, "Allow me."

And I watch as he maneuvers between the couch and table in such a way that clearly *avoids* Riley's dangling legs.

Then she gapes at me, and I gawk at her, and the next thing I know she's disappeared.

"All set," Damen says, tossing me the bottle and moving freely through the space that, just a moment ago, he navigated so carefully. And when he catches me gawking, he smiles and says, "What?"

But I just shake my head and stare at the TV, telling myself it was merely a coincidence. That there's no possible way he could've seen her.

"So would you please just explain how you do it?"

We're sitting outside, curled up on the lounge chair, having just devoured almost an entire pizza, most of which was eaten by me, since Damen eats more like a supermodel than a guy. You know—pick, pick—move the food around—take a bite— pick some more, but mostly he just sipped his drink.

"Do what?" he asks, arms wrapped loosely around me, chin resting on my shoulder.

"Do *everything*! Seriously. You never do homework, yet you know all the answers, you pick up a brush, dip it in paint, and voilà, the next thing you know you've created a Picasso that's even better than Picasso! Are you bad at sports? Painfully unco-ordinated? Come on, tell me!"

He sighs. "Well, I've never been much good at baseball," he says, pressing his lips to my ear. "But I am a world-class soccer player, and I'm fairly skilled at surfing, if I say so myself."

"Must be music, then. Got a tin ear?"

"Bring me a guitar and I'll strum you a tune. Or even a piano, violin, or saxophone will do."

"Then what is it? Come on, everyone sucks at something! Tell me what you're bad at."

"Why do you want to know this?" he asks, pulling me closer. "Why do you want to wreck this perfect illusion you have of me?"

"Because I hate feeling so pale and meager in comparison. Se- riously, I'm so mediocre in so many ways, and I just want to know that you suck at something too. Come on, it'll make me feel better."

"You're not mediocre," he says, his nose in my hair, his voice far too serious.

But I refuse to give up, I need something to go on, something that'll humanize him, if only a little. "Just one thing, please? Even if you have to lie, it's for a good cause—my self-esteem."

I try to turn so that I can see him, but he grips me tighter and holds me in place, kissing the tip of my ear as he whispers, "You really want to know?"

I nod, my heart beating wildly, my blood pulsing electric.

"I suck at love."

I stare into the firepit, wondering what he could possibly mean. And even though I seriously wanted him to answer, that doesn't mean I wanted him to answer so seriously. "Um, care to elaborate?" I ask, laughing nervously, not sure if I really do want to hear it. Fearing it might have something to do with Drina—a subject I'd rather avoid.

He presses against me, his breath drawn out and deep. And he stays like that for so long I wonder if he's ever going to speak. But when he finally does, he says, "I just always end up—disappointing." He shrugs, refusing to explain any further.

"But you're only seventeen." I move out of his arms and face him.

He shrugs.

"So how many *disappointments* could there be?"

But instead of answering, he turns me back around and brings his lips to my ear, whispering, "Let's go for a swim."

———

One more sign of how perfect Damen is—he keeps a pair of trunks in his car.

"Hey, this is California, you never know when you'll need them," he says, standing at the edge of the pool and smiling at me. "Got a wet suit in the trunk too; should I get it?"

"I can't answer that," I say, wading in the deep end, steam rising up all around. "You just have to see for yourself."

He inches toward the very edge and pretends to dip his big toe.

"No testing, only jumping," I scold.

"May I dive?"

"Cannonball, belly flop, whatever." I laugh, watching as he executes the most gorgeous arcing dive, before popping up beside me.

"Perfect," he says, his hair slicked back, his skin wet and glistening, as tiny drops of water cling to his lashes. And just when I think he's going to kiss me, he ducks back under the water and swims away.

So I take a deep breath, swallow my pride, and follow.

"Much better," he says, holding me close.

"Scared of the deep end?" I smile, my toes barely touching the bottom.

"I was referring to your outfit. You should dress like this more often."

I gaze down at my white body in my white bikini and try not to feel overly insecure next to his perfectly sculpted, bronzed self.

"Definitely a big improvement over the hoodies and jeans." He laughs.

I press my lips together, unsure of what to say.

"But I guess you gotta do what you gotta do, *right?*"

I search his face. Something about the way he just said that seemed like he meant something more, like he might actually know why I dress the way I do.

He smiles. "Obviously it protects you from the wrath of Stacia and Honor. They're not too keen on competition." He tucks my hair behind my ear and smoothes the side of my face.

"Are we competing?" I ask, remembering the flirting, the rosebud retrieving, our brawl today at school, the threat I've no doubt she'll make good on. Watching as he looks at me for the longest time, so long that my mood has changed, and I move away.

"Ever, there was never any contest," he says, following me.

But I duck underwater and swim toward the ledge, grabbing hold and wriggling out, knowing I need to act fast if I'm going to have my say, because the moment he comes near, the words will evaporate.

"How can I possibly know anything when you run so hot and cold?" I say, my hands trembling, my voice shaky, wishing I could just stop, let it go, reclaim the nice, romantic evening we were having. But knowing this needed to be said, despite whatever consequences it brought. "I mean, one minute you're gazing at me in—in that way that you do—and the next thing I know you're all over Stacia." I press my lips together and wait for him to respond, watching as he climbs out of the pool and moves toward me, so gorgeous, wet, and glistening. I fight to catch my breath.

"Ever, I—" He closes his eyes and sighs. And when he opens them again, he takes another step toward me and says, "It was never my intention to hurt you. Truly. Never." He slides his arms around me and tries to make me face him. And when I do, when I finally give in, he looks into my eyes and says, "Not once did I set out to hurt you. And I'm sorry if you feel that I played with your feelings. I told you I'm not so good at this sort of thing." He smiles, burying his fingers in my wet hair, before coming away with a single red tulip.

I stare at him, taking in his strong shoulders, defined chest, washboard abs, and bare hands. No sleeves for hiding things under, no pockets to stow anything in. Just his glorious half-naked body, dripping-wet swim trunks, and that stupid red tulip in hand.

"How do you do it?" I ask, holding my breath, knowing damn well it didn't come from my ear.

"Do what?" He smiles, his arms encircling my waist, pulling me closer.

"The tulips, the rosebuds, all of it?" I whisper, trying to ignore the feel of his hands on my skin, how his touch makes me warm, sleepy, verging on dizzy.

"It's magic." He smiles.

I pull away and reach for a towel, wrapping it tightly around me. "Why can't you ever be serious?" I ask, wondering what I've gotten myself into, and if there's still time to retreat.

"I am serious," he mumbles, pulling on his T-shirt and reaching for his keys as I shiver in my cold damp towel, watching speechless as he heads for the gate, waves over his shoulder, and calls, "Sabine's home," before blending into the night.

nineteen

The next day, when I pull into the parking lot, Damen's not there. And as I climb out of my car, sling my bag over my shoulder, and head for class, I give myself a pep talk and prepare for the worst.

But the moment I reach the classroom, I'm completely immobile. Staring stupidly at the green painted door, unable to open it.

Since my psychic abilities evaporate wherever Damen's concerned, the only thing I can actually *see* is the nightmare I craft in my head. The one where Damen's perched on the edge of Stacia's desk, laughing and flirting, retrieving rosebuds from all manner of places, as I slump by and head for my seat, the warm sweet flicker of his gaze skimming right over me as he turns his back so he can focus on *her.*

And I just can't go through with it. I seriously can't bear it. Because even though Stacia's cruel, mean, horrible, and sadistic, she happens to be cruel, mean, horrible, and sadistic in a straightforward way. Holding no secrets, cloaking no mysteries, her unkindness is out there, clearly displayed.

While I'm just the opposite: paranoid, secretive, lurking behind sunglasses and a hoodie, and hoarding a burden so heavy there's nothing simple about me.

I reach for the handle again, scolding myself: *This is ridiculous. What are you gonna do—drop out of school? You've got another year and a half to deal with this, so just suck it up and go inside already!*

But my hand starts to shake, refusing to obey, and just as I'm about to make a run for it, this kid comes up from behind, clears his throat, and says, "Uh—you gonna open that?" Completing the question in his head with an unspoken—*You fuckin' freak!*

So I take a deep breath, open the door, and slink right inside. Feeling worse than I ever could've imagined, when I see Damen's not there.

The second I enter the lunch area, I scan all the tables, searching for Damen, but when I don't see him, I head for my usual spot, arriving at the same time as Haven.

"Day six and no word on Evangeline," she says, dropping her cupcake box on the table before her and sitting across from me.

"Have you asked around the anonymous group?" Miles slides in beside me and twists the cap off his VitaminWater.

Haven rolls her eyes. "They're *anonymous*, Miles."

Miles rolls his eyes. "I was referring to her *mentor*."

"They're called *sponsors*. And yeah, she's no help, hasn't heard a thing. Drina thinks I'm overreacting though, says I'm making way too big a deal."

"She still here?" Miles peers at her.

My eyes dart between them, alerted by the edge in his voice and waiting for more. Since most everything to do with Damen and Drina is psychically off limits, I'm as curious to hear the answer as he is.

"Um, yeah, Miles, she *lives* here now. Why? Is that a problem?" She narrows her eyes.

Miles shrugs and sips his drink. "No problem." Though his thoughts say otherwise and his yellow aura turns dark and opaque as he struggles with saying what he wants, versus not saying anything at all. "There's just . . ." he starts.

"Just what?" She stares at him, eyes narrowed, lips pinched.

"Well . . ."

I stare at him, thinking: *Do it, Miles, say it! Drina's arrogant, awful, a bad influence, pure trouble. You're not the only one who sees it, I see it too, so go ahead and say it—she's the worst!*

He hesitates, the words forming on his tongue as I suck in my breath, anticipating their release. Then he exhales loudly, shakes his head, and says, "Never mind."

I glance at Haven, seeing her enraged face, her aura flaring, the edges sparking and flaming all around, forecasting a major meltdown scheduled to start in just *three-two-one*—

"Excuse me, Miles, but I'm so not buying that. So if you have something to say, then just say it." She glares at him, cupcake forgotten as she drums her fingers against the fiberglass table. And when he doesn't respond, she continues. "Whatever, Miles. You too, Ever. Just because you're not saying anything doesn't make you any less guilty."

Miles peers at me, eyes wide, brow raised, and I know I should say something, do something, make a show of asking just what exactly it is that I'm guilty of. But the truth is, I already know. I'm guilty of not liking Drina. Of not trusting her. Of sensing something suspicious, sinister even. And not doing nearly enough to hide those suspicions.

She shakes her head and rolls her eyes, and she's so upset she practically spits out the words, "You guys don't even know her! And you have no right to judge her! For your information, I happen to like Drina. And in the short time I've known her she's been a way better friend to me than either of you!"

"That's so not true!" Miles shouts, eyes blazing. "That's such total bullsh—"

"Sorry Miles, but it *is* true. You guys tolerate me, you go along with me, but you don't really get me like she does. Drina and I like the same things, we share the same interests. She doesn't secretly want me to change like you do. She likes me just as I am."

"Oh, is that why you changed your entire look, because she accepts you for who you really are?"

I watch as Haven closes her eyes and takes a slow breath, then she looks at Miles and rises from her seat, gathering her things as she says, "Whatever, Miles. Whatever, both of you."

"And now, ladies and gentlemen, behold the big dramatic exit!" Miles scowls. "I mean, are you *kidding*? All I did was ask if she was still here! That's it! And you turn it into this major ordeal. Jeez, sit down, find your happy place, and chillax already, would you?"

She shakes her head and grips the table, the small elaborate tattoo on her wrist now finished, but still red and inflamed.

"What do you call that?" I ask, gazing at the ink rendering of the snake eating its own tail, knowing there's a name for it, that it's some sort of mythical creature, but forgetting which one.

"Ouroboros." And when she rubs it with her finger I swear I saw its tongue flicker and move.

"What does it mean?"

"It's an ancient alchemy symbol for eternal life, creation out of destruction, life out of death, immortality, something like that," Miles says.

Haven and I gaze at him, but he just shrugs. "What? So I'm well read."

Then I look at her and say, "It looks infected. Maybe you should have it looked at."

But as soon as it's out I know it was the wrong thing to say, and I watch as she yanks down her sleeve, as her aura sparks and flames. "My tattoo is fine. I'm fine. And excuse me for saying so, but I can't help but notice how neither one of you is freaking out over Damen, who, by the way, never comes to school anymore. I mean, what's up with that?"

Miles gazes down at his Sidekick, and I just shrug. It's not like she doesn't have a point. And we watch as she shakes her head, snatches her cupcake box, and storms away.

"Can you tell me what just happened?" Miles says, watching her slalom through the maze of lunch tables, in a big hurry to nowhere.

But I just shrug, unable to shake the image of the snake on her wrist, how it turned its head, focused its beady eyes, and looked right at me.

The moment I pull into my drive, I see Damen, leaning against his car, smiling.

"How was school?" he asks, coming around to open my door.

I shrug and reach for my books.

"Ah, so you're still angry," he says, following me to the front door. And even though he's not touching me, I can feel his emanating heat.

"I'm not angry," I mutter, opening the door and tossing my backpack onto the floor.

"Well that's a relief. Because I've made reservations for two, and if you're not angry, then I assume you'll be joining me."

I look at him, my eyes grazing over his dark jeans, boots, and soft black sweater that can only be cashmere, wondering what he could possibly be up to now.

He removes my sunglasses and earbuds and sets them on the entryway table. "Trust me, you really don't need all those *defenses*," he says, lowering my hood, tucking his arm through mine, and leading me out the front door and over to his car.

"Where are we going?" I ask, settling onto the passenger seat, complacent, spineless, always so eager to go along with whatever he says. "I mean, what about my homework? I have a ton of catching up to do."

But he just shakes his head and climbs in beside me. "Relax, you can do it later, I promise."

"How much later?" I peer at him, wondering if I'll ever get used to his amazing dark beauty, the warmth of his gaze, and his ability to talk me into just about anything.

He smiles, starting the car without even turning the key. "Before the stroke of midnight, I promise. Now buckle in, we're going for a ride."

Damen drives fast. Really fast. So when he pulls into the parking lot and leaves his car with the valet, it seems as though only a few minutes have passed.

"Where are we?" I ask, gazing at the green buildings and the sign marked EAST ENTRANCE. "East entrance to what?"

"Well, this should explain it." He laughs, pulling me toward him as four shiny sweaty Thoroughbreds trot by with their grooms, followed by a jockey in a pink-and-green jacket, thin white pants, and muddy black boots.

"The racetrack?" I gape. Like Disneyland, it's pretty much the last place I expected.

"Not just any racetrack, it's Santa Anita," he nods. "One of the nicer ones. Now come on, we've got a three-fifteen reservation at the FrontRunner."

"The *what*?" I ask, standing my ground.

"Relax, it's just a restaurant." He laughs. "Now, come on, I don't want to miss post."

"Um, isn't this illegal?" I say, knowing I sound like the worst kind of goody-good, but still, he's just so—lawless and reckless and—*random*.

"Eating is illegal?" He smiles, but I can tell his patience is running thin.

I shake my head. "Betting, gambling, whatever, *you know*."

But he just laughs and shakes his head. "It's horse racing, Ever, not cockfighting. Now come on." He squeezes my hand and leads me to the elevator bank.

"But don't you have to be twenty-one?"

"Eighteen," he mumbles, going inside and pressing *five*.

"Exactly. I'm sixteen and a half."

He shakes his head and leans in to kiss me. "Rules should always be bent, if not broken. It's the only way to have any fun. Now come," he says, leading me down a hall and into a large room decorated in varying shades of green, stopping before the front podium and greeting the maitre d' like a long lost friend.

"Ah, Mr. Auguste, so wonderful to see you! Your table is ready, follow me."

Damen nods and takes my hand, leading me through a room full of couples, retirees, single men, groups of women, a father and his young son—not an empty seat in the house. Eventually stopping at a table just across from the finish line, with a beautiful view of the track and the green hills beyond.

"Tony will be right over to take your orders. Should I bring you champagne?"

Damen glances at me then shakes his head. His face flushing slightly when he says, "Not today."

"Very well then, five minutes 'til post."

"Champagne?" I whisper, raising my brows, but he just shrugs and unfolds his racing program.

"What do you think about Spanish Fly?" He looks at me. Smiling when he says, "The horse, not the aphrodisiac."

But I'm too busy gazing around to answer, struggling to take it all in. Because this room is not only huge, but it's also completely full—in the middle of the week—the middle of the day even. All these people playing hooky and betting. It's like a whole other world I never knew existed. And I can't help but wonder if this is where he spends all his free time.

"So what do you say? You wanna bet?" He glances at me briefly, before making a series of notes with his pen.

I shake my head. "I wouldn't even know where to begin."

"Well, I could give you the whole lowdown on odds, percentages, stats, and who sired who. But since we're short on time, why don't you just look this over, and tell me what you *feel*, which names you're drawn to. It's always worked for me." He smiles.

He tosses me the racing form and I look it over, surprised to find three distinct names jump out at me, in a one-two-three order. "How about Spanish Fly to win, Acapulco Lucy second, and

Son of Buddha third," I say, having no idea how I got there, but feeling pretty confident in my picks.

"Lucy to place, Buddha to show," he mumbles, scribbling it down. "And how much would you like to wager on that? Minimum bet's two, but you can certainly go higher."

"Two's good," I say, suddenly losing confidence and unwilling to empty my wallet on a whim.

"You sure?" he asks, looking disappointed.

I nod.

"Well, I think you've got some sound picks so I'm betting five. No, make that ten."

"Don't bet ten," I say, pressing my lips. "I mean, I just picked 'em, I don't even know why."

"Looks like we're about to find out," he says, standing as I reach for my wallet. But he just waves it away. "You can reimburse me when you collect your winnings. I'm going to post. If the waiter comes by, order whatever you want."

"What should I get for you?" I call, but he moves so fast he doesn't even hear me.

By the time he returns, the horses are all in the gate, and when the shot goes off, they bolt from their stalls. At first appearing like shiny dark blurs, as they take the corner and race for the finish, I spring from my seat, watching as my three favorite picks jockey for position, then jumping and shouting and screaming with glee when they all cross the finish in my perfect one-two-three.

"Omigod, we won! We won!" I say, smiling as Damen leans in to kiss me. "Is it always this exciting?" I gaze down at the track, watching as Spanish Fly trots into the winner's circle and gets draped with flowers, preparing for his photo op.

"Pretty much." Damen nods. "Though there's nothing like that first big win, that's always the best."

"Well, I'm not sure how big it will be," I say, wishing I'd had a little more faith in my abilities, at least enough to broaden the stakes.

He frowns. "Well, since you only bet two, I'm afraid you won somewhere around eight."

"Eight dollars?" I squint, more than a little disappointed.

"Eight hundred." He laughs. "Or, eight hundred and eighty dollars and sixty cents to be exact. You won a trifecta, meaning win, place, and show, in that exact order."

"All that on just two *dollars*?" I say, suddenly knowing why he has a regular table.

He nods.

"What about you? What did you win?" I ask. "Did you bet the same as me?"

He smiles. "As it just so happens I lost. I lost big. I got a little greedy and went for the superfecta, which means I added a pony that didn't quite make it. But don't worry, I plan to make up for it on the next race."

And did he ever. Because when we went to the window, after the eighth and final race, I collected a total of one thousand six hundred and forty-five dollars and eighty cents, while Damen pocketed significantly more, having won the Super High Five, meaning he picked all five horses in the exact order they finished. And since he was the only one to have done so, for the last several days, he won five hundred and thirty-six *thousand* dollars and forty-one cents—all on a ten-dollar bet.

"So what do you think of the races?" He asks, his arm tucked around mine as he leads me outside.

"Well, now I get why you're not all that into school. I guess it can't really compete, can it?" I laugh, still feeling high from my winnings, thinking I've finally found a profitable outlet for my psychic *gift*.

"Come on, I want to buy you something to celebrate my big win," he says, leading me into the gift shop.

"No, you don't have to—" I start.

But he squeezes my hand, his lips on my ear as he says, "I insist. Besides, I think I can afford it. But there's one condition."

I look at him.

"Absolutely no sweatshirts or hoodies." He laughs. "But anything else, just say the word."

After joking around and insisting on a jockey cap, a model horse, and a huge bronze horseshoe to hang on my bedroom wall, we settle on a silver horse-bit bracelet instead. But only after I made sure that the crystal bits were really just crystal, not diamonds, because that would be too much, no matter how much money he won.

"This way, no matter what happens, you'll never forget this day," he says, closing the clasp on my wrist as we wait for the valet to bring us the car.

"How could I possibly forget?" I ask, gazing at my wrist, then at him.

But he just shrugs as he climbs in beside me and there's something so sad, so bereft in his eyes, I hope that's the one thing I do forget.

Unfortunately, the ride home seems even quicker than the one to the track and when he pulls into my driveway, I realize how reluctant I am for the day to end.

"Would you look at that?" he says, motioning to the clock on his dash. "Well before midnight, just like I promised." And when he leans in to kiss me, I kiss him back with so much enthusiasm I practically pull him onto my seat.

"Can I come in?" he whispers, tempting me with his lips as they make their way down my ear, my neck, and all along my collarbone.

And I surprise myself by pushing him away and shaking my head. Not just because Sabine's inside and I have homework to do, but because I need to get a backbone already, stop giving in to him so dang easily.

"I'll see you at school," I say, climbing out of his car, before he can change my mind. "You remember, Bay View? That high school you used to attend?"

He averts his gaze and sighs.

"Don't tell me you're ditching—*again?*"

"School is so dreadfully boring. I don't know how you do it."

"You don't know how *I* do it?" I shake my head and glance toward the house, seeing Sabine peek through the blinds and then pulling away. Then I turn back to Damen and say, "Well, I guess I do it the same way you used to do it. You know, you get up, get dressed, and just go. And sometimes, if you pay attention, you actually learn a thing or two while you're there." But the second it's out of my mouth, I know it's a lie. Because the truth is, I haven't learned a damn thing all year. I mean, it's hard to actually learn anything when you just sort of *know* everything instead. Though it's not like I share that with him.

"There's got to be a better way," he groans, his eyes wide, pleading with mine.

"Well, just for the record, truancy and dropping out? *Not* a better way. Not if you want to go to college, and make something of your life." More lies. Because with a few more days like that at the track, one could live very well. Better than well.

But he just laughs. "Fine. We'll play it your way. For now. See you tomorrow, Ever."

And I've barely made it through the front door when he's already driven away.

twenty

The next morning, as I'm getting ready for school, Riley's perched on my dresser, dressed as Wonder Woman, and spilling celebrity secrets. Having grown bored with watching the everyday antics of old neighbors and friends, she's set her sights on Hollywood, which allows her to dish the dirt better than any supermarket tabloid.

"No *way*!" I gape at her. "I can't believe it! Miles will flip when he hears this!"

"You have no idea." She shakes her head, her black curls bouncing from side to side, looking jaded, world weary, like one who's seen too much—and then some. "*Nothing's* what it seems. Seriously. It's just one big illusion, as fake as the movies they make. And believe me, those publicists work their butts off keeping all of their dirty little secrets—*secret*."

"Who else have you spied on?" I ask, eager to hear more. Wondering why it never occurred to me to try to tune in to their energies while I'm watching TV or flipping through a magazine. "What about—"

I'm just about to ask if the rumors about my favorite actress are true, when Sabine pokes her head in my room and says, "What about what?"

I glance at Riley, seeing she's bent over laughing, and clear my throat as I say, "Um, nothing, I didn't say anything."

Sabine gives me an odd look, as Riley shakes her head and says, "Good one, Ever. *Real* convincing."

"Did you need something?" I ask, turning my back on Riley and focusing on the real purpose behind Sabine's visit—she's been invited away for the weekend and isn't sure how to tell me.

She walks into my room, her posture too straight, her gait unnaturally stiff, then she takes a deep breath and sits on the edge of my bed, her fingers nervously picking at a loose thread on my blue cotton duvet as she considers just how to broach it. "Jeff invited me away for the weekend." She merges her brows. "But I thought I should run it by you first."

"Who's Jeff?" I ask, inserting my earrings and turning to look at her. Because even though I already know, I still feel like I should still ask.

"You met him at the party. He came as Frankenstein." She glances at me, her mind clouded with guilt, feeling like a negligent guardian, a bad role model, though it hasn't affected her aura, which is still a bright happy pink.

I cram my books into my backpack, stalling for time, as I decide what to do. On the one hand, Jeff isn't the guy she thinks. Not even close. Though from what I can *see,* he truly does like her and means her no harm. And it's been so long since I've seen her happy like this, I can't bear to tell her. Besides, how would I even go about it?

Um, excuse me, but that Jeff guy? Mr. Swanky Investment Banker? So not the man you think he is. In fact, he still lives with his mom! Just don't ask how I know what I know—just trust that I know.

No. Uh-uh. Can't do it. Besides, relationships have a way of working themselves out—in their own way—in their own good time. And it's not like I don't have my own relationship issues to deal with. I mean, now that things are starting to stabilize with Damen, now that we're growing closer and I'm feeling more like a couple, I've been thinking that maybe it's time I stop pushing him away. Maybe it's time we take the next step. And with Sabine out of town for the next couple days, well, it's an opportunity that may not come around again.

"Go! Have fun!" I finally say, trusting she'll eventually learn the truth about Jeff and move on with her life.

She smiles, with equal amounts of excitement and relief. Then she gets up from my bed and moves toward the door, pausing as she says, "We're leaving today, after work. He's got a place up in Palm Springs, and it's less than a two-hour drive, so if you need anything, we won't be too far."

Correction, his mom *has a place in Palm Springs.*

"We'll be back Sunday. And Ever, if you want to have your friends over that's fine, though—do we need to talk about that?"

I freeze, knowing exactly where this conversation is headed and wondering if she's somehow read my mind. But realizing she's just trying to be a responsible adult and fulfill her new role as "parent," I shake my head and say, "Trust me, it's all been covered."

Then I grab my bag and roll my eyes at Riley who's dancing on top of my dresser, singing, *"Par-ty! Par-ty!"*

Sabine nods, clearly relieved at having avoided the S-E-X talk almost as much as me. "See you Sunday," she says.

"Yup," I say, heading down the stairs. "See you then."

"Swear to God he's on your team," I say, pulling into the parking lot, feeling the warm, sweet tingle of Damen's gaze long before I actually see him.

"I *knew* it!" Miles nods. "I knew he was gay. I could just tell. Where'd you hear that?"

I stall, knowing there's no way I can divulge my true source, admitting that my dead little sister is now the ultimate Hollywood insider. "Um, I don't remember," I mumble, climbing out of my car. "I just know that it's true."

"What's true?" Damen asks smiling as he brings his lips to my cheek.

"Jo—" Miles starts.

But I shake my head and cut him off, unwilling to display my celebrity-obsessing shallow side so early in the game. "Nothing, we just, um, did you hear Miles is playing Tracy Turnblad in *Hairspray*?" I ask, going into a full-blown discourse of jumbled phrases and disjointed nonsense until Miles finally waves good-bye and heads off to class.

As soon as he's gone, Damen stops and says, "Hey, I have a better idea. Let's go have breakfast."

I shoot him the *you're crazy* look and continue walking, but I don't get very far before he's squeezing my hand and pulling me back.

"Come on," he says, his eyes on mine, laughing in a way that's contagious.

"We can't," I whisper, glancing around anxiously, knowing we're seconds from being late and not wanting it to get any worse. "Besides, I already had breakfast."

"Ever, please!" He drops to his knees, palms pressed together, eyes wide and pleading. "*Please* don't make me go in there. If you have any kindness at all, you won't make me do it."

I press my lips and try not to laugh. Watching my gorgeous, elegant, sophisticated boyfriend begging on his knees is a sight I never thought I'd see. But still, I just shake my head and say, "Come on, get up, bell's about to—" And I don't even finish the sentence before it's already rung.

He smiles, rising to his feet, wiping his jeans, and then tucking his arm around my waist as he says, "You know what they say, better a no-show than a tardy."

"Who's *they*?" I ask, shaking my head. "Sound more like *you*."

He shrugs. "Hmmm, maybe it is me. Nonetheless, I guarantee there are much better ways to spend a morning. Because Ever," he says, squeezing my hand, "we don't have to do this. And, *you* don't have to wear this." He removes my sunglasses and lowers my hood. "The weekend starts now."

And even though I can think of a million good and valid reasons why we absolutely should not ditch, why the weekend should wait until three o'clock just like any other Friday, when he gazes at me, his eyes are so deep and inviting, I don't think twice, I just dive right in.

Barely recognizing the sound of my own voice when I hear myself say, "Hurry before they lock the gate."

We take separate cars. Because even though it went unspoken, it's pretty obvious we have no plans to return. And as I follow Damen up the sweeping curves of Coast Highway, I gaze out at the dramatic stretch of coastline, the pristine beaches, the navy blue waters, and my heart swells with gratitude, feeling so lucky to live here, to call this amazing place home. But then I remember how I ended up here—and just like that, the thrill is gone.

He makes a quick right and I pull into the space beside him, smiling as he comes around to open my door. "Have you been here yet?" he asks.

I gaze at the white clapboard hut and shake my head.

"I know you said you weren't hungry, but their shakes are the best. You should definitely try the date malt, or the chocolate peanut butter shake, or both, it's my treat."

"Dates?" I crinkle my nose and make a face. "Um, I hate to say it, but that sounds *awful.*"

But he just laughs and pulls me toward the counter, ordering one of each, and then carrying them over to the painted blue bench where we take a seat and gaze down at the beach.

"So which one's your favorite?" he asks.

I try them each again, but they're both so thick and creamy, I remove their lids and use a spoon. "They're both really good," I say. "But surprisingly, I think I like the date one best." But when I slide it toward him so he can taste too, he shakes his head and pushes it back. And something about that small simple act pierces straight through me.

There's just something about him, something more than just the strange magic tricks and disappearing acts. I mean, for one thing, this guy *never eats.*

But no sooner have I thought it than he reaches for the straw and takes a long deep pull, and when he leans in to kiss me his lips are icy cold.

"Let's head down to the beach, shall we?"

He takes my hand and we walk along the trail, shoulders bumping into each other, as we pass the milkshakes back and forth, even though I'm doing most all of the slurping. And as we make our way down to the beach, we remove our shoes, roll up our hems, and walk along the shore, allowing the frigid water to wash over our toes and splash on our shins.

"Do you surf?" he asks, taking the empty cups and placing one inside the other.

I shake my head, and step over a pile of rocks.

"Would you like a lesson?" He smiles.

"In this water?" I head toward a bank of dry sand, my toes numb and blue from just that quick dip. "No thanks."

"Well, I was thinking we'd wear wet suits," he says, coming up behind me.

"Only if they're fur lined." I laugh, smoothing the sand with my foot, making a flat space for us to sit.

But he takes my hand and leads me away, all the way past the tide pools, and into a hidden natural cave.

"I had no idea this was here," I say, gazing around at the smooth rock walls, the recently raked sand, and the towels and surfboards piled up in the corner.

"Nobody does." He smiles. "That's why all my stuff is still here. Blends into the rock; most people walk right by without even seeing it. But then, most people live their whole lives without ever noticing what's directly in front of them."

"So how'd you find it?" I ask, settling onto the large green blanket he's laid out in the middle.

He shrugs. "I guess I'm not like most people."

He lies down beside me, then pulls me down too. Resting his cheek on the palm of his hand, he gazes at me for so long, I can't help but squirm.

"Why do you hide under those baggy jeans and hoodies?" he whispers, his fingers stroking the side of my face, pushing my hair behind my ear. "Don't you know how beautiful you are?"

I press my lips together and look away, liking the sentiment but wishing he'd stop. I don't want to go down this road of having to explain myself, defend why I am the way I am. Obviously he'd prefer the old me, but it's too late for that. That girl died and left me in her place.

A tear escapes down my cheek, and I try to turn, not wanting him to see. But he holds me tight and won't let me go, erasing my sadness with a brush of his lips before merging with mine.

"Ever," he groans, voice thick, eyes burning, shifting until he's draped right across me, the weight of his body providing the most comforting warmth that soon turns to heat.

I run my lips along the line of his jaw, the square of his chin, my breath coming in short shallow gasps as his hips press and circle with mine, eliciting all of the feelings I've fought so hard to deny. But I'm tired of fighting, tired of denying. I just want to be normal again. And what could be more normal than *this*?

I close my eyes as he removes my sweatshirt, surrendering, yielding, allowing him to unbutton my jeans and remove them too. Consenting to the press of his palm and push of his fingers, telling myself that this glorious feeling, this dreamy exuberance surging inside me could only be one thing—could only be *Love*.

But when I feel his thumbs anchored in the elastic of my panties, guiding them down, I sit up abruptly and push him away. Part of me wanting to continue, to pull him back to me—only not here, not now, not in this way.

"Ever," he whispers, his eyes searching mine. But I just shake my head and turn away, feeling his warm wonderful body mold around mine, his lips on my ear saying, "It's all right. Really. Now sleep."

"Damen?" I roll over, squinting in the dim light, as my hand explores the empty space beside me. Patting the blanket again and again, until I'm convinced he's truly not there. "Damen?" I call again, glancing around the cave, the distant sound of crashing waves the only reply.

I slip on my sweatshirt and stumble outside, staring into the fading afternoon light, scanning the beach, expecting to find him.

But when I don't see him anywhere, I head back inside, seeing the note he left on my bag, and unfolding it to read:

Gone surfing.
Be back soon.
—D

I run back outside, note still in hand, rushing up and down the shore, scanning for surfers, one in particular. But the only two out there are so blond and pale, it's clear they're not Damen.

twenty-one

When I pull into the driveway I'm surprised to see someone sitting on the front steps, but when I get closer, I'm even more surprised to see that it's Riley.

"Hey," I say, grabbing my bag and slamming the car door, a little harder than planned.

"Sheesh!" she says, shaking her head and staring at me. "I thought you were gonna run me over."

"Sorry, I thought you were Damen," I say heading for the front door.

"Oh no, what'd he do now?" She laughs.

But I just shrug and unlock the door. I'm certainly not going to fill her in on the details. "What happened, you get locked out?" I ask, leading her inside.

"Very funny." She rolls her eyes and heads into the kitchen, taking a seat at the breakfast bar as I drop my bag on the counter and stick my head in the fridge.

"So, what's up?" I glance at her, wondering why she's so quiet, thinking maybe my bad mood is contagious.

"Nothing." She rests her chin in her hand and gazes at me.

"Doesn't seem like nothing." I grab a bottle of water instead of the quart of ice cream I really want, and lean against the granite counter, noticing how her black hair is tangled, and the Wonder Woman costume more than a little droopy.

She shrugs. "So, what are you gonna do?" she asks, leaning back on the stool in a way that makes me cringe, even though she can't possibly fall and get hurt. "I mean, this is like a teen dream come true, right? House to yourself, no chaperones." She wiggles her brows in a way that seems false, like she's trying too hard to put up a good front.

I take a swig of water and shrug, part of me wanting to confide in her, unburden my secrets, the good, bad, and the completely revolting. It would be so nice to get it off my chest, not bear all this weight on my own. But when I look at her again, I remember how half her life was spent waiting to turn thirteen, viewing each passing year as the one that brought her closer to the *important* double digits. And I can't help but wonder if that's why she's here. Since I robbed her of her dream, she's left with no choice but to live it through me.

"Well, I hate to disappoint you," I finally say. "But I'm sure you've already guessed what a colossal failure I am in the teen dream department." I gaze up at her shyly, my face flushing when she nods in agreement. "All that promise I showed back in Oregon? With the friends, and the boyfriend, and the cheerleading? Gone. Kaput. O-V-E-R. And the two friends I managed to make at Bay View? Well, they're not speaking to each other. Which, unfortunately means they're barely speaking to me. And even though through some weird, unexplainable, unimaginable fluke I managed to snag a gorgeous, sexy boyfriend, well the truth is, it's not all it's cracked up to be. Because when he's not acting weird, or vanishing into thin air, well, then he's convincing me to ditch school and bet at the tracks and all sorts of sordid business like that. He's kind of a bad influence." I cringe, realizing too late that I shouldn't have shared any of that.

But when I look at her again, it's clear she's not listening. She's staring at the counter, fingers tracing the black granite swirls, as her mind wanders in some other place.

"Please don't be mad," she finally says, gazing at me with eyes so wide and somber it's like a punch in the gut. "But I spent the day with Ava."

I press my lips, thinking: *I don't want to hear this. I absolutely do not want to hear this!* I grip the counter and brace for what follows.

"I know you don't like her, but she has some good points, and she's really making me think about things. You know, the choices I've made. And, well, the more I think about it, the more I realize she just might be right."

"What could she possibly be right about?" I ask, talking past the lump in my throat, thinking this day's gone from really bad, to extremely bad and it's a long way from over.

Riley looks at me, then glances away, her fingers still tracing those random swirls, as she says, "Ava says I shouldn't be here. That I'm not *supposed* to be here."

"And what do you say?" I suck in my breath, wishing she'd stop talking and take it all back. There's no way I can lose her, not now, not ever. She's all I have left.

Her fingers stop moving as she looks up at me. "I say I like being here. I say that even though I'll never get to be a teenager, at least I can kind of live it through you. You know, vicariously."

And even though her comment makes me feel guilty and horrible, and confirms all my thoughts, I try to lighten the load when I say, "Jeez, Riley, you couldn't have picked a worse example."

She rolls her eyes and groans. "Tell me." But even though she laughs, the light in her eyes is quickly extinguished when she says,

"But what if she's right? I mean, what if it *is* wrong for me to be here all the time?"

"Riley—" I start, but then the doorbell rings, and when I glance at her again, she's gone. "Riley!" I yell, gazing around the kitchen. "Riley!" I shout, hoping she'll reappear. I can't leave it like that. I refuse to leave it like that. But the more I shout, yell, and scream for her to return, the more I realize I'm shouting at air.

And as the doorbell continues to ring, one time, followed by two, I know Haven's outside, and I need to let her in.

"The gate guard waved me through," she says, storming into the house, her face a mess of mascara and tears, her newly red hair a tangled-up mess. "They found Evangeline. She's dead."

"What? Are you sure?" I start to shut the door behind her when Damen drives up, leaps from his car, and runs toward us. "Evangeline—" I start, so shocked by the news I've forgotten I've decided to hate him.

He nods and moves toward Haven, peering at her as he says, "Are you okay?"

She shakes her head and wipes her face. "Yeah, I mean, it's not like I knew her all that well, we only hung out a few times, but still. It's *so* awful, and the fact that I may have been the last one to see her . . ."

"Surely you weren't the *last* to see her."

I gape at Damen, wondering if he meant it as some kind of sick joke, but his face is deadly serious, and his gaze far away.

"I just—I just feel so responsible," she mumbles, burying her face in her hands, groaning *oh God, oh God, oh God,* over and over again.

I move toward her, wanting to comfort her in some way, but then she lifts her head, wipes her eyes, and says, "I—I just thought you should know, but I should get going, I need to get to Drina's." She raises her hand and jangles her keys.

Hearing her say that is like fuel for the fire, and I narrow my eyes at Damen, staring accusingly. Because even though Haven's friendship with Drina seems like a fluke, I'm sure that it isn't. I can't shake the feeling it's somehow connected.

But Damen ignores me as he grabs Haven's arm and peers at her wrist. "Where'd you get that?" he says, his voice tight, controlled, but with an undercurrent of edge, reluctantly letting go as she yanks free and covers it with her hand.

"It's fine," she says, clearly annoyed. "Drina gave me something to put on it, some salve, said it would take about three days to work."

Damen clenches his jaw so tight his teeth gnash together. "Do you happen to have it with you? This—*salve*?"

She shakes her head and moves for the door. "No, I left it at home. I mean, jeez, what's with you guys, anyway? Any more questions?" She turns, her eyes darting between us, her aura a bright flaming red. "Because I don't appreciate being interrogated like this. I mean, the only reason I stopped by in the first place was because I thought you might want to know about Evangeline, but since all you want to do is gawk at my tattoo and make stupid comments, I think I'll just go." She storms toward her car.

And even though I call after her, she just shakes her head and ignores me. And I can't help but wonder what happened to my friend. She's so moody, so distant, and I realize she's been lost to me for a while now. Ever since she met Drina, I feel like I hardly even know her.

I watch as she gets in her car, slams the door, and backs down the drive. Then I turn to Damen and say, "Well, that was pleasant. Evangeline's dead, Haven hates me, and you left me alone in a cave. I hope you at least caught some *killer* waves." I fold my arms across my chest and shake my head.

"As a matter of fact, I did," he says, gazing at me intently. "And when I returned to the cave I saw you had left and I raced right over."

I look at him, my eyes narrowed, my lips pressed together. I can't believe he actually expects me to believe that. "Sorry, but I looked, and there were only two surfers out there. Two *blond* surfers, which pretty much rules out either one of them being you."

"Ever, would you look at me?" he says. "*Really* look at me. How do you think I got this way?"

So I do, I lower my glare to take it all in. Noticing his wet suit that's dripping salt water all over the floor.

"But I checked. I ran up and down the beach, I looked *every-where*," I say, convinced of what I saw, or in this case, *didn't* see.

But he just shrugs. "Ever, I don't know what to tell you, but I didn't abandon you. I was surfing. *Really*. Now, can you please get me a towel, and maybe another for the floor?"

We head into the backyard so he can hose down his wet suit, while I sit on the lounge chair and watch him. I was so sure he'd ditched me. I looked everywhere. But maybe I did miss him. I mean, it *is* a long beach. And I *was* really angry.

"So how'd you know about Evangeline?" I ask, watching as he drapes his wet suit over the outdoor bar, unwilling to let go of my anger quite so easily. "And what's up with Drina and Haven and that creepy tattoo? And, just for the record, I'm not sure I buy your story about surfing, *seriously*. Because believe me, I checked, and you were *nowhere* in sight."

He looks at me, his deep dark eyes obscured by a rim of lush lashes, his lean, sinuous body wrapped in a towel. And when he moves toward me, his step is so light and sure, he's as graceful as any jungle cat. "This is my fault," he finally says, shaking his head as he sits down beside me, folding my hands into his, but then dropping them just as quickly. "I'm not sure how much . . ." he starts, and when he finally looks at me, his eyes are sadder than I ever could've imagined. "Maybe we shouldn't do this," he finally says.

"Are you—*are you breaking up with me?*" I whisper, the wind rushing right out of me, like an ill-fated balloon. All my suspicions confirmed: Drina, the beach, all of it. *Everything.*

"No, I just . . ." He turns away, leaving both the sentence, and me, to dangle.

And when it's clear he has no plans to continue I say, "You know, it would really be nice if you'd stop talking in code, finish a sentence, and tell me what the heck is going on. Because all I know is that Evangeline is dead, Haven's wrist is a red oozing mess, you ditched me at the beach because I wouldn't go all the way, and now you're breaking up with me." I glare at him, waiting for some confirmation that these seemingly random events are easily explained and not at all related. Even though my gut says otherwise.

He's silent for a while, staring at the pool, but when he finally looks at me he says, "None of it's related."

Though he hesitated for so long I'm not sure I believe him.

Then he takes a deep breath and continues. "They found Evangeline's body in Malibu canyon. I was on my way here when I heard it on the radio," he says, his voice becoming sure, steady, as he visibly relaxes and regains control. "And yes, Haven's wrist does appear to be infected, but sometimes those things happen." He breaks my gaze and I suck in my breath, waiting for the rest, the part about me. Then he grabs my hand and covers it with his, flipping it over and tracing the lines on my palm as he says, "Drina can be charismatic, charming—and Haven's a bit of a lost soul. I'm sure she just likes the attention. I thought you'd be glad she transferred her affections to Drina from me." He squeezes my fingers and smiles. "Now there's no one standing between us."

"But maybe there's *something* standing between us?" I ask, my voice barely a whisper. Knowing I should be more concerned with Haven's wrist and Evangeline's death, but unable to focus on anything other than the planes of his face, his smooth dark skin, his deep narrowed eyes, and the way my heart surges, my blood rushes, and my lips swell in anticipation of his.

"Ever, I didn't ditch you today. And I'd never push you to do anything you weren't ready for. Believe me." He smiles, cradling my face in the palms of his hands as his lips part against mine. "I know how to wait."

twenty-two

Even though Haven refused to answer our calls, we managed to get ahold of Miles. And after convincing him to stop by after rehearsals, he showed up with Eric, and the four of us spent a really fun night eating and swimming and watching bad scary movies. And it was so nice to hang out with my friends in such a nice relaxed way, that it *almost* made me forget about Riley, Haven, Evangeline, Drina, the beach—and all of that afternoon's drama.

Almost made me oblivious to the faraway look Damen got whenever he thought no one was looking.

Almost made me ignore the undercurrent of worry bubbling just under the surface.

Almost. But not quite.

And even though I made it perfectly clear that Sabine was out of town and Damen was more than welcome to stay, he stayed just long enough for me to fall asleep, then he quietly let himself out.

So the next morning, when he shows up on my doorstep with coffee, muffins, and a smile, I can't help but feel a little relieved.

We try to call Haven again, and even leave a message or two, but it's not like it takes a psychic to know she doesn't want to speak to either of us. And when I finally call her house and talk to her little brother, Austin, I can tell he's not lying when he says he hasn't seen her.

So after a full day of lounging outside by the pool, I'm just about to order another pizza when Damen grabs the phone out of my hand and says, "I thought I'd make dinner."

"You can cook?" I ask, though I don't know why I'm surprised, because the truth is, I've yet to find anything he can't do.

"I'll let you be the judge of that." He smiles.

"Do you need help?" I offer, even though my kitchen skills are severely limited to boiling water and adding milk to cereal.

But he just shakes his head and heads for the stove, so I go upstairs to shower and change, and when he calls me down for dinner, I'm amazed to find the dining room table dressed with Sabine's finest china, linens, candles, and a large crystal vase filled with dozens of—big surprise—red tulips.

"Mademoiselle." He smiles and pulls out my chair, his French accent lilting and perfect.

"I can't believe you did this." I gaze at the heaping platters lined up before me, so piled with food I wonder if we're expecting guests.

"It's all for you." He smiles, answering the question I hadn't yet asked.

"Just me? Aren't you going to have any?" I watch as he fills my plate with perfectly prepared vegetables, finely grilled meats, and a sauce so rich and complex I don't even know what it is.

"Of course." He smiles. "But mostly I made it for you. A girl can't live on pizza alone, you know."

"You'd be surprised." I laugh, cutting into a juicy piece of grilled meat.

While we eat, I ask questions. Taking advantage of the fact that he's barely touching his food by asking all of the things I've been dying to know but always seem to forget the moment he looks in my eyes. Things about his family, his childhood, the constant moves, the emancipation—partly because I'm curious, but mostly because it feels weird to be in a relationship with someone I know so little about. And the more we talk, the more surprised I am by how much we share in common. For one thing, both of us are orphaned, though he at a much younger age. And even though he's a little sketchy on the details, it's not like I volunteer to talk about my situation either, so I don't really push it.

"So where'd you like best?" I ask, having just cleaned my plate of every last morsel and feeling the beginnings of a nice languid fullness.

"Right here." He smiles, having barely eaten a thing but making a pretty good show of moving his food all around.

I squinch my eyes, not quite believing it. I mean, sure, Orange County's nice, but it can't possibly compare to all of those exciting European cities, *can it?*

"Seriously. I'm very happy here." He nods, looking right at me.

"And you weren't happy in Rome, Paris, New Delhi, or New York?"

He shrugs, his eyes suddenly tinged with sadness as they drift away from mine and he takes a sip of his strange red drink.

"And what exactly is that?" I ask, peering at the bottle.

"You mean this?" he smiles, holding it up for me to see. "Secret family recipe." He swirls the contents around, and I watch as the color glows and sparks as it runs up the sides and splashes back down. Looking like a cross between lightning, wine, and blood mixed with the tiniest hint of diamond dust.

"Can I try it?" I ask, not entirely sure that I want to, but still curious.

He shakes his head. "You won't like it. Tastes just like medicine. But that's probably because it is medicine."

My stomach sinks as I gape at him, imagining a whole host of incurable diseases, horrible afflictions, grave ailments—*I knew he was too good to be true.*

But he just shakes his head and laughs as he reaches for my hand. "No worries. I just get a little low on energy sometimes. And this helps."

"Where do you get it?" I squint, searching for a label, an imprint, some kind of mark, but the bottle is clear, smooth, and appears almost seamless.

He smiles. "I told you, secret family recipe," he says, taking a long deep swig and finishing it off. Then he pushes away from the table and his still-full plate, as he says, "Shall we go for a swim?"

"Aren't you supposed to wait an hour after eating?" I ask, peering at him.

But he just smiles and reaches for my hand. "Don't worry. I won't let you drown."

Since we spent most of the day in the pool, we decide to hang in the Jacuzzi instead. And when our fingers and toes start to resemble small prunes, we wrap ourselves in oversized towels and head up to my room.

He follows me into my bathroom. I drop my damp towel on

the floor, then he comes up behind me, pulls me to him, and holds me so close our bodies meld right together. And when his lips brush across the nape of my neck, I know I better lay down some ground rules while my brain is still working.

"Um, you're welcome to stay," I mumble, pulling away, my cheeks burning with embarrassment when I meet his amused gaze. "I mean, what I meant to say was, I *want* you to stay. I do. But, well, I'm not sure that we should—*you know*—"

Oh god, what am I saying? Um, hello, like he doesn't know what I mean. Like he wasn't the one getting pushed away in the cave and just about everywhere else. What is with you? What are you doing? Any girl would kill for a moment like this, a long, lazy weekend with no parents or chaperones—and yet, here I am, enforcing some stupid set of rules—for no good reason—

He places his finger under my chin and lifts my face until it's level with his. "Ever, please, we've been over this," he whispers, tucking my hair behind my ear and bringing his lips to my neck. "I know how to wait, really. I've already waited this long to find you—I can wait even more."

With Damen's warm body curled around mine, and his reassuring breath in my ear, I fall right to sleep. And even though I was worried I'd be way too freaked by his presence to get any rest, it's the warm secure feeling of having him right there beside me that helps me drift off.

But when I wake at 3:45 A.M., only to discover he's no longer there, I throw the covers aside and rush to the window, reliving that moment in the cave all over again as I search the drive for his car, surprised to find it's still there.

"Looking for me?" he asks.

I turn to find him standing in the doorway, my heart beating wildly, my face gone crimson. "Oh, I—I rolled over and you weren't there, and—" I press my lips, feeling ridiculous, small, embarrassingly needy.

"I went downstairs for some water." He smiles, taking my hand and leading me back to the bed.

But as I lay down beside him, my hand drifts to his side, brushing across sheets so cold and abandoned, it seems he's been gone for a much longer time.

The second time I wake, I'm alone again. But when I hear Damen banging around in the kitchen, I pull on my robe and head downstairs to investigate.

"How long have you been up?" I ask, gazing at a spotless kitchen, the previous night's mess having vanished, replaced by a lineup of donuts, bagels, and cereals that didn't originate in my cupboard.

"I'm an early riser." He shrugs. "So I thought I'd clean up a bit before running to the store. I may have gone a little overboard, but I didn't know what you'd want." He smiles, coming around the counter and kissing me on the cheek.

I sip from the glass of fresh-squeezed orange juice he sets before me and ask, "Want some? Or are you still fasting?"

"Fasting?" He lifts his brow and gazes at me.

I roll my eyes. "Please. You eat less than anyone I know. You just sip your . . . medicine and push your food all around. I feel like a complete pig next to you."

"Is this better?" He smiles, picking up a donut and biting it in half, his jaw working overtime to break down the glazed, doughy mass.

I shrug and gaze out the window, still unused to this California weather, a seemingly endless succession of warm sunny days, even though soon it will officially be winter. "So, what should we do today?" I ask, turning to look at him.

He gazes at his watch and then back at me. "I need to take off soon."

"But Sabine won't be back until late," I say, hating how my voice sounds so whiny and needy, and the way my stomach curls when he jangles his keys.

"I need to get home and take care of a few things. Especially if you want to see me at school tomorrow," he says, his lips grazing my cheek, my ear, the nape of my neck.

"Oh, school. Do we still go there?" I laugh, having successfully avoided thinking about my recent bout of truancy, and the repercussions to follow.

"You're the one who thinks it's important." He shrugs. "If it was up to me, every day would be Saturday."

"But then Saturday wouldn't be special. It'd all be the same," I say, picking off a piece of glazed donut. "A never-ending flow of long lazy days, nothing to work toward, nothing to look forward to, just one hedonistic moment after another. After a while, it wouldn't be so great."

"Don't be so sure." He smiles.

"So what exactly are these mysterious chores of yours, anyway?" I ask, hoping to get a glimpse into his life, of the more mundane things that occupy his time when he's not with me.

He shrugs. "You know, *stuff.*" And even though he laughs when he says it, it's pretty obvious he's ready to leave.

"Well, maybe I can—" But before I can even finish the sentence he's already shaking his head.

"Forget it. You are *not* doing my laundry." He shifts his weight from one foot to the other, as though warming up for a race.

"But I want to see where you live. I've never been in the home of someone who's emancipated, and I'm curious." And even though I tried to sound lighthearted, it came out more whiny and desperate.

He shakes his head and gazes at the door as though it's a potential lover he can't wait to meet.

And even though it's obviously time to wave my white flag and cry *uncle,* I can't keep from giving it one last go when I say, "But *why?*" Then I peer at him, waiting for a reason.

He looks at me, his jaw tense when he says, "Because it's a mess. A horrible filthy mess. And I don't want you to see it like that and get the wrong idea about me. Besides, I'll never be able to straighten it up with you around; you'll only distract me." He smiles, but his lips are stretched tight and his eyes are impatient, and it's clear they're just words meant to fill up the space between now and when he finally gets to leave. "I'll call you tonight," he says, showing me his back as he heads for the door.

"And what if I decide to follow you? What will you do then?" I ask, my nervous laughter halting the second he turns back to me.

"Don't follow me, Ever."

And the way he says it makes me wonder if he said, *Don't follow me ever,* or *Don't follow me, Ever.* But either way, it means the same thing.

———

When Damen leaves, I pick up the phone and try to call Haven, but when it goes straight into voice mail, I don't bother with leaving another message. Because the truth is, I've left several already, and now it's up to her to call me. So after I head upstairs and shower, I sit at my desk, determined to get through my homework, but not getting very far before my thoughts return to Damen, and all of his weird, mysterious quirks that I can no longer ignore.

Stuff like: How does he always seem to know just what I'm thinking when I can't get the slightest read on him? And how, in just seventeen short years, did he find time to live in all of those exotic places, mastering art, soccer, surfing, cooking, literature, world history, and just about every other subject I can think of? And what's up with the way he moves so fast he actually blurs? And what about the rosebuds and tulips and magical pen? Not to mention how one minute he's talking like a normal guy, and the next he sounds like Heathcliff, or Darcy, or some other character from a Brontë sister's book. Add to that the time he acted like he saw Riley, the fact that he has no aura, the fact that Drina has no aura, the fact that I *know* he's hiding something about how he really knows her—and now he doesn't want me to know where he lives?

After we slept together?

Okay, maybe all we did was *sleep,* but still, I think I deserve answers to at least some (if not all) of my questions. And even though I'm not really up for breaking into the school and searching for his record, I know someone who is.

Only I'm not sure I should involve Riley in this. Not to mention how I don't even know how to summon her since I've never had to before. I mean, do I call out her name? Light a candle? Close my eyes and make a wish?

Since lighting a candle seems a little hokey, I settle for just stand-ing in the middle of my room, eyes shut tight, as I say, "Riley? Riley, if you can hear me I really need to talk to you. Well, actually I kind of need a favor. But if you don't want to do it, then I totally under-stand, and there will be no hard feelings, since I know it's a little weird, and um, I feel kind of dumb right now, standing here talk-ing to myself, so if you can hear me, could you maybe give me some kind of sign?"

And when my stereo suddenly blasts the Kelly Clarkson song she always used to sing, I open my eyes and see her standing be-fore me, laughing hysterically.

"Omigod—you looked like your were two seconds away from closing the blinds, lighting a candle, and pulling the Ouija board out from under the bed!" She shakes her head and looks at me.

"Oh jeez, I feel like an idiot," I say, my face turning red.

"You kind of looked like an idiot." She laughs. "Okay, so let me get this straight, you want to corrupt your little sister by making her spy on your boyfriend?"

"How'd you know?" I stare at her, amazed.

"Please." She rolls her eyes and plops down on my bed. "You think you're the only one around here who can read minds?"

"And how'd you know *that*?" I ask, wondering what else she might know.

"Ava told me. But please don't be mad, because it really does explain some of your more recent fashion blunders."

"And what about your more recent fashion blunders?" I say, motioning to her *Star Wars* getup.

But she just shrugs. "So you wanna know where to find your boyfriend or not?"

I move to the bed and sit down beside her. "Honestly? I'm not sure. I mean, yeah I want to know, but I don't feel right about involving you."

"But what if I already did it? What if I already know?" she says, wiggling her brows.

"You broke into the school?" I ask, wondering what else she's been up to since we last talked.

But she just laughs. "Even better, I followed him home."

I gape at her. "But when? And how?"

She shakes her head. "Come on, Ever, it's not like I need wheels to get where I want to go. Besides, I know how you're all in love with him, and it's not like I blame you, he is pretty dreamy. But remember that day when he acted like he saw me?"

I nod. I mean, how could I forget?

"Well, it freaked me out. So, I decided to do a little investigation."

I lean toward her. *"And?"*

"And, well, I'm not sure how to say this, and I hope you won't take it the wrong way, but—he's a little odd." She shrugs. "I mean, he lives in this big house over in Newport Coast, which is strange enough considering his age and all. I mean where does he get the money? Because it's not like he works."

I remember that day at the track. But decide not to mention it.

"But that's not even the strangest part," she continues. "Because what's really weird is that the house is completely *empty*. Like, no furniture whatsoever."

"Well, he is a guy," I say, wondering why I feel the need to defend him.

She shakes her head. "Yeah, but I'm talking seriously weird. I mean, the only things in there are one of those iPod wall docks and a flat-screen TV. Seriously. That's it. And believe me, I checked the whole house. Well, other than this one room that was locked."

"Since when do locked rooms stop you?" I say, having seen her walk through plenty of walls this past year.

"Believe me, it wasn't the door that stopped me. It was *me* that stopped me. I mean, jeez, just because I'm dead doesn't mean I can't get scared." She shakes her head and scowls at me.

"But, he hasn't really lived here all that long," I say, rushing to make more excuses, like the worst kind of codependent fool. "So maybe he just hasn't gotten around to furnishing it yet. I mean, that's probably why he doesn't want me to come over; he doesn't want me to see it like that." And when I replay my words in my head, I can't help but think: *Oh, God, I'm even worse than I thought.*

Riley shakes her head and looks at me like she's about to let me in on the truth behind the tooth fairy, the Easter bunny, and Santa, all in one sitting. But then she just shrugs and says, "Maybe you should see for yourself."

"What do you mean?" I ask, knowing she's holding something back.

But she gets up from the bed and goes over to the mirror, gazing at her reflection and adjusting her costume.

"Riley?" I say, wondering why she's acting so mysterious.

"Listen," she says, finally turning toward me. "Maybe I'm wrong. I mean, what do I know, I'm just a kid." She shrugs. "And it's probably nothing, but . . ."

"But . . ."

She takes a deep breath. "But I think you should see for yourself."

"So how do we get there?" I ask, already up and reaching for the keys.

She shakes her head. "No way. Forget it. I'm convinced he can see me."

"Well we know he can see *me*," I remind her.

But she stands firm. "*So* not happening. But I'll draw you a map."

Since Riley's not so great at drawing maps, she settles for making a list of street names instead, indicating their left and right turns, since north, south, east, and west always confuse me.

"Sure you don't want to come?" I offer, grabbing my bag and heading out of my room.

She nods and follows me downstairs. "Hey, Ever?"

I turn.

"You could've told me about all the psychic stuff. I feel bad about making fun of your clothes."

I open the front door and shrug. "Can you really read my mind?"

She shakes her head and smiles. "Only when you're trying to communicate with me. I figured it was just a matter of time before you'd want me to spy on him." She laughs. "But, Ever?"

I turn to look at her again.

"If I don't come around for a while, it's not because I'm mad at you or trying to punish you or anything like that, okay? I promise I'll still look in and make sure you're all right and stuff, but, well, I might be gone for a while. I might be kind of busy."

I freeze, the first hint of panic beginning to stir. "You *are* coming back though, right?"

She nods. "It's just, well . . ." She shrugs. "I promise I'll be back, I just don't know when." And even though she smiles, it's obviously forced.

"You're not leaving me, are you?" I hold my breath, exhaling only when she shakes her head. "Okay, well, good luck then," I say, wishing I could hug her, hold her, convince her to stay, but knowing that's not possible, I head for my car and start the engine instead.

twenty-three

Damen lives in a gated community. A detail Riley failed to reveal. I guess since the presence of big iron gates and uniformed guards could never stop someone like her, it didn't seem very important. Though I guess it doesn't really stop someone like me either, since I just smile at the attendant, and say, "Hi, I'm Megan Foster. I'm here to see Jody Howard." Then I watch as she scrolls down her computer screen, searching for the name I just happen to know is listed as entry number three.

"Leave this in your window, on the driver's side," she says, handing me a piece of yellow paper, the word VISITOR and the date clearly marked on its front. "And no parking on the left side of the street, right side only." She nods, returning to her booth as I drive through the open gate, hoping she won't notice when I pass right by Jody's street as I make my way toward Damen's.

I've almost reached the top of the hill when I see the next street on my list, and after making a left, quickly followed by another, I stop at the end of his block, kill the engine, and realize I've lost all my nerve.

I mean, what kind of psycho girlfriend am I? Who in their

right mind would even think of enlisting their dead little sister to help spy on their boyfriend? But then again, it's not like anything in my life is remotely normal, so why should my relationships be any different?

I sit in my car, focusing on my breath, fighting to keep it slow and steady despite the fact that my heart is pounding like crazy and my palms are slick with sweat. And as I gaze around his clean, tidy, affluent neighborhood I realize I couldn't have picked a worse day to do this.

First of all, it's hot, sunny, and glorious, which means everyone's either riding their bikes, walking their dogs, or working in their gardens, which pretty much makes for some of the worst spying conditions you could ask for. And since I spent the entire drive just concentrating on getting here and not even considering what I'd do once I made it, it's not like I have a plan.

Though it probably doesn't matter much anyway. I mean, what's the worst that can happen? I get caught and Damen confirms I'm a freak? After my clingy, needy, desperate act this morning, he's probably already there.

I climb out of my car and head toward his house, the one at the very end of the cul-de-sac with the tropical plants and manicured lawn. But I don't creep, or skulk, or do anything that will draw unwanted attention, I just stroll right along, as though I have every right to be there, until I'm standing before his large double doors wondering what to do next.

I take a step back and gaze up at the windows, their blinds drawn, drapes closed, and even though I've no idea what I'll say, I bite down on my lip, push the bell, hold my breath, and wait.

But after a few minutes pass with no answer, I ring again. And when he still doesn't answer, I turn the handle, confirm that it's locked, then I head down the walk, making sure none of the neighbors are watching as I slip through the side gate and slink around back.

I stay close to the house, barely glancing at the pool, the plants, and the amazing white water view, as I go straight for the sliding glass door, which, of course, is locked too.

Then just as I'm ready to cut my losses and head home, I hear this voice in my head urging—*the window, the one by the sink*. And sure enough, I find it cracked just enough to slip my fingers under and open the rest of the way.

I place my hands on the ledge and use all of my strength to hoist myself in. And the second my feet hit the floor I've officially crossed over the line.

I shouldn't continue. I have no right to do this. I should climb right back out and make a run for my car. Get back to my safe quiet house while I still can. But that little voice in my head is urging me on, and since it got me this far, I figure I may as well see where it leads.

I explore the large empty kitchen, the bare den, the dining room devoid of table and chairs, and the bathroom with only a small bar of soap and a single black towel, thinking how Riley was right—this place is vacant in a way that seems abandoned and creepy, with no personal mementos, no photos, no books. Nothing but dark wood floors, off-white walls, bare cupboards, a fridge stuffed with countless bottles of that weird red liquid, and nothing more. And when I get to the media room, I see the flat-screen TV Riley mentioned, a recliner she didn't mention, and a large pile of foreign-language DVDs whose titles I can't translate. Then I pause at the bottom of the stairs knowing I should leave, that I've seen more than enough, but something I can't quite define urges me on.

I grip the banister, cringing as the stairs groan beneath me, their high-pitched protest alarmingly loud in this vast vacant space. And when I make my way to the landing, I come face to face with the door Riley found locked. Only this time it's left open, pushed slightly ajar.

I creep toward it, summoning the voice in my head, desperate for some kind of guidance. But the only answer I get is the sound of my own beating heart as I press my palm flat against it, then gasp as it opens to a room so ornate, so formal, so grand, it seems straight out of Versailles.

I pause in the doorway, struggling to take it all in. The finely woven tapestries, the antique rugs, the crystal chandeliers, the golden candelabras, the heavy silk draperies, the velvet settee, the marble-topped table piled with tomes. Even the walls, the entire area between the wainscoting and crown molding is covered by large gilt-framed paintings—all of them capturing Damen in costumes that span several centuries, including one of him astride a white stallion, silver sword by his side, wearing the exact same jacket he wore Halloween night.

I move toward it, my eyes seeking the hole on the shoulder, the frayed spot he jokingly blamed on artillery fire. Startled to find it right there in the picture, as I run my finger along it, spellbound, mesmerized, wondering what kind of freaky elaborate ruse he's concocted as my fingertips graze all the way down to the small brass plaque at the bottom that reads:

DAMEN AUGUSTE ESPOSITO, MAY 1775

I turn to the one beside it, my heart racing as I gaze at a portrait of an unsmiling Damen, cloaked in a severe dark suit, surrounded by blue, its plaque bearing the words:

DAMEN AUGUSTE AS PAINTED BY PABLO PICASSO IN 1902

And the one next to that, its heavily textured swirls forming the likeness of

DAMEN ESPOSITO AS PAINTED BY VINCENT VAN GOGH

And on it goes, all four walls displaying Damen's likeness as painted by all the great masters.

I sink onto the velvet settee, eyes bleary, knees weak, my mind racing with a thousand possibilities, each of them equally ridiculous. Then I grasp the book nearest to me, flip to the title page, and read:

For Damen Auguste Esposito.

Signed by William Shakespeare.

I drop it to the floor and reach for the next, *Wuthering Heights, for Damen Auguste,* signed by Emily Brontë.

Every book made out to *Damen Auguste Esposito,* or *Damen Auguste,* or just *Damen.* All of them signed by an author who's been dead for more than a century.

I close my eyes, trying to concentrate on slowing my breath as my heart races, my hands shake, telling myself it's all some kind of joke, that Damen's some freaky history buff, antique collector, an art counterfeiter who's gone too far. Perhaps these are prized family heirlooms, left from a long line of great, great, great, grandfathers, all bearing the same name and uncanny resemblance.

But when I look around again, the chill down my spine tells the undeniable truth—these aren't merely antiques, nor are they heirlooms. These are Damen's personal possessions, the favored treasures he's collected through the years.

I stagger to my feet and stumble into the hall, feeling shaky, unstable, desperate to escape this creepy room, this hideous, gaudy, overstuffed mausoleum, this crypt-like house. Wanting to put as much distance between us as I possibly can, and to never, ever, under any circumstances, come back here again.

I've just reached the bottom stair when I hear a loud piercing scream followed by a long muffled moan, and without even thinking, I turn and race toward it, following the sound to the end of the hall and rushing through the door, finding Damen on the floor, his clothes torn, his face dripping with blood, while Haven thrashes and moans underneath him.

"Ever!" he shouts, springing to his feet and holding me back as I lunge, fight, and kick, desperate to get to her.

"What have you done to her?" I shout, glancing between them, seeing her pale skin, her eyes rolling back in her head, and knowing there's no time to waste.

"Ever, please, stop," he says, his voice sounding too sure, too measured for the incriminating circumstances he's in.

"WHAT HAVE YOU DONE TO HER?" I scream, kicking, hitting, biting, screaming, scratching, using every ounce of my strength, but it's no match for him. He just stands there, holding me with one hand, while absorbing my blows with barely a grimace.

"Ever, please, let me explain," he says, dodging my furiously kicking feet that are aiming right for him.

As I stare at my friend who's bleeding profusely, grimacing in pain, a terrible realization sweeps right through me—*this is why he tried to keep me away!*

"No! That's not it at all. You've got it all wrong. Yes, I didn't want you to see this, though it's not what you think."

He holds me up high, my legs dangling like a rag doll, and despite all my punching and fighting, he hasn't even broken a sweat.

But I don't care about Damen. I don't even care about me. All I care about is Haven, whose lips are turning blue, as her breath grows alarmingly weak.

"What have you done to her?" I glare at him with all the hate I can muster. *"What have you done to her, you freak?"*

"Ever, please, I need you to listen," he pleads, his eyes begging mine.

And despite all my anger, despite my adrenaline, I can still feel that warm languid tingle of his hands on my skin, and I fight like hell to ignore it. Yelling and screaming and kicking my feet, aiming for his most vulnerable parts, but always missing since he's so much quicker than me.

"You can't help her, trust me, I'm the only one who can."

"You're not helping her, you're killing her!" I shout.

He shakes his head and looks at me, his face appearing tired when he whispers, "Hardly."

I try to pull away again, but it's no use, I can't beat him. So I stop, allowing myself to go limp as I close my eyes in surrender.

Thinking: *So this is how it happens. This is how I disappear.*

And the moment he relaxes his grip, I kick my foot as hard as I can, my boot hitting its target as he loosens his grip and I drop to the floor.

I spring toward Haven, my fingers slipping to her blood-covered wrist as I search for a pulse, my eyes fixed on the two small holes in the center of her creepy tattoo, as I beg her to keep breathing, to hang on.

And just as I reach for my cell, intending to call 911, Damen comes up behind me, grabs the phone out of my hand, and says, "I was hoping I wouldn't have to do this."

twenty-four

When I wake, I'm lying in bed with Sabine looming over me, her face a mask of relief, her thoughts a maze of concern.

"Hey," she says, smiling and shaking her head. "You must've had *some* weekend."

I squint first at her and then at the clock. Then I spring out of bed when I realize the time.

"Are you feeling okay?" she asks, trailing behind me. "You were already asleep when I got home last night. You're not sick are you?"

I head for the shower, not sure how to answer. Because even though I don't feel sick, I can't imagine how I slept so long and so late.

"Anything I should know about? Anything you need to tell me?" she asks, standing outside the door.

I close my eyes and rewind the weekend, remembering the beach, Evangeline, Damen staying over and making me dinner, followed by breakfast—"No, nothing happened," I finally say.

"Well, you better hurry if you want to make it to school on time. You sure you're all right?"

"Yes," I say, trying to sound clear-cut, unambiguous, sure as sure can be, as I turn on the taps and step into the spray, not sure if I'm lying or if it's true.

The whole way to school Miles talks about Eric. Giving me the lowdown, the entire step-by-step of their Sunday night text-message breakup, trying to convince me that he couldn't care less, that he is completely and totally over him, which pretty much proves that he's not.

"Are you even listening to me?" He scowls.

"Of course," I mumble, stopping at a light, just a block from school, my mind running through my own weekend events, and always ending at breakfast. No matter how hard I try, I can't remember anything after that.

"Could've fooled me." He smirks and looks out the window. "I mean, if I'm boring you, just say so. Because believe me, I am *so* over Eric. Did I ever tell you about that time when he—"

"Miles, have you talked to Haven?" I ask, glancing at him briefly before the light turns green.

He shakes his head. "You?"

"I don't think so." I press down on the gas, wondering why just saying her name fills me with dread.

"You don't *think* so?" His eyes go wide as he shifts in his seat.

"Not since Friday."

I pull into the parking lot, my heart beating triple time when I see Damen in his usual spot, leaning against his car, waiting for me.

"Well, at least one of us has a shot at happily ever after," Miles says, nodding at Damen who comes around to my side, a single red tulip in hand.

"Good morning." He smiles, handing me the flower and kissing my cheek, as I mumble an incoherent reply and head for the gate. The bell rings as Miles sprints toward class and Damen takes my hand and leads me into English. "Mr. Robins is on his way," he whispers, squeezing my fingers as he leads me past Stacia, who scowls at me and sticks out her foot, before moving it out of my way at the very last second. "He's off the sauce, trying to get his wife back." His lips curve against my ear as I pick up the pace and move away.

I slide onto my seat and unload my books, wondering why my boyfriend's presence is making me feel so edgy and weird, then reach inside my iPod pocket and panic when I realize I left it at home.

"You don't need that," Damen says, reaching for my hand and smoothing my fingers with his. "You have me now."

I close my eyes, knowing Mr. Robins will be here in just three, two, one—

"Ever," Damen whispers, his fingers tracing over the veins on my wrist. "You feeling okay?"

I press my lips together and nod.

"Good." He pauses. "I had a great weekend, I hope you did too."

I open my eyes just as Mr. Robins walks in, noticing how his eyes aren't as puffy, his face not as red, though his hands are still a little shaky.

"Yesterday was fun, don't you think?"

I turn to Damen, gazing into his eyes, my skin infused with warmth and tingle merely because his hand is on mine. Then I nod in agreement, knowing it's the response he wants, even though I'm not sure that it's true.

The next couple of hours are a blur of classes and confusion, and it's not until I get to the lunch table that I learn the truth about yesterday.

"I can't believe you guys went in the water," Miles says, stirring his yoghurt and looking at me. "Do you have any idea how cold it is?"

"She wore a wet suit." Damen shrugs. "In fact, you left it at my house."

I unwrap my sandwich, not remembering any of it. I don't even own a wet suit. *Do I?* "Um, wasn't that Friday?" I ask, blushing when *all* the events of that day come rushing back to me.

Damen shakes his head. "You didn't surf on Friday, I did. Sunday was when I gave you a lesson."

I peel the crust off my sandwich, and try to remember, but it keeps coming up blank.

"So, was she any good?" Miles asks, licking his spoon and gazing from Damen to me.

"Well, it was pretty flat so there wasn't much to surf. Mostly we just lay on the beach, under some blankets. And yeah, she's pretty good at that." He laughs.

I gaze at Damen wondering if my wet suit was on or off under those blankets, and what, if anything happened under there. *Is it possible that I tried to make up for Friday, then blocked it out so I can't even remember it?*

Miles looks at me, brows raised, but I just shrug and take a bite of my sandwich.

"Which beach?" he asks.

But since I can't remember, I turn to Damen.

"Crystal Cove," he says, sipping his drink.

Miles shakes his head and rolls his eyes. "Please tell me you're not turning into one of those couples where the guy does all the talking. I mean, does he order for you in restaurants too?"

I look at Damen, but before he can answer Miles goes, "No, I'm asking *you,* Ever."

I think back to our two restaurant meals, one that wonderful day at Disneyland that ended so strangely, and the other at the racetrack when we won all that money. "I order my own meals," I say. And then I look at him and go, "Can I borrow your Side-kick?"

He pulls it from his pocket and slides it toward me. "Why? You forget your phone?"

"Yeah and I want to text Haven and see where she is. I have the weirdest feeling about her." I shake my head, not knowing how to explain it to myself, much less to them. "I can't stop thinking about her," I say, fingers tapping the tiny keyboard.

"She's at home, sick," Miles says. "Some kind of flu. Plus she's sad about Evangeline, though she swears she no longer hates us."

"I thought you said you hadn't talked to her." I pause and gaze up at him, sure that's what he said in the car.

"I sent her a text in history."

"So she's okay?" I stare at Miles, my stomach a jumble of nerves though I can't begin to grasp why.

"Puking her guts out, mourning the loss of her friend, but yeah, basically fine."

I return the Sidekick to Miles, figuring there's no use in both-ering her if she's not feeling well. Then Damen puts his hand on my leg, Miles goes on about Eric, and I pick at my lunch, going through the motions of nodding and smiling, but unable to shake my unease.

Wouldn't you know it, the one day Damen decides to spend the whole day at school just happens to be the day I wish he would've ditched. Because every time I get out of class, I find him standing right outside the door, anxiously waiting, and asking if I'm feeling okay. And it's really starting to get on my nerves.

So after art, when we're walking to the parking lot and he offers to follow me home, I just look at him and say, "Um, if it's okay with you, I need to be by myself for a while."

"Is everything okay?" he asks for the millionth time.

But I just nod and climb inside, anxious to close the door and put some distance between us. "I just need to catch up on a few things, but I'll see you tomorrow, okay?" And not giving him a chance to reply, I back out of my space and drive away.

When I get home, I'm so incredibly tired I head straight for my bed, planning to take a short nap before Sabine comes home and starts worrying about me again. But when I wake up in the middle of the night, with my heart pounding and my clothes soaked with sweat, I have this undeniable feeling I'm not alone in my room.

I reach for my pillow, grasping it tightly as though those soft downy feathers will serve as some sort of shield, then I peer into the dark space before me, and whisper, "Riley?" Even though I'm pretty sure it's not her.

I hold my breath, hearing a soft muffled sound, like slippers on carpet, over by the french doors, and I surprise myself by whispering, "Damen?" as I peer into the dark, unable to make out anything other than a soft swishing sound.

I fumble for the light switch, squinting against the sudden brightness, and searching for the intruder, so sure I had company, so positive I wasn't alone, that I'm almost disappointed when I find my room empty.

I climb out of bed, still clutching my pillow, as I lock the french doors. Then I peek into my closet and under my bed, like my dad used to do those long-ago nights he reported for boogey-man duty. But not finding anything, I crawl back in bed, wonder-ing if it was possibly my dream that sparked all these fears.

It was similar to the one I had before, where I was running through a dark windswept canyon, my filmy white dress a poor defense against the cold, inviting the wind to lash at my skin, chilling me straight through to my bones. And yet I barely no-ticed, I was so focused on running, my bare feet carving into the damp, muddy earth, heading toward a hazy refuge I couldn't quite see.

All I know is that I was running toward a soft glowing light.

And away from Damen.

twenty-five

The next day at school, I park in my usual space, jump out of my car, and run right past Damen, heading for Haven who's waiting by the gate. And even though I normally do everything possible to avoid physical contact, I grab onto her shoulders and hug her right to me.

"Okay, okay, I love you too." She laughs, shaking her head and pushing me away. "I mean, jeez, it's not like I was going to stay mad at you guys forever."

Her dyed red hair is dry and limp, her black nail polish is chipped, the hollows under her eyes seem darker than usual, and her face is decidedly pale. But even though she assures me she's okay, I can't help but reach out and hug her again.

"How're you feeling?" I ask, eyeing her carefully, trying to get a read, but other than her aura appearing gray, weak, and translucent, I can't *see* much of anything.

"*What* is going on with you?" she says, shaking her head and pushing me away. "What's with all the love and affection? I mean *you* of all people, you of the eternal iPod-hoodie combo."

"I heard you were sick, and then when you weren't at school yesterday—" I stop, feeling ridiculous to be hovering like this.

But she just laughs. "I know what's going on here." She nods. "This is your fault, isn't it?" She points at Damen. "You just had to come along and thaw out my icy cold friend, turning her into a sentimental, warm, fuzzy sap."

And even though Damen laughs, it doesn't quite reach his eyes.

"It was just the flu," she says as Miles loops his arm through hers and we head past the gate. "And I guess being all depressed about Evangeline made it that much worse. I mean, I was so feverish, I actually blacked out a few times."

"Seriously?" I break away from Damen so I can walk alongside her.

"Yeah, it was the weirdest thing. Every night I would go to bed wearing one thing, and when I woke up I'd be wearing something entirely different. And when I'd go looking for what I had on before, I couldn't find it. It was like it'd vanished or something."

"Well, your room is pretty messy." Miles laughs. "Or maybe you were hallucinating; you know that can happen when you have a monster fever."

"Maybe." She shrugs. "But all my black scarves were gone, so I had to borrow this one from my brother." She lifts the end of her blue wool scarf and waves it around.

"Was anyone there to take care of you?" Damen asks, coming up beside me and taking my hand, his fingers intertwining with mine, sending a flood of warmth through my system.

Haven shakes her head and rolls her eyes. "Are you kidding? I may as well be emancipated like you. Besides, I had my door locked the whole time. I could've *died* in there and nobody would've known."

"What about Drina?" I ask, my stomach clenching at the mention of her name.

Haven gives me a strange look and says, "Drina's in New York. She left Friday night. Anyway, I hope you guys don't get it, because even though some of the dream-state stuff was pretty cool, I know you guys wouldn't be into it." She stops near her class and leans against the wall.

"Did you dream about a canyon?" I ask, dropping Damen's hand, and moving so close I'm right up in her face again.

But Haven just laughs and pushes me away. "Um, excuse me, boundaries!" She shakes her head. "And no, there were no canyons. Just some wild goth stuff, hard to explain, though plenty of blood and gore."

And the second she says that, the second I hear the word "blood," everything goes black as my body tilts toward the floor.

"Ever?" Damen cries, catching me just seconds before I crash to the ground. "Ever," he whispers, his voice tinged with worry.

And when I open my eyes to meet his, something about his expression, something about the intensity of his gaze seems so familiar. But just as the memory begins to form, it's erased by the sound of Haven's voice.

"That's exactly how it starts." She nods. "I mean, I didn't pass out until later, but still, it definitely started with a major dizzy spell."

"Maybe she's pregnant?" Miles says, loud enough for several passing students to hear.

"Not likely," I say, surprised by how much better I feel, now that I'm wrapped in Damen's warm, supportive arms. "I'm okay, really." I stagger to my feet and move away.

"You should take her home," Miles says, looking at Damen. "She looks awful."

"Yeah." Haven nods. "You should rest, seriously. You *so* don't want to catch it."

But even though I insist on going to class, nobody listens to me. And the next thing I know, Damen's arm is wrapped around my waist and he's leading me back to his car.

"This is ridiculous," I say, as he pulls out of the parking lot and heads away from school. "Seriously, I'm fine. Not to mention that we're totally gonna get busted for ditching again!"

"No one's getting busted." He glances at me briefly, before focusing back on the road. "May I remind you that you fainted back there? You're lucky I caught you in time."

"Yes, but that's the thing, you *did* catch me in time. And now I'm fine. Seriously. I mean, if you're really so worried about me, then you should've taken me to the school nurse. You didn't have to kidnap me."

"I'm not *kidnapping* you," he says, clearly annoyed. "I just want to look after you, make sure you're okay."

"Oh, so now you're a doctor?" I shake my head and roll my eyes.

But he doesn't say anything. He just cruises up Coast Highway, passing right by the street that leads to my house until eventually stopping before a big imposing gate.

"Where are you taking me?" I ask, watching as he nods at a familiar attendant, who smiles and waves us right through.

"My house," he mumbles, driving up a steep hill before making a series of turns that lead into a cul-de-sac and a big empty garage at the end.

Then he takes my hand and leads me through a well-appointed kitchen and into the den where I stand, hands on hips, taking in all of his beautiful furnishings, the exact opposite of the frat-house chic I expected.

"Is this really all yours?" I ask, running my hand over a plush chenille sofa as my eyes tour exquisite lamps, Persian rugs, a collection of abstract oil paintings, and the dark wood coffee table covered in art books, candles, and a framed photo of me. "When'd you take this?" I lift it off the table and study it closely, having absolutely no memory of the moment.

"You act like you've never been here before," he says, motioning for me to sit.

"I haven't." I shrug.

"You *have*," he insists. "Last Sunday? After the beach? I've even got your wet suit hanging upstairs. Now sit." He pats the sofa cushion. "I want to see you resting."

I sink down into the overstuffed cushions, still clutching the photo and wondering when it was taken. My hair is long and loose, my face is slightly flushed, and I'm wearing a peach-colored hoodie I'd forgotten I had. But even though I appear to be laughing, my eyes are sad and serious.

"I took that one day at school. When you weren't looking. I prefer candid shots, it's the only way to really capture the essence of a person," he says, removing it from my grip and retuning it to the table. "Now, close your eyes and rest, while I make you some tea."

When the tea is ready he places the cup in my hands, then busies himself with the thick wool throw, tucking it in all around me.

"This is really nice and all, but it's not necessary," I say, placing the cup on the table and glancing at my watch, thinking if we leave right now, I can still make it to second period in time. "Seriously. I'm fine. We should get back to school."

"Ever, you *fainted*," he says, sitting down beside me, his eyes searching my face as he touches my hair.

"Stuff happens." I shrug, embarrassed by all the fussing, especially when I know nothing's wrong.

"Not on my watch," he whispers, moving his hand from my hair to the scar on my face.

"Don't." I pull away just before he can touch it, watching as his hand falls back to his side.

"What's wrong?" he asks, peering at me.

"I don't want you to catch it," I lie, not wanting to admit to the truth—that the scar is for me, and me only. A constant reminder, ensuring I'll never forget. That's why I refused the plastic surgeon, refused to let him "fix" it. Knowing what happened could never be fixed. It's my fault, my private pain, which is why I hide it under my bangs.

But he just laughs when he says, "I don't get sick."

I close my eyes and shake my head, and when I open them I say, "Oh, so now you don't get sick?"

He shrugs and brings the cup to my lips, urging me to drink.

I take a small sip then turn my head and push it away, saying, "So let's see, you don't get sick, you don't get in trouble for truancy, you get straight A's despite said truancy, you pick up a paint brush and *voilà*, you make a Picasso better than Picasso. You can cook a meal as good as any five-star chef, you used to model in New York—which was right before you lived in Santa Fe, which came after you lived in London, Romania, Paris, and Egypt—you're unemployed and emancipated, yet you somehow manage to live in a luxuriously decorated multimillion-dollar dream home, you drive an expensive car, and—"

"Rome," he says, giving me a serious look.

"What?"

"You said I lived in Romania, when it was actually Rome."

I roll my eyes. "Whatever, the point is—" I stop, my words caught in my throat.

"Yes?" He leans toward me. "The point is . . ."

I swallow hard and avert my gaze, my mind grasping the edges of something, something that's been gnawing at me for some time. Something about Damen, something about that almost, *otherworldly,* quality of his—*is he a ghost like Riley? No, that's impossible, everyone can see him.*

"Ever," he says, his palm on my cheek, turning my head so I'm facing him again. "Ever, I—"

But before he can finish, I'm off the couch and out of his reach, tossing the throw from my shoulders and refusing to look at him when I say, "Take me home."

twenty-six

The second Damen pulls into my drive, I jump out of the car and hit the ground running, racing through the front door and taking the stairs two at a time, hoping and praying that Riley will be there. I need to see her, need to talk to her about all the crazy thoughts that are building inside me. She's the only one I can even begin to explain it to, the only one who just might understand.

I check my den, my bathroom, my balcony, I stand in my room and call out her name, feeling strange, hectic, shaky, panicked in a way that I can't quite explain.

But when she fails to appear, I crumble onto my bed, curl my body into a small tight ball, and relive her loss all over again.

"Ever, honey, are you okay?" Sabine drops her bags and kneels down beside me, her palm cool and sure against my hot clammy skin.

I close my eyes and shake my head, knowing that despite the fainting spell, despite my recent bout of exhaustion, I'm not sick. At least not in the way that she means. It's more complicated than that, and not so easily cured.

I roll onto my side, using the edge of my pillowcase to wipe at my tears, then I turn to her and say, "Sometimes—sometimes it just hits me, you know? And, it's not getting any easier," I choke, my eyes flooding all over again.

She gazes at me, her face softened by sorrow as she says, "I'm not sure that it will. I think you just get used to the feeling, the hollowness, the loss, and somehow learn to live around it." She smiles, removing my tears with her hand.

And when she lies down beside me, I don't pull away. I just close my eyes and allow myself to feel her pain, and my pain, until it's all mixed together, raw and deep with no beginning or end. And we stay like that, crying and talking and sharing in the way we should've done long ago. If only I'd let her in. If only I hadn't pushed her away.

And when she finally gets up to make us some dinner, she pilfers through her tote bag and says, "Look what I found in the trunk of my car. I borrowed it ages ago after you first moved here. I didn't realize I had it all this time."

Then she tosses me the peach hoodie.

The one I'd forgotten all about.

The one I haven't worn since the first week of school.

The one I was wearing in the picture on Damen's coffee table even though we hadn't yet met.

The next day at school, I drive right past Damen, and that stupid spot he always saves for me, and park in what seems like the other side of the world.

"What the *hell*?" Miles says, gaping incredulously. "You drove right past it! And now look how far we have to walk!"

I slam my door and storm across the lot, marching right past Damen who's leaning against his car, waiting for me.

"Um, hel-*lo*! Tall dark and handsome at three o'clock, you walked right by him! What is going on with you?" Miles says, grabbing my arm and looking at me. "Are you guys in a fight?"

But I just shake my head and pull away. "*Nothing's* going on," I say, striding toward the building.

Even though the last time I checked Damen was well behind me, when I walk into class and head for my seat, he's already there. So I raise my hood and switch on my iPod, making a point to ignore him, while I wait for Mr. Robins to call roll.

"Ever," Damen whispers, as I stare straight ahead, focusing on Mr. Robins's receding hairline, just waiting for my turn to say "here."

"Ever, I know you're upset. But I can explain."

I stare straight ahead, pretending not to hear.

"Ever, *please*," Damen begs.

But I just act like he's not even there. And just when Mr. Robins gets to my name, Damen sighs, closes his eyes, and says, "Fine. Just remember, you asked for it."

And the next thing I know, a horrible *thwonk!* resonates throughout the room, as nineteen heads hit the tops of their desks.

Everyone's head but Damen's and mine.

I gaze all around, mouth gaping, eyes trying to comprehend, and when I finally turn back to Damen, staring accusingly, he just shrugs and says, "This is exactly what I'd hoped to avoid."

"What've you done?" I stare at all the limp bodies, a terrible understanding beginning to emerge. "Omigod, you killed them! You killed everyone!" I shout, my heart pounding so fast I'm sure he can hear it.

But he just shakes his head and says, "Come on, Ever. What do you take me for? Of course, I didn't kill them. They're just taking a little . . . siesta, that's all."

I scoot to the edge of my seat, my eyes fixed on the door, plotting my escape.

"You can try, but you won't get very far. You see how I beat you to class even though you had a head start?" He crosses his legs and gazes at me, his face calm, voice steady as can be.

"You can read my mind?" I whisper, recalling some of my more embarrassing thoughts, my cheeks growing hot as my fingers grip the edge of my desk.

"Usually." He shrugs. "Well, pretty much always, yes."

"For how long?" I stare at him, part of me wanting to take my chance on escape, while the other part wants to get a few questions answered before my most certain demise.

"Since the first day I saw you," he whispers, his gaze locked on mine, sending a flood of warmth through my body.

"And when was that?" I ask, voice trembling, remembering the photo on his table, and wondering just how long he's been stalking me.

"I'm not stalking you." He laughs. "At least not in the way that you think."

"Why should I believe you?" I glare, knowing better than to trust him, no matter how trivial.

"Because I've never lied to you."

"You're lying now!"

"I've never lied to you about anything important," he says, averting his gaze.

"Oh really? What about the fact that you took a photo of me long before you were even enrolled here? Where does that fall on your list of important things to share in a relationship?" I glare.

He sighs, his eyes appearing tired when he says, "And where does being a clairvoyant who hangs out with her dead little sister fall upon yours?"

"You don't know anything about me." I stand, hands sweaty and shaky, heart slam-dancing in my chest, as I stare at all of the slumped-over bodies, Stacia with her mouth hanging open, Craig snoring so loud he's vibrating, Mr. Robins looking more happy and peaceful than I've ever seen him. "Is it the whole school? Or just this room?"

"I can't be sure, but I'm guessing it's the whole school." He nods, smiling as he glances around, clearly pleased with his handiwork.

And without another word, I spring from my seat, race out the door, sprint down the hall, across the quad, and through the office. Fleeing past all the slumped-over secretaries and administrators sleeping at their desks, before bursting through the door and into the parking lot, running toward my little red Miata, where Damen is already waiting, my bag dangling from the very tips of his fingers.

"I told you." He shrugs, returning my backpack.

I stand before him, sweaty, frantic, completely freaked out. All of those long-forgotten moments flashing before me—his blood-covered face, Haven thrashing and moaning, that weird creepy room—and I know he did something to my mind, something to keep me from remembering. And even though I'm no match for someone like him, I refuse to go down without a fight.

"Ever!" he cries, reaching toward me, then letting his hand

fall to his side. "You think I did all of this so that I can kill you?" His eyes are full of anguish, frantically searching my face.

"Isn't that the plan?" I glare. "Haven thinks it's all some wild, goth, fever dream. I'm the only one who knows the truth. I'm the only one who knows just how big of a monster you really are. The only thing I don't get is why you didn't just kill us both while you had the chance? Why bother suppressing the memory and keeping me alive?"

"I would *never* hurt you," he says, his eyes pinched with pain. "You've got it all wrong, I was trying to *save* Haven, not harm her. You just wouldn't listen."

"Then why did she look like she was on the brink of death?" I press my lips together to stop them from quivering, my eyes fixed on his but refusing their heat.

"Because she *was* on the brink of death," he says, sounding annoyed. "That tattoo on her wrist was infected in the worst way—it was killing her. When you walked in on us I was suck-ing the infection right out of her, like you do with a snake bite."

I shake my head. "I know what I saw."

He closes his eyes, pinching the bridge of his nose with his fingers and taking a long deep breath before he looks at me and says, "I know how it looks. And I know you don't believe me. But I've been trying to explain and you just wouldn't let me, so I did all of this to get your attention. Because, Ever, trust me, you've got it all wrong."

He looks at me, his eyes dark and intense, his hands relaxed and open, but I'm not buying it. Not a single word. He's had hundreds, maybe thousands of years to perfect such an act, re-sulting in a really good show, but still only a show. And even though I can't believe I'm about to say it, even though I can't quite get my mind wrapped around it, there's only one explanation, no matter how crazy.

"All I know is that I want you to go back to your coffin, or your coven, or wherever it is that you lived before you came here and—" I gasp for breath, feeling like I'm trapped in some horrible nightmare, wishing I'd wake up soon. "Just leave me alone—just go away!"

He closes his eyes and shakes his head, stifling a laugh as he says. "I'm not a vampire, Ever."

"Oh, yeah? Prove it!" I say, my voice shaky, my eyes on his, fully convinced I'm just a rosary, garlic clove, and wooden stake short of ending all this.

But he just laughs. "Don't be ridiculous. There's no such thing."

"I know what I saw," I tell him, picturing the blood, Haven, that strange and creepy room, knowing that as soon as I *see* it, he'll see it too. Wondering how he'll possibly try to explain his friendship with Marie Antoinette, Picasso, Van Gogh, Emily Brontë, and William Shakespeare—when they lived centuries apart.

He shakes his head, then looks at me and says, "Well, for that matter, I was also a good friend of Leonardo da Vinci, Botticelli, Francis Bacon, Albert Einstein, and John, Paul, George, and Ringo." He pauses, seeing the blank look on my face and groaning when he says, "Christ, Ever, the *Beatles!*" He shakes his head and laughs. "God, you make me feel old."

I just stand there, barely breathing, not comprehending, but when he reaches for me, I still have the good sense to pull away.

"I'm not a vampire, Ever. I'm an immortal."

I roll my eyes. "Vampire, immortal, same difference," I say, shaking my head and fuming under my breath, thinking how ridiculous it is to argue over a label.

"Ah, but it happens to be a label worth arguing over, as there *is* a big difference. You see, a vampire is a *fictional, made-up* creature that exists only in books, and movies, and, in your case, overactive imaginations." He smiles. "Whereas *I* am an immortal. Which means I've roamed the earth for hundreds of years in one continuous life cycle. Though, contrary to the fantasy you've conjured in your head, my immortality is not reliant on bloodsucking, human sacrifice, or whatever unsavory acts you've imagined."

I squint, suddenly remembering his strange red brew and wondering if that has something to do with his longevity. Like it's some kind of immortal juice or something.

"Immortal juice." He laughs. "Good one. Imagine the marketing possibilities." But when he sees I'm not laughing, his face softens when he says, "Ever, please, you've no need to fear me. I'm not dangerous, or evil, and I would never do anything to hurt you. I'm simply a guy who's lived *a very long time.* Maybe too long, who knows? But that doesn't make me bad. Just immortal. And I'm afraid . . ."

He reaches for me, but I back away, my legs shaky, unstable, refusing to hear any more. "You're lying!" I whisper, my heart filled with rage. "This is crazy! *You're crazy!*"

He shakes his head and gazes at me, eyes filled with unfathomable regret. Then he takes a step toward me and says, "Remember the first moment you saw me? Right here in the parking lot? And how the second your eyes met mine you felt an immediate rush of recognition? And the other day, when you fainted? How you opened your eyes and looked right into mine, and you were so close to remembering, on the very verge of recollection, but then you lost the thread?"

I stare at him, immobile, transfixed, sensing exactly what he's about to say, but refusing to hear it. "No!" I mumble, taking another step back, my head dizzy, my body off balance as my knees begin to buckle.

"I'm the one who found you that day in the woods. I'm the one who *brought you back!*"

I shake my head, my eyes blurred with tears. *No!*

"The eyes you looked into, on your—*return*—were mine, Ever. I was there. I was right there beside you. I brought you back. I *saved* you. I know you remember. I can see it in your thoughts."

"*No!*" I scream, covering my ears and closing my eyes. "Stop it!" I yell, not wanting to hear any more.

"Ever." His voice invades my thoughts, my senses. "I'm sorry but it's true. Though you have no reason to fear me."

I crumble to the ground, face pressed against my knees, as I break into violent, gasping, shoulder-shaking sobs. "You had no right to come near me, no right to interfere! It's your fault I'm a freak! It's your fault I'm stuck with this horrible life! Why didn't you just leave me alone, why didn't you just let me die?"

"I couldn't stand to lose you again," he mumbles, kneeling down beside me. "Not this time. *Not again.*"

I lift my gaze to his, having no idea what he means, but hoping he won't try to explain it. I've heard about all I can take, and I just want it to stop. I just want it to end.

He shakes his head, a pained expression masking his face. "Ever, please don't think that way, please don't—"

"So—so you just randomly decide to bring me back while my whole family dies?" I say, gazing up at him, my sorrow consumed by a crushing rage. "*Why?* Why would you do such a thing? I mean, if what you say is true, if you're so powerful you can raise the dead, then why didn't you save them too? *Why only me?*"

He winces at the hostility in my gaze, tiny arrows of hate directed at him. Then he closes his eyes when he says, "I'm not that powerful. And it was too late, they'd already moved on. But you—you lingered. And I thought that meant you wanted to live."

I lean against my car, closing my eyes, gasping for breath, thinking: *So it really is my fault. Because I procrastinated, lingered, wandered through that stupid field, distracted by those pulsating trees and flowers that shivered. While they moved on, crossed over, and I fell for his bait . . .*

He looks at me briefly, then averts his gaze.

And wouldn't you know it, the one time I'm so angry I could actually kill someone, my anger's directed at the one person who claims to be, well, *un-killable*.

"Go away!" I finally say, ripping the crystal-encrusted horseshoe bracelet from my wrist and throwing it at him. Wanting to forget about that, about him, about *everything*. Having seen and heard more than I can take. "Just—go away. I never want to see you again."

"Ever, please don't say that if you don't really mean it," he says, his voice pleading, sorrowful, weak.

I place my head in my hands, too weary to cry, too shattered to speak. And knowing he can hear the thoughts in my head, I shut my eyes and think:

You say you'd never harm me, but look what you've done! You've ruined everything, wrecked my whole life, and for what? So I could be alone? So I could live the rest of my life as a freak? I hate you—I hate you for what you've done to me—I hate you for what you've made me— I hate you for being so selfish! And I never, ever want to see you again!

I stay like that, head in my hands, rocking back and forth against the wheel of my car, allowing the words to flow through me, over and over again.

Just let me be normal, please just let me be normal again. Just go away, leave me alone. Because I hate you—I hate you—I hate you—I hate you—

When I finally look up, I'm surrounded by tulips—hundreds of thousands of tulips, all of them red. Those soft waxy petals glinting in the bright morning sun, filling up the parking lot and covering all the cars. And as I struggle to my feet and brush myself off, I know without looking: their sender is gone.

twenty-seven

It's weird in English, not having Damen beside me, holding my hand, whispering in my ear, and acting as my *off* switch. I guess I'd grown so used to having him around I'd forgotten just how mean Stacia and Honor could be. But watching them smirk, as they text each other with messages like—*Stupid freak, no wonder he left*—I know I'm back to relying on my hoodie, sunglasses, and iPod again.

Though it's not like I don't see the irony. It's not like I don't get the joke. Because for someone who sobbed in a parking lot, begging her immortal boyfriend to disappear so that she could feel normal again, well, obviously, the punch line is *me*.

Because now, in my new life without Damen, all of the random thoughts, the profusion of colors and sounds, are so overwhelming, so tremendously crushing, my ears constantly ring, my eyes continuously water, and the migraines appear so quickly, invading my head, hijacking my body, and rendering me so nauseous and dizzy I can just barely function.

Though it is funny how I was so worried about mentioning our breakup to Miles and Haven that a full week passed by before his name was even mentioned. And even then, I'm the one who brought it up. I guess they'd gotten so used to his erratic attendance they didn't see anything unusual about his latest extended absence.

So one day, during lunch, I cleared my throat, glanced between them, and said, "Just so you know, Damen and I broke up." And when their mouths dropped open and they both started to speak, I held up my hand and said, "And, he's gone."

"*Gone?*" they said, four eyes bugging, two jaws dropping, both of them reluctant to believe it.

And even though I knew they were concerned, even though I knew I owed them a good explanation, I just shook my head, pressed my lips together, and refused to say anything further.

Though Ms. Machado wasn't so easy. A few days after Damen left, she walked right up to my easel, did her best to avoid direct eye contact with my Van Gogh disaster, and said, "I know you and Damen were close, and I know how hard this must be for you, so I thought you should have this. I think you'll find it extraordinary."

She pushed a canvas toward me, but I just leaned it against the leg of my easel and kept painting. I had no doubt about its being extraordinary; everything Damen did was extraordinary. But then again, when you've roamed the earth for hundreds of years, you've plenty of time to master a few skills.

"Aren't you going to look at it?" she asked, confused by my lack of interest in Damen's masterpiece replica of a masterpiece.

But I just turned to her, forcing my face into a smile when I said, "No. But thank you for giving it to me."

And when the bell finally rang, I dragged it out to my car, tossed it into my trunk, and slammed down the hood, without once even looking.

And when Miles asked, "Hey, what was that?" I just jammed the key in the ignition and said, "Nothing."

But the one thing I didn't expect was how lonely I felt. I guess I failed to realize just how much I relied on Damen and Riley to fill up the gaps, to seal all the cracks in my life. And even though Riley warned me she wouldn't be around all that much, when it hit the three-week mark, I couldn't help but panic.

Because saying good-bye to Damen, my gorgeous, creepy, quite possibly evil, immortal boyfriend, was harder than I'll ever admit. But not getting to say good-bye to Riley is more than I can possibly bear.

Saturday, when Miles and Haven invite me to tag along on their annual Winter Fantasy pilgrimage, I accept. Knowing it's time to get out of the house, out of my slump, and rejoin the living. And since it's my first time there, they're pretty excited about showing me around.

"It's not as good as the summer Sawdust Festival," Miles says, after we buy our tickets and head through the gates.

"That's because it's better," Haven says, skipping ahead and turning to smile at us.

Miles smirks. "Well, other than the weather it doesn't really matter since they both have glassblowers, and that's always my favorite part."

"Big surprise." Haven laughs, looping her arm through Miles's as I follow alongside them, my head spinning from the crowd-generated energy, all of the colors, sights, and sounds swirling around me, wishing I'd had the good sense to just stay home where it's quieter, safer.

I've just lifted my hood and am about to insert my earbuds

when Haven turns to me and says, "Really? You're seriously doing that here?"

And I stop, and slip them back into my pocket. Because even though I want to drown everyone out, I don't want my friends to think I'm trying to drown them out too.

"Come on, you've *got* to see the glassblower, he's amazing," Miles says, leading us past an authentic-looking Santa and several silversmiths before stopping in front of some guy crafting beautiful, multicolored vases using only his mouth, a long metal tube, and fire. "I have *got* to learn how to do that." He sighs, completely transfixed.

I stand beside him, watching the swirl of liquid colors mold and take shape, then I head over to the next booth, where some really cool purses are displayed.

I hoist a small brown bag off its shelf and stroke its soft buttery leather, thinking it might make a good Christmas gift for Sabine, since it's something she'd never buy for herself, but might secretly want.

"How much for this one?" I ask, wincing as my voice reverberates through my head in a never-ending percussion.

"One hundred and fifty."

I gaze at the woman, taking in her blue batik tunic, faded jeans, and silver peace-sign necklace, knowing she's prepared to go lower, much lower. But my eyes are stinging so bad, and the throbbing in my head's so severe I don't have the strength to barter. In fact, I just want to go home.

I put it back where I found it and start to turn away, when she says, "But for you, one thirty."

And even though I'm well aware that she's still at the top of her offer, that there's plenty more room to bargain, I just nod and move away.

Then someone behind me says, "Now you and I both know her absolute bottom line is ninety-five. So why'd you give up so easily?"

And when I turn, I see a petite auburn-haired woman surrounded by the most brilliant purple aura.

"Ava." She nods, extending her hand.

"I know," I say, making a point to ignore it.

"How've you been?" she asks, smiling as though I didn't just do something incredibly cold and rude, which makes me feel even worse for having done it.

I shrug, glancing over to the glassblower, searching for Miles and Haven, and feeling the first hint of panic when I don't see them.

"Your friends are standing in line at Laguna Taco. But don't worry, they're ordering for you too."

"I *know*," I tell her, even though I didn't. My head hurts far too much to get a read on anyone.

And just as I start to move away again, she grabs hold of my arm and says, "Ever, I want you to know my offer still stands. I'd really like to help you." She smiles.

My first instinct is to pull away, to get as far from her as possible, but the moment she placed her hand on my arm, my head stopped pounding, my ears stopped ringing, and my eyes stopped manufacturing tears. But when I look in her eyes, I remember who she really is—the horrible woman who's stolen my sister. And I narrow my gaze and yank my arm free, glaring at her as I say, "Don't you think you've *helped* enough already?" I press my lips together and glare. "You've already stolen Riley, so what more could you possible want?" I swallow hard and try not to cry.

She looks at me, brows merging with concern, her aura a beautiful vibrant beacon of violet. "Riley was never anyone's to take. And she'll always be with you, even if you can't actually *see* her," she says, reaching for my arm.

But I refuse to listen. And I refuse to let her touch me again, no matter how calming. "Just—just stay out of my life," I say, moving away. "Just leave me alone. Riley and I were fine until you came along."

But she doesn't leave. She doesn't go anywhere. She just stays right there, gazing at me in that horribly annoying, soft, caring way. "I know about the headaches," she whispers, her voice light and soothing. "You don't have to live like this, Ever. Really, I can help."

And even though I'd love a break from the onslaught of noise and pain, I turn on my heel and storm away, hoping I never see her again.

"Who was that?" Haven asks, plunging a tortilla chip into a tiny cup of salsa as I sit down beside her and shrug.

"No one," I whisper, cringing as my words vibrate in my ears.

"Looks like that psychic lady from the party."

I reach for the plate Miles slides toward me and pick up a plastic fork.

"We didn't know what you wanted so we got a little of everything," he says. "Did you buy a purse?"

I shake my head, then immediately regret it since it only intensifies the pounding. "Too expensive," I say, covering my mouth as I chew, the crunch reverberating so badly my eyes fill with tears. "You get a vase?" But I already know that he didn't, and not just because I'm psychic, but because there's no bag.

"No, I just like to watch 'em blow." He laughs, taking a sip of his drink.

"Hey you guys, shh! Is that my phone?" Haven digs through her oversized, overstuffed bag that often stands in for her closet.

"Well, since you're the only one at this table with a Marilyn Manson ring tone . . ." Miles shrugs, ignoring his taco shell and eating only the insides.

"Off the carbs?" I ask, watching as he picks at his food.

He nods. "Just because Tracy Turnblad's fat doesn't mean I have to be."

I take a sip of my Sprite and gaze at Haven. And when I see the elated expression on her face, I *know*.

She turns away from us, covers her other ear, and says, "Omigod! I totally thought you'd vanished—I'm out with Miles— yeah, Ever's here too—yeah, they're right here—okay." She covers the mouthpiece and turns toward us, her eyes lighting up when she says, "Drina says hi!" Then she waits for us to say *hi* back. But when we don't, she rolls her eyes, gets up, and walks away, saying, "They say hi too."

Miles shakes his head and looks at me. "I didn't say *hi*. Did you say *hi*?"

I shrug and mix my beans into my rice.

"Trouble," he says, gazing after her and shaking his head.

And even though I sense that it's true, I'm wondering what exactly he means. Because the energy in this place is bubbling and swirling like a big cosmic soup, too lumpy to slog through or try to tune in. "What do you mean?" I ask, squinting against the glare.

"Isn't it obvious?"

I shrug, my head pounding so badly I can't get inside his.

"There's something just so—*creepy* about their friendship. I mean, a harmless girl crush is one thing. But this—this just doesn't make any sense. Major creep factor."

"Creepy how?" I tear a piece off my taco shell and look at him.

He ignores his rice and favors the beans. "I know this is going to sound horrible, and trust me, I don't mean it to be, but it's almost like she's turning Haven into an acolyte."

I raise my brows.

"A follower, a worshipper, a clone, a Mini-Me." He shrugs. "And, it's just so—"

"Creepy," I provide.

He sips his drink and glances between Haven and me. "Look at how she's started dressing like her, the contacts, the hair color, the makeup, the clothing, she acts like her too—or at least she tries to."

"Is it just that, or is there something else?" I ask, wondering if he knows anything specific, or if it's just a general sense of doom.

"You need more?" He gapes.

I shrug, dropping my taco onto my plate, no longer hungry.

"But between you and me, that whole tattoo thing takes it to a whole new level. I mean, *what the hell?*" he whispers, glancing at Haven, making sure she can't hear. "What's it even supposed to *mean?*" He shakes his head. "I mean, okay, I *know* what it means, but what does it mean to *them?* Is it the latest in vampire chic? Because Drina's not exactly goth. I'm not sure what she's trying to be with her fitted silk lady dresses and purses that match her shoes. Is it a cult? Some kind of secret society? And don't get me started on that infection. Na-*sty*. And, by the way, *so* not normal like she thinks. It's probably what made her so sick."

I press my lips and stare at him, not sure how to respond, how much to share. And yet, wondering why I'm so determined to keep Damen's secrets—secrets that bring *creepy* to a whole new level. Secrets that, when I think about it, have nothing to do with *me.* But I hesitate for too long, and Miles continues, ensuring the vault stays locked, at least for today.

"The whole thing is just so—*unhealthy.*" He cringes.

"What's unhealthy?" Haven asks, plopping down beside me and tossing her phone back into her purse.

"Not washing your hands after you go to the bathroom," Miles quips.

"And *that's* what you guys were talking about?" She eyes us suspiciously. "Like I'm supposed to believe that?"

"I'm telling you, Ever refuses to suds up, and I was just trying to warn her of the dangers she's exposing herself to. Exposing *all of us* to." He shakes his head and looks at me.

I roll my eyes, my face turning crimson even thought it's *not* true. Watching as Haven digs through her bag, pushing past stray tubes of lipstick, a cordless curling iron, stray breath mints—their wrappers long gone—before coming across a small silver flask, unscrewing the top, and dumping a fair amount of clear, odorless liquid into each of our drinks.

"Well, that's all very amusing, but it's obvious you were talking about *me.* But you know what? I'm so freaking happy I don't even care." She smiles.

I reach for her hand, determined to stop her from pouring. Ever since the night I puked my guts out at cheerleading camp, after drinking more than my share of the contraband bottle Rachel smuggled into our cabin, I've sworn off the vodka. But the moment I touch her I'm overcome with dread, seeing a calendar flash before me with December 21 circled in red.

"Jeez, relax, already. Stop being so *clenched.* Live a little, will ya?" She shakes her head and rolls her eyes. "Aren't you going to ask me why I'm so happy?"

"No, because I know you'll tell us anyway," Miles says, discarding his plate, having eaten all of the protein and saving the rest for the pigeons.

"You're right, Miles, you're absolutely right. Though it's always nice to be asked. Anyway, that was Drina. She's still in New York, enjoying a major shopping spree. She even bought a bunch of stuff for me, if you can believe it." She looks at us, her eyes wide, but when we don't respond, she makes a face and continues. "Anyway, she said *hi* even though you couldn't be bothered to say *hi* back. And don't think she didn't know it," she says, scowling at us. "But, she's heading back soon, and she just invited me to this really cool party and I totally cannot wait!"

"When?" I ask, trying not to sound as panicked as I feel. Wondering if it could possibly be on the twenty-first of December.

But she just smiles and shakes her head. "Sorry, no say. I promised not to tell."

"Why?" Miles and I both say.

"Because it's super exclusive, invitation only, and they don't need a bunch of crashers showing up."

"And that's how you see us? As party crashers?"

Haven shrugs and takes a hearty sip of her drink.

"Now that's just wrong." Miles shakes his head. "We're your best friends, so by law, you have to tell us."

"Not this," Haven says. "I'm sworn to secrecy. Just know that I'm so excited I could burst!"

I gaze at her, sitting before me, face flushed with a happiness that sets me on edge, but my head hurts so badly, and my eyes are really tearing, and her aura's so merged with everyone else's, I can't get a read.

I take a sip of my drink, forgetting about the vodka until a trail of hot liquid slips down my throat, courses into my bloodstream, and makes my head sway.

"You still sick?" Haven asks, shooting me a worried look. "You should take it easy. Maybe you're not completely over it."

"Over what?" I squint, taking another sip, and then another, my senses blunted a little more with each taste.

"The fever-dream flu! Remember how you fainted that day at school? I told you the whole dizzy nausea thing is just the beginning. Just promise to tell me if you have the dreams, because they're *amazing.*"

"What dreams?"

"Didn't I tell you?"

"Not in detail." I take another sip, noting how my head feels woozy yet clear, all the visions, random thoughts, colors, and sounds suddenly shrinking and fading away.

"They were wild! And don't get mad, but Damen was in some of them, though it's not like anything happened. It wasn't *that* kind of dream. It was more like he was saving me, like he was fighting these evil forces to save my life. So bizarre." She laughs. "Oh, speaking of, Drina saw Damen in New York."

I stare at Haven, my body growing cold, despite the alcohol blanketing my insides. But when I take another sip, the chill slips away, taking my pain and anxiety with it.

So I take another.

And then another.

Then I squint at her and say, "Why did you just tell me that?"

But Haven just shrugs. "Drina just wanted you to know."

twenty-eight

After the festival, we pile into Haven's car, make a quick stop at her house to refill her flask, then head into town where we park on the street, stuff the meter full of quarters, and storm the sidewalks, three across, arms linked, making all the other pedestrians move out of our way, as we sing "(You Never) Call Me When You're Sober," at the top of our lungs and wildly off-key. Staggering in fits of laughter every time someone snickers and shakes their head at us.

And when we pass one of those New Age bookstores advertising psychic readings, I just roll my eyes and avert my gaze, thrilled that I'm no longer part of that world, now that the alcohol's released me, now that I'm free.

We cross the street to Main Beach, and stumble past Hotel Laguna, until we fall onto the sand, legs overlapping, arms entwined, passing the flask back and forth, and mourning its loss the moment it's empty.

"Crap!" I mumble, tilting my head all the way back and tapping hard on the bottom and sides, straining for every last drop.

"Jeez, take it easy." Miles looks at me. "Just sit back and enjoy the buzz."

But I don't want to sit back. And I am enjoying the buzz. I just want to make sure it continues. Now that my psychic bonds have been broken, I want to ensure they stay broken. "Wanna go to my house?" I slur, hoping Sabine's not at home so we can get to the leftover Halloween vodka and keep the buzz rolling.

But Haven shakes her head. "Forget it," she says. "I'm wrecked. I'm thinking of ditching the car and crawling back home."

"Miles?" I gaze at him, my eyes pleading, not wanting the party to end. This is the first time I've felt so light, so free, so un-encumbered, so normal, since—well, since Damen went away.

"Can't." He shakes his head. "Family dinner. Seven-thirty sharp. Tie optional. Straightjacket required." He laughs, falling onto the sand, as Haven topples over and joins him.

"Well, what about me? What am I supposed to do?" I cross my arms and glare at my friends, not wanting to be left on my own, watching as they laugh and roll around together, oblivious to me.

The next morning, even though I oversleep, the first thing I think when I open my eyes is: *My head's not pounding!*

At least not in the usual way.

Then I roll over, reach under my bed, and retrieve the bottle of vodka I stashed there last night, taking a long deep swig and closing my eyes as its warm wonderful numbness blankets my tongue and sinks down my throat.

And when Sabine peeks her head in my room to see if I'm up, I'm thrilled to see her aura has vanished from sight.

"I'm awake!" I say, shoving the bottle under a pillow and rushing over to hug her. Anxious to see what kind of energy exchange there will be, and elated when there is none. "Isn't it a beautiful day?" I smile, my lips feeling clumsy and loose as they unveil my teeth.

She gazes out the window and back at me. "If you say so." She shrugs.

I look past my french doors and into a day that's gray, overcast, and rainy. But then again, I wasn't referring to the weather. I was referring to me. The new me.

The new, improved, nonpsychic me!

"Reminds me of home." I shrug, slipping out of my nightgown and into the shower.

The second Miles gets in my car he takes one look at me, and goes, "What *the*—?"

I gaze down at my sweater, denim mini, and ballet flats, relics Sabine saved from my old life, and smile.

"I'm sorry, but I don't accept rides from strangers," he says, opening the door and pretending to climb back out.

"It's me, really. Cross my heart and hope to—well, just trust that it's me." I laugh. "And close your door already, I don't need you falling out and making us late."

"I don't get it," he says, gaping at me. "I mean, when did this happen? *How* did this happen? Just yesterday you were practically wearing a burka, and now it looks like you've raided Paris Hilton's closet!"

I look at him.

"Only classier, way classier."

I smile, pushing down on the gas, my wheels sliding and lifting off the soggy wet street and easing up only when I remember how my internal cop radar is gone and Miles starts screaming.

"Seriously, Ever, *what the hell?* Omigod, are you still drunk?"

"No!" I say, a little too quickly. "I'm just, you know, coming out of my shell, that's all. I can be kind of—shy, for the first—several—months." I laugh. "But trust me, this is the *real* me." I nod, hoping he buys it.

"Do you realize you've picked the wettest, most miserable day of the year to *come out of your shell?*"

I shake my head and pull into the parking lot as I say, "You have no idea how beautiful it is. Reminds me of home."

I park in the closest available space, then we race for the gate, backpacks held over our heads like makeshift umbrellas, as the soles of our shoes splash water onto our legs. And when I see Haven shivering under the eaves, I feel like jumping with glee when I see she's aura-free.

"What *the*—?" she says, eyes bugging as she looks me up and down.

"You guys really need to learn how to finish a sentence." I laugh.

"Seriously, who *are* you?" she says, still gawking at me.

Miles laughs, wraps his arms around both of us, and leads us past the gate, saying, "Don't mind Miss Oregon, she happens to think it's a beautiful day."

When I walk into English, I'm relieved that I can no longer see or hear anything I'm not meant to. And even though Stacia and Honor are whispering back and forth, scowling at my clothes, my shoes, my hair, even the makeup I wear on my face, I just shrug it off and mind my own business. Because while I'm sure they're not saying anything remotely kind, the fact that I no longer have access to the actual words makes a whole world of difference. And when I catch them both looking at me again, I just smile and wave until they're so freaked out they turn away.

But by third-period chemistry, the buzz is nearly gone. Giving way to a barrage of sights, colors, and sounds that threaten to overwhelm me.

And when I raise my hand and ask for the hall pass, I'm barely out the door before I'm taken over completely.

I stagger toward my locker, spinning the dial around and around, trying to remember the correct number sequence.

Is it 24-18-12-3? Or 12-18-3-24?

I glance around the hall, my head pounding, my eyes tearing, and then I hit it—*18-3-24-12.* And I dig through a pile of books and papers, knocking them all to the ground but paying no attention as they splay around my feet, just wanting to get to the water bottle I've hidden inside, longing for its sweet liquid release.

I unscrew the cap and tilt my head back, taking a long deep pull, soon followed by another, and then another, and another. And hoping to make it through lunch, I'm taking one last swig when I hear:

"Hold it—smile—no? That's okay, I still got it."

And I watch in horror as Stacia approaches, camera held high, an image of me, guzzling vodka, clearly displayed.

"Who would've thought you'd be so photogenic? But then again, it's so rare we get the chance to see you without your hood." She smiles, her eyes grazing over me, from my feet to my bangs.

I stare at her, and even though my senses are blunted from drink, her intentions are clear.

"Who would you prefer I send this to first? Your mom?" She lifts her brows and covers her mouth in mock horror, as she says, "Oh, so sorry, my apologies. What I meant to say was your *aunt*? Or perhaps one of your teachers? Or maybe *all* of your teachers? No? No, you're right, this should go straight to the principal, one bird, one stone, a quick and easy kill, as they say."

"It's a *water* bottle," I tell her, leaning down to pick up my books and shoving them back in my locker, striving for nonchalance, acting as though I don't even care, knowing she can sniff out fear better than any police-trained bloodhound. "All you have is a photo of me, drinking from a water bottle. Big effin' deal."

"A *water* bottle." She laughs. "Yes, and so it is. And so *very* original I might add. I'm sure you're the absolute very first person to ever think of pouring vodka into a water bottle." She rolls her eyes. "Please. You are *so* going down, Ever. One quick sobriety test, and it's good-bye Bay View, hello Academy for Losers and Abusers."

I gaze at her standing before me, so sure, so smug, so completely overconfident, and I know she has every right to be, she caught me red-handed. And even though the evidence may appear circumstantial, we both know that it isn't. We both know that she's right.

"What do you want?" I finally whisper, figuring everybody has a price, I just need to find hers. I've heard enough thoughts over the past year, seen enough visions, to confirm this is true.

"Well, for starters, I want you to quit bothering me," she says, folding her arms across her chest, anchoring the evidence snugly under her armpit.

"But I don't bother you," I say, the words slightly slurred. "*You* bother *me*."

"*Au contraire.*" She smiles, looking me over, eyes scathing. "Just having to look at you day after day is a bother. A huge horrible bother."

"You want me to transfer out of English?" I ask, still holding that stupid bottle, unsure what to do with it. If I leave it in my locker, she'll nark and have it confiscated—and if I stow it in my backpack, same thing.

"You know you still owe me for that dress you destroyed in your spastic rampage."

So that's it, blackmail. Good thing I won all that money at the track.

I dig through my backpack and locate my wallet, more than willing to reimburse her if it'll put an end to all this. "How much?" I say.

She looks me over, trying to calculate my immediate net worth. "Well, like I said, it was *designer*—and not so easily replaced—so—"

"A hundred?" I pick off a Ben Franklin and offer it to her.

She rolls her eyes. "While I totally get how you're completely clueless about fashion and all things worth having, you really need to up the offer. Aim a little higher, a tad bit steeper," she says, eyeballing my wad.

But since blackmailers have a way of returning and constantly upping the ante, I know it's better just to deal with it now, before it can go any further. So I look at her and say, "Since we both know you bought that dress at the outlet mall, on your way home from Palm Springs"—I smile, remembering what I *saw* that day in the hall—"I'll reimburse you for the cost of the dress, which, if memory serves, was eighty-five dollars. In which case, a hundred seems like a pretty generous deal, wouldn't you say?"

She looks me over, her face twisting into a grin, as she takes the bill and shoves it deep into her pocket. Then she glances between the water bottle and me, and smiles when she says, "So, aren't you going to offer me a drink?"

If someone had told me just yesterday that I'd be hanging in the bathroom, getting whacked with Stacia Miller, I never would've believed it. But sure enough, that's exactly what I did. Trailed her right inside so we could huddle in the corner and suck down a water bottle full of vodka.

Nothing like shared addictions and hidden secrets to bring people together.

And when Haven walked in and found us like that, her eyes bugged out when she said, "What the *fug*?"

And I fell over in fits of howling laughter, as Stacia squinted at her and slurred, "Welthome gosh girthl."

"Am I missing something?" Haven asked, gazing between us, eyes narrowed, suspicious. "Is this supposed to be funny?"

And the way she looked, the way she stood there so authoritative, so derisive, so serious, so *not* amused, made us laugh even more. Then as soon as the door slammed behind her, we got back to drinking.

But getting tanked in the bathroom with Stacia does not ensure access to the VIP table. And knowing better than to even try, I head for my usual spot, my head so polluted, my brain so fuzzy, it takes a moment before I realize I'm not welcome there either.

I plop myself down, squint at Haven and Miles, then start laughing for no apparent reason. Or at least not one that's apparent to them. But if they could only see the looks on their faces, I know they'd laugh too.

"What's up with her?" Miles asks, glancing up from his script.

Haven scowls. "She's bent, totally and completely bent. I caught her in the bathroom, getting twisted with, of all people, Stacia Miller."

Miles gapes, his forehead all scrunched in a way that makes me start laughing all over again. And when I won't quiet down, he leans toward me, pinches my arm, and says, "Shh!" He glances all around and then back at me. "Seriously, Ever. Are you crazy? Jeez, ever since Damen left you've been—"

"Ever since Damen left—*what?*" I pull away so fast I lose my balance and nearly fall off the bench, righting myself just in time to see Haven shake her head and smirk. "Come on, Miles, spit it out already." I glare at him. "You too, Haven, spit it out." Only it comes out more like, *schthpititowt,* and don't think they don't notice.

"You want us to *schthpititowt?*" Miles shakes his head as Haven rolls her eyes. "Well, I'm sure we'd be happy to if we only knew what it meant. Do you know what it means?" He looks at Haven.

"Sounds German," she says, glaring at me.

I roll my eyes, and get up to leave, only I don't coordinate it so well, and I end up banging my knee. *"Owww!"* I cry, slumping back onto the bench, gripping my leg as my eyes squinch in pain.

"Here, drink this," Miles urges, pushing his VitaminWater toward me. "And hand over your keys, because you are *so* not driving me home."

Miles was right. I *so* did not drive him home. That's because he drove himself home.

I got a ride from Sabine.

She gets me settled in the passenger seat, then goes around to her side, and when she starts the engine and pulls out of the lot, she shakes her head, clenches her jaw, glances at me, and says, *"Expelled?* How do you go from honor roll to expelled? Can you please explain that to me?"

I close my eyes and press my forehead against the side window, the smooth, clean glass cooling my skin. "Suspended," I mumble.

"Remember? You pleaded it down. And quite impressively, I might add. Now I know why you earn the big bucks." I peer at her from the corner of my eye just as the shock of my words transform her face from concern to outrage, rearranging her features in a way I've never seen. And even though I know I should feel bad, ashamed, guilty, and worse—the fact is, it's not like I asked her to litigate. It's not like I asked her to plead *extenuating circumstances*. Claiming that my drinking on school grounds was: *clearly mitigated by the gravity of my situation, the huge toll of losing my entire family.*

And even though she said it in good faith, even though she truly believes it to be true, that doesn't mean that it *is* true.

Because the truth is, I wish she hadn't said anything. I wish she'd just let them expel me.

The moment they caught me in front of my locker, the buzz faded and the day's events came rushing right back like a preview for a movie I'd rather not see. Pausing on the frame where I forgot to make Stacia delete that photo, and playing it over and over again. Then later, in the office, when I learned that it was actually Honor's phone that was used, that Stacia had gone home sick with an unfortunate bout of "food poisoning" (though not before arranging for Honor to share the photo, along with her "concerns" to Principal Buckley), well, I have to admit, that even though I was in big trouble, I mean, big, huge, *you can be sure this will go on your permanent record* kind of trouble, there was still this small part of me that admired her. This part that shook its tiny head and thought:

Bravo! Well done!

Because despite the trouble I'm facing, not only with the school, but Sabine too, Stacia not only made good on her promise to destroy me, but she managed to bag one hundred dollars and the afternoon off for her troubles. And that is seriously admirable.

At least in a calculating, sadistic, sinister kind of way.

And yet, thanks to Stacia, Honor, and Principal Buckley's coordinated efforts, I don't have to go to school tomorrow. Or the next day. Or the day after that. Which means I'll get the whole house to myself, all day, every day, allowing me plenty of privacy to continue my drinking and build up my tolerance, while Sabine's busy at work.

Because now that I've found my path to peace, nobody's gonna stand in my way.

"How long has this been going on?" Sabine asks, unsure how to approach me, how to handle me. "Do I have to hide all the alcohol? Do I need to ground you?" She shakes her head. "Ever, I'm speaking to you! What *happened* back there? What is going *on* with you? Would you like for me to arrange for you to speak with someone? Because I know this great counselor who specializes in grief therapy . . ."

I can feel her looking at me, can actually feel the concern emanating off her face, but I just close my eyes and pretend to sleep. There's no way I can explain, no way I can unload the whole sordid truth about auras and visions and spirits and immortal ex-boyfriends. Because even though she hired a psychic for the party, she did it as a joke, a lark, a spooky bit of good clean fun. Sabine is left-brained, organized, compartmentalized, operating on pure black-and-white logic and avoiding all gray. And if I was ever dumb enough to confide in her, to reveal the real secrets of my life, she'd do more than just arrange for me to *speak with someone*. She'd have me committed.

———

Just like she promised, Sabine hides all the alcohol before she heads back to work, but I just wait till she's gone, then slink downstairs and head for the pantry, retrieving all the bottles of vodka left over from the Halloween party, the ones she shoved in the back and forgot all about. And after I haul 'em up to my room, I plop down on my bed, thrilled by the prospect of three full weeks without any school. Twenty-one long glorious days all sprawled out before me like food before an overfed cat. One week for my pleaded-down suspension, and two for the conveniently scheduled winter break. And I plan to make the most of every single moment, spending each long lazy day in a vodka-fueled haze.

I lean back against the pillows and unscrew the cap, determined to pace myself by limiting each sip, allowing the alcohol to trail all the way down my throat and into my bloodstream before taking another. No guzzling, no gulping, no chugging allowed. Just a slow and steady stream until my head starts to clear and the whole world grows brighter. Sinking down into a much happier place. A world without memories. A home without loss.

A life where I only *see* what I'm supposed to.

twenty-nine

On the morning of December 21, I make my way downstairs. And despite being dizzy, bleary eyed, and completely hungover, I put on a pretty good show of brewing coffee and making breakfast, wanting Sabine to leave for work convinced all is well, so I can return to my room and sink back into my liquid haze.

And the second I hear her car leave the drive, I pour the Cheerios down the drain and head upstairs to my room, retrieving a bottle from under the bed and unscrewing the cap, anticipating the rush of that warm sweet liquid that will soothe my insides, erase all my pain, gnaw away my anxieties and fears until nothing remains.

Though for some reason, I can't stop staring at the calendar hanging over my desk, the date jumping out at me, shouting and waving and nudging like an annoying poke in the ribs. So I get up and move toward it, peering at its blank empty square, no obligations, no appointments, not a birthday reminder in sight, just the words WINTER SOLSTICE in tiny black type, a date the publisher deems important, though it means nothing to me.

I plop back down on my bed, my head propped on a mound of pillows as I take another long pull from the bottle. Closing my eyes as that warm wonderful heat courses right through me, flushing my veins and soothing my mind—like Damen used to do with merely a gaze.

I take another sip, and then another, too fast, too reckless, not at all like I've practiced. But now that I've resurrected his memory, I only want to erase it. So I continue like that, drinking, sipping, guzzling, gulping—until I can finally rest, until he's finally faded away.

When I wake, I'm filled with the warmest, most peaceful feeling of all-consuming love. Like I'm bundled in a ray of golden sunlight, so safe, so happy, so secure, I want to stay in that place and live there forever. I clench my eyes shut, grasping the moment, determined to hang on, until a tickle on my nose, an almost imperceptible flutter, makes me open them again and bolt from my bed.

I clutch at my chest, my heart pounding so hard I can feel it, as I gaze at the single black feather that was left on my pillow.

The same black feather I wore the night I dressed as Marie Antoinette.

The same black feather Damen took as a *souvenir*.

And I know he was here.

I glance at the clock, wondering how I could've possibly slept for so long. And when I gaze across the room, I see the painting I'd left in the trunk of my car is now propped against the far wall, left for me to see. But instead of Damen's version of *Woman with Yellow Hair* I expected, I'm confronted with an image of a pale blond girl running through a dark, foggy canyon.

A canyon just like the one in my dream.

And without knowing why, I grab my coat, shove my feet

into some flip-flops, then race into Sabine's room, retrieving the car keys she hid in her drawer, before sprinting downstairs and into the garage, no idea where I'm going, or why. I just know I have to get there, and that I'll know it when I see it.

I drive north on PCH, heading straight for downtown Laguna. Weaving my way through the usual Main Beach bottleneck, before turning on Broadway and dodging pedestrians. And the moment I'm free of those overcrowded streets, I punch the gas and drive on instinct, burying some miles between me and downtown, before cutting in front of an oncoming car, braking in the lot for the wilderness park, pocketing my keys and cell phone, and rushing toward the trail.

The fog is rolling in fast, making it hard to see, and even though there's this part of me telling me to turn back, go home, that being here in the dark, all by myself, is nothing but crazy, I can't stop, I'm compelled to move on, as though my feet are moving of their own accord, and all I can do is just follow.

I bury my hands in my pockets, shivering against the cold, as I stumble along, with no idea where I'm going, no destination in mind, it's the same as how I got here, I'll just know it when I see it.

And when I stub my toe on a rock, I fall to the ground, howling with pain. But by the time my cell phone rings, I've toned it down to barely a whimper.

"Yeah?" I say, struggling to stand, my breath coming shallow and quick.

"Is that how you answer your phone these days? Because that is so not working for me."

"What's up, Miles?" I brush myself off and continue down the trail, this time with a little more caution.

"I just wanted you to know that you're missing a pretty wild party. And since we all know how much you like to party these days, I thought I'd invite you. Though, to be honest, I shouldn't build it up so much because it's really more funny than fun. I mean, you should see it, there's like, hundreds of goths filling up the canyon, it looks like a Dracula convention or something."

"Is Haven there?" I ask, my stomach involuntarily clenching when I say her name.

"Yeah, she's searching for Drina. Remember the big secret event? Well, this is pretty much it. That girl cannot keep a secret, even her own."

"I thought they weren't into goth anymore?"

"So did Haven, and believe me, she's pretty pissed about getting the dress code all wrong."

I've just made it to the crest of a hill when I see the valley flooded with light. "Did you say you're in the canyon?"

"Yeah."

"Me too. In fact, I'm almost there," I say, starting down the other side.

"Wait—*you're here?*"

"Yeah, I'm heading toward the light as we speak."

"Did you go through a tunnel first? Ha-ha, get it?" And when I don't respond, he says, "How'd you even know about it?"

Well, I woke up in a drunken stupor with a black feather tickling my nose and an eerily prophetic painting propped against my wall, so I did what any insane person would do, I grabbed a coat, slipped on some flip-flops, and ran out of the house in my nightgown!

Knowing I can't exactly say that, I don't say anything. Which only makes him even more suspicious.

"Did Haven tell you?" he asks, a definite edge to his voice. "Because she swore I was the only one she told. I mean, no offense or anything. *But still.*"

"No, Miles, I swear she didn't tell me, I just found out. Anyway, I'm almost there, so I'll see you in a minute—if I don't get lost in the fog . . ."

"Fog? There's no fo—"

And before he can finish, the phone is yanked out of my hand, as Drina smiles and says, "Hello, Ever. I told you we'd meet again."

thirty

I know I should run, scream, do *something*. But instead I just freeze, my rubber flip-flops sticking to the ground as though they've grown roots. And I stare at Drina, wondering not only how I ended up here, but what she could possibly have in mind.

"Ain't love a bitch?" She smiles, head cocked to the side as she looks me over. "Just when you meet the man of your dreams, a guy who seems too good to be true, *just like that,* you find out he *is* too good to be true. At least too good for *you*. And the next thing you know you're miserable and alone, and well, let's face it, drunk a good deal of the time. Though I must say, I have enjoyed watching your descent into adolescent addiction. So predictable, so—*textbook*. You know what I mean? The lying, the sneaking, the stealing, all of your energy focused on securing your fix. Which only made my task that much easier. Because every drink you took just weakened your defenses, blunted all the stimuli, yes, but it also left your mind vulnerable, open, and easier for me to manipulate." She grabs hold of my arm, her sharp nails pressing into my wrist, as she pulls me right to her. And even though I try to yank free, it's no use. She's freakishly strong.

"You mortals." She purses her lips. "You're such fun to tease, such easy targets. You think I set up this whole elaborate ruse just to end it so soon? Sure, there are easier ways to do this. Hell, if I wanted, I could've done away with you in your bedroom, while I was setting the stage. It would've been so much quicker, less time consuming, though clearly, not nearly as fun. For either of us, don't you agree?"

I gape at her, taking in her flawless face, coiffed hair, perfectly tailored black silk dress, nipping and flowing in all the right places, all of it highlighting her breathtaking beauty, and when she runs her hand through her shiny copper-tinged hair, I see her ouroboros tattoo. But as soon as I blink, it's vanished again.

"So let's see, you thought Damen was leading you here, summoning you, against your will. Sorry to disappoint you, Ever, but it was me, the whole elaborate ruse, created by me. I just love December twenty-first, don't you? The winter solstice, or longest night, all of those ridiculous goths partying in some dopey canyon." She shrugs, her elegant shoulders rising and falling, the tattoo on her wrist coming in and out of view. "Pardon my flair for the dramatic. Though it does keep life interesting, don't you agree?"

I try to pull away again, but she grips me that much tighter, her nails digging in, eliciting a terrible sharp ache as they pierce right through my flesh.

"Now let's just say that I did let you go. What would you do? Run away? I'm faster. Look for your friend? Oops, my bad. Haven's not even here. It seems I've sent her to the *wrong* party, in the *wrong* canyon. She's wandering around as we speak, pushing and shoving through hundreds of ridiculous vampire wannabes, looking for me." She laughs. "I thought we'd enjoy a smaller, more intimate gathering." She smiles, her eyes sweeping over me. "And it looks like our guest of honor is here."

"What do you want?" I say, gritting my teeth as she tightens her hold, the bones in my wrist giving way, crushing against each other in unbearable pain.

"Don't rush me." She narrows her amazing green eyes on mine. "All in good time. Now where was I before you so rudely interrupted? Ah, yes, we were talking about *you,* how you ended up here, and how it's not turning out anything like you expected. But then, nothing in your life is what you expected, is it? And, truth be told, it never has, was, or I suspect, will be. You see, Damen and I go way back. I'm talking way, way, way, way—well, you get the picture. And yet, despite all of those years together, despite our *longevity,* you just keep showing up and getting in the way."

I gaze at the ground, wondering how I could've been so stupid, so naïve. None of this was ever about Haven—it was all about me.

"Aw, don't be so hard on yourself. This isn't the first time you've made this mistake. I've been responsible for your demise, for, let's see—how many lifetimes?" She shrugs. "Well, I guess I lost count."

And suddenly I remember what Damen said, in the parking lot, about not being able to lose me *again.* But when I look at her and see her face harden and change, I clear my mind of such thoughts, knowing she can read them.

She walks around me, swinging my arm as she goes, making me spin in circles before her as she clucks her tongue against the inside of her cheek. "Let's see, if memory serves, and it *always* does, then the last few times we played a little game called *Trick or Treat.* And I think it's only fair to inform you up front that it didn't really work out so well for you. Still, you never seem to tire of it, so I thought perhaps you'd like to try it again?"

I gaze at her, dizzy from the spinning, the residual alcohol clinging to my veins, her thinly veiled threat.

"Ever watch a cat kill a mouse?" She smiles, eyes glowing, as her tongue snakes around the outside of her lips. "How they toy with their poor pathetic prey for the longest time, until they finally get bored and finish the job?"

I close my eyes, not wanting to hear any more. Thinking that if she's so intent on killing me then why doesn't she just hurry up and do it already?

"Well that would be the *treat*, at least for me." She laughs. "And the *trick*? Aren't you curious about the trick?" And when I don't respond, she sighs. "Well, you're rather dull, aren't you? Though I suppose I'll tell you anyway. You see, the *trick* is—I pretend to let you go, then I stand back and watch as you run around in circles, trying to evade me, until you finally wear yourself out, and I proceed toward the *treat*. So what'll it be? Slow death? Or agonizingly slow death? Come on, hurry up, clock's ticking!"

"Why do you want to kill me?" I look at her. "Why can't you just let me be? Damen and I aren't even a couple, I haven't seen him for weeks!"

But she just laughs. "Nothing personal, Ever. But Damen and I always seem to get along so much better once you've been— *eliminated*."

And even though I thought I wanted a quick demise, I've now changed my mind. I refuse to give up without a fight. Even if it's one I'm destined to lose.

She shakes her head and looks at me, disappointment marring her face. "And so it is. You choose trick, right?" She shakes her head. "Very well then, off you go!"

She lets go of my arm and I flee through the canyon, knowing there's probably nothing that can save me, but knowing I still have to try.

I push the hair from my eyes and race blindly through the fog, hoping to locate the trail, get back to where I started. My lungs threatening to explode in my chest, as my flip-flops break and abandon my feet, but still I run. Running as the sharp cold rocks slice into my soles. Running as a searing hot pain burns a hole through my ribs. Running past trees whose sharp, unadorned branches snatch at my jacket and rip it right off me. Running for my life—even though I'm not sure it's worth living.

And as I'm running, I remember another time I ran like this. But also like my dream, I have no idea how it ends.

I've just reached the edge of the clearing that leads back to the trail, when Drina steps out of the mist and stands right before me.

And even though I dodge, and try to move past her, she lifts one languid leg and assists me in a face plant.

I lie on the ground, blinking into a pool of my own blood, listening to the derisive laughter she directs right at me. And when I tentatively touch my face, my nose flops to the side, and I know that it's broken.

I struggle to stand, spitting rocks from my mouth, cringing in dismay as a stream of blood and teeth tumble out too. And I watch as she shakes her head and says, "Wow, you look *awful*, Ever." She grimaces in disgust. "Seriously awful. One wonders what Damen ever saw in you."

My body's racked with pain, my breath's shallow, unsteady, as mouthfuls of blood coat my tongue with a taste that's metallic and bitter.

"Well, I suppose you'll want all the details, even though you won't remember them the next time around. Still, it's always fun to see the shock on your face when I explain it to you." She laughs. "I don't know why, but for some reason, I never bore of this particular episode, no matter how many times we re-run it. Plus, if I'm going to be perfectly honest, then I have to admit it allows for a deliciously prolonged pleasure. Kind of like foreplay, not that *you* would know anything about *that*. All these lifetimes and somehow you always die a virgin. Which would be so sad, if it wasn't so funny." She scoffs. "So, where to begin, where to begin?" She looks at me, lips pursed, red-manicured nails tapping the sides of her hips. "Okay, well, as you know, I'm the one who swapped the picture from the one in your trunk. I mean, *you* as the woman with the yellow hair? I. Don't. Think. So. And between you and me, Picasso would've been *furious*. Still, I do love him. Damen, that is. Not that old dead artist." She laughs. "Anywho, let's see, I planted the feather." She rolls her eyes. "Damen can be so—*maudlin*. Oh, I even planted that dream in your head. How's *that* for months of mysterious foreshadowing? And no, I'm not going to explain all the hows and whys because that would take too long, and, quite frankly, it's hardly important where you're going. Too bad you didn't just die in that accident, because you could've saved us both a lot of trouble. Do you have any idea how much damage you've caused? I mean, because of you Evangeline is dead and Haven—well, look how close she came. I mean, really Ever, how selfish of you."

She looks at me but I refuse to respond. Wondering if that qualifies as an admission of guilt.

She laughs. "Well, you're about to exit now, so yes, no harm in confessing." She lifts her right hand as though solemnly swearing. "I, Drina Magdalena Auguste"—she raises her brow at me when she says that last part—"effectively eliminated Evangeline a.k.a. June Porter, who, by the way, was contributing nothing and only taking up space so it's not nearly as sad as you think. I needed to get her out of the way so I'd have full access to Haven." She smiles, her eyes grazing over me. "Yes, just like you suspected, I purposely stole your friend Haven. Which is so easy to do with those lost and unloved ones who are so desperately craving attention they'll do just about anything for someone who gives them the time of day. And yes, I convinced her to get a tattoo that nearly killed her, but only because I couldn't decide if I should *kill her–kill her,* or kill her so that I could bring her back and make her immortal. It's been so long since I last had an acolyte, and I must say, I really did enjoy it. But, then again, indecisiveness has always been a weakness of mine. When you have so many options spread out before you and an eternity to see them played out, well, it's hard not to get greedy and want to choose them all!" She smiles, like a child who's simply been naughty, but nothing more. "Still, I waited too long, and then Damen stepped in—well-meaning, altruistic sap that he is—and, well, you know the rest. Oh, and I got Miles that part in *Hairspray*. Though, in all fairness, he probably could've nailed it himself, because the kid has *loads* of talent. Still, I couldn't take any chances, so I climbed inside the director's head and swung the vote in his favor. Oh, and Sabine and Jeff? My bad. But still, it worked out beautifully, don't you think? Imagine, your smart, successful, savvy aunt falling for that loser." She laughs. "Pathetic, and yet, quite funny, don't you think?"

But why? Why would you do this? I think, no longer able to speak since I'm missing most of my teeth and gagging on my own blood, but knowing it's not necessary, knowing she can hear the thoughts in my head. *Why involve everyone else, why not just go after me?*

"I wanted to show you how lonely your life can be. I wanted to demonstrate how easy it is for people to abandon you in favor of something better, more exciting. You're all alone, Ever. Isolated, unloved, alone. Your life is pathetic and hardly worth living. So, as you can see, I'm doing you a favor." She smiles. "Though I'm sure you won't thank me."

I gaze at her, wondering how someone so amazingly beautiful could be so ugly inside. Then I stare into her eyes and take a tiny step back, hoping she won't notice.

I'm not even with Damen anymore. We broke up a long time ago. So why don't you go find him, we can go our separate ways, and forget this ever happened! I think, hoping to distract her.

She laughs and rolls her eyes. "Trust me, you're the only one who will forget this ever happened. Besides, it's really not that simple. You have no idea how this works, do you?"

She's got me there.

"You see, Damen is mine. And he's *always* been mine. But unfortunately, you keep showing up, in your stupid, boring, repetitive soul recycle. And since you insist on doing that, it's become my job to track you down and kill you each time." She takes a step toward me as I take a step back, the bloody sole of my foot landing on a pointy sharp rock as I close my eyes and wince in unbearable pain.

"You think *that* hurt?" She laughs. "Just wait."

I glance around the canyon, eyes darting furiously, scanning for a way out, some kind of escape. Then I take another step back and stumble again. My hand brushing the ground as my fingers curl around a sharp rock that I hurl at her face, smacking her square in the jaw and tearing a chunk from her cheek.

She laughs, the hole in her face spurting blood and revealing two missing teeth. Then I watch in horror as it rights itself again, returning her back to her pure seamless beauty.

"This again." She sighs. "Come on, try something new, see if you can amuse me for a change."

She stands before me, hands on hips, brows raised, but I refuse to run. I refuse to make the next move. I refuse to give her the satisfaction of yet another fool's race. Besides, everything she said is true. My life really is a lonely horrible mess. And everyone I touch gets dragged down in it too.

I watch as she advances on me, smiling in anticipation, knowing my end is near. So I close my eyes and remember the moment right before the accident. Back when I was healthy and happy and surrounded by family. Imagining it so vividly I can *feel* the warm leather seat beneath my bare legs, I can *sense* Buttercup's tail thumping against my thigh, I can *hear* Riley singing at the top of her lungs, her voice inharmonious, horribly off-key. I can *see* my mom's smile as she turns in her seat, her hand reaching out to chuck Riley's knee. I can *see* my dad's eyes, both of us gazing into the rearview mirror, his smile knowing, kind, and amused—

I hold on to that moment, cradling it in my mind, experiencing the feel, the scents, the sounds, the emotions, as though I'm right there. Wanting this to be the last moment I see before I go, reliving the last time I was truly happy.

And just when I'm so far in, it's as though I'm right there, I hear Drina gasp. "What the *hell*?"

And I open my eyes to see the shock on her face, her eyes sweeping over me, her mouth hanging open. Then I gaze down at a gown that's no longer torn, feet that are no longer bloody, knees that are no longer scraped, and when I run my tongue around a full set of teeth and bring my hand to my nose, I know that my face is healed too. And even though I've no idea what it means, I know I need to act fast, before it's too late.

And as Drina steps back, her eyes wide, full of questions, I move toward her, not sure what the next step will bring, or the one after that. All I know is that I'm running out of time, as I rush forward and say, "Hey Drina, trick or treat?"

thirty-one

At first she just stares, green eyes wide and unbelieving, then she lifts her chin and bares her teeth. But before she can attack, I lunge toward her. Determined to get to her first, to take her down while I can. But just as I spring forward, I see this shimmering veil of soft golden light, a luminous circle just off to the side, glowing and beckoning, like the one in my dream. And even though Drina planted those dreams, even though it's probably a trap, I can't help but veer toward it.

I tumble through a brilliant haze, a shower of light so loving, so warm, so intense, it calms my nerves and soothes all my fears. And when I land in a field of vibrant green grass, the blades hold me, support me, and cushion my fall.

I gaze at the meadow around me, its flowers blooming with petals that seem lit from within, surrounded by trees that reach far into the sky, their branches sagging with ripe juicy fruit. And as I lie there quietly, taking it all in, I can't help but feel like I've been here before.

"Ever."

I spring to my feet, poised and ready to fight. And when I see that it's Damen, I take a step back, having no idea whose side he's really on.

"Ever, relax. It's okay." He nods, smiling as he offers his hand.

But I refuse to take it, refuse to fall for his bait. So I take another step back as my eyes search for Drina.

"She's not here." He nods, his eyes fixed on mine. "You're safe, it's just me."

I hesitate, debating whether or not to believe him, doubting he could ever be thought of as *safe*. Staring at him, while weighing my options (which are admittedly few), until I finally ask, "Where are we?" In place of my actual question: *Am I dead?*

"I assure you, you're not dead." He laughs, reading my thoughts. "You're in Summerland."

I look at him, without even a hint of understanding.

"It's a sort of—place between places. Like a waiting room. Or a rest stop. A dimension between the dimensions, if you will."

"Dimensions?" I squint, the word sounding foreign, unfamiliar, at least in the way that he uses it. And when he reaches for my hand, I quickly pull away, knowing it's impossible to see anything clearly whenever he touches me.

He gazes at me, then shrugs, motioning for me to follow him through a meadow where every flower, every tree, every single blade of grass bends and sways and twists and curves like partners in an infinite dance.

"Close your eyes," he whispers. And when I don't he adds, "Please?"

I close them. Halfway.

"Trust me." He sighs. "Just this once."

So I do. "Now what?"

"Now imagine something."

"What do you mean?" I ask, immediately picturing a giant elephant.

"Imagine something else," he says, "quickly."

I open my eyes, startled to see a ginormous elephant charging right at us, then I gasp in amazement when I transform him into a butterfly—a beautiful Monarch butterfly that lands right on the tip of my finger. "How—?" I glance between Damen and the butterfly, its black antennae twitching at me.

Damen laughs. "Want to try again?"

I press my lips and look at him, trying to think of something good, something better than an elephant or a butterfly.

"Go ahead," he urges. "It's so much fun. It never gets old."

I close my eyes and imagine the butterfly turning into a bird, and when I open them again a colorful majestic macaw is perched on my finger. But when a messy trail of bird poop drips down my arm, Damen hands me a towel and says, "How about something with a little less—cleanup?"

I set the bird down and watch it fly away, then I close my eyes, fervently wishing, and when I open them again, Orlando Bloom has taken his place.

Damen groans and shakes his head.

"Is he real?" I whisper, gaping in amazement as Orlando Bloom smiles and winks at me.

Damen shakes his head. "You can't manifest actual people, only their likeness. Luckily, it won't be long before he fades."

And when he does, I can't help but feel a little sad.

"What's going on?" I ask, looking at Damen. "Where are we? And how is this even possible?"

Damen smiles and makes a beautiful white stallion appear. After getting me mounted and settled, he makes a black one for him. "Let's go for a ride," he says, leading me down a trail.

We ride side by side, down a beautiful, manicured path, cutting right through the valley of flowers and trees and a sparkling stream the color of rainbows. And when I see my parrot perched next to a cat I veer from the trail, ready to shoo him away, but Damen grabs the reins and says, "No worries. There are no enemies. All is at peace here."

We ride in silence as I gape at the surrounding beauty, struggling to take it all in, though it's not long before my mind starts reeling with all sorts of questions and no clue where to begin.

"The veil you saw? The one you were drawn to?" He looks at me. "I put it there."

"In the canyon?"

He nods. "And in your dream."

"But Drina says she created the dream." I look at him, seeing how he rides with such confidence, so sure in the saddle. But then I remember the painting on his wall, the one of him mounted on the white stallion, sword by his side, and I figure he's been at it for a while.

"Drina showed you the location, I showed you the exit."

"Exit?" I say, my heart pounding again.

He shakes his head and smiles. "Not *that* kind of exit. I already told you, you're *not* dead. In fact, you're more alive than ever. Able to manipulate matter and manifest anything you want. The ultimate in instant gratification." He laughs. "But don't come here too often. Because I'm warning you, it's addictive."

"So you *both* created my dreams?" I ask, squinting at him, trying to get a handle on all these bizarre events. "Like—like a *collaboration?*"

He nods.

"So I don't even control my own dreams?" I say, my voice rising, not liking the sound of any of this.

"Not that particular dream, no."

I scowl at him, shaking my head when I say, "Well, excuse me, but don't you think that's just *a little* invasive? I mean, jeez! And why didn't you try to stop it, if you knew it was coming?"

He looks at me, his eyes tired and sad. "I didn't know it was Drina. I was just observing your dreams, you were frightened by something, so I showed you the way here. This is always a safe place to come to."

"So why didn't Drina follow me?" I say, looking around for her again.

He reaches for my hand and squeezes my fingers. "Because Drina can't see it, only you could see it."

I squint at him. Everything's so weird, so strange, and none of it makes any sense.

"Don't worry, you'll get it. But for now, why not just try to enjoy it?"

"Why does it seem so familiar?" I say, feeling the tug of recognition, but unable to place it.

"Because this is where I found you."

I look at him.

"I found your body outside the car, true. But your soul had already moved on and was lingering here." He stops both our horses, and helps me dismount, then he leads me to a warm patch of grass, so brilliant and sparkling in the warm golden light that doesn't seem to emanate from any one place, and the next thing I know he's manifested a big cushy couch and a matching ottoman for our feet.

"Care to add anything?" He smiles.

I close my eyes and imagine a coffee table, some lamps, a few knickknacks, and a nice Persian rug, and when I open them again we're in a fully furnished outdoor living room.

"What happens if it rains?" I ask.

"Don't—"

But it's too late, we're already soaked.

"Thoughts create," he says, making a giant umbrella, the rain sloping steadily off the sides and onto the rug. "It's the same on Earth, it just takes a lot longer. But here in Summerland, it's instant."

"That reminds me of what my mom used to say—*'Be careful what you wish for, you just might get it!!'*" I laugh.

He nods. "Now you know where that originates. Care to make this rain stop, so we can dry off?" He shakes his wet hair at me.

"How—"

"Just think of someplace warm and dry." He smiles.

And the next thing I know we're lying on a beautiful pink-sand beach.

"Let's leave it at this? Shall we?" He laughs as I make us a plushy blue towel and a turquoise ocean to match.

And when I lie back and close my eyes against the warmth, he confirms it. Not that I didn't already start to figure it out for myself, but still not having it stated in a complete sentence. One that begins with:

"I'm an immortal."

And ends with:

"And you are too."

Is not something you hear every day.

"So, we're both immortals?" I say, opening one eye to peer at him, wondering how I could have such a bizarre conversation in such a normal tone of voice. But then again, I'm in Summerland, and it doesn't get more bizarre than that.

He nods.

"And you *made* me an immortal when I died in the crash?"

He nods again.

"But how? Does it have something to do with that weird red drink?"

He takes a deep breath before answering. "Yes."

"But how come I don't have to drink it all the time, like you do?"

He averts his gaze and looks out toward the sea. "Eventually you will."

I sit up picking at a loose string on my towel, still unable to fully wrap my mind around this. Remembering a time in the not-so-distant past when I thought just being psychic was a curse, and *now* look.

"It's not as bad as you think," he says, placing his hand over mine. "Look around, it doesn't get any better than this."

"But *why*? I mean, did it ever occur to you that maybe I don't want to be an immortal? That maybe you should've just let me go?"

I watch as he cringes, averting his gaze, looking all around, focusing on everything but me. Then he turns to me and says, "First of all, you're right. I was selfish. Because the truth is, I saved you more for myself than for you. I couldn't bear to lose you again, not after . . ." He stops and shakes his head. "But still, I wasn't sure if it worked. Obviously I knew I'd brought you back, but I wasn't sure for how long. I wasn't sure I'd actually turned you until I saw you in the canyon just now—"

"You were watching me in the canyon?" I stare at him incredulously.

He nods.

"You mean you were *there*?"

"No, I was watching you *remotely*." He rubs his jaw. "It's a lot to explain."

"So let me get this straight. You were watching me, *remotely*, but still, you could see everything going on, and yet *you didn't try to save me?*" And when I say it out loud I'm so mad I can barely breathe.

He shakes his head. "Not until you wanted to be saved. That's when I made the veil appear, and urged you to move toward it."

"You mean you were going to let me die?" I scoot away from him, not wanting to be anywhere near him.

He looks at me, his face completely serious when he says, "If that's what you wanted, then yes." He shakes his head. "Ever, the last time we spoke, in the parking lot, you said you hated me for what I had done, for being selfish, for separating you from your family, for bringing you back. And even though your words really stung, I knew you were right. I had no business interfering. But then, in the canyon, when you filled yourself with such love, well, that love is what saved you, restored you, and it's then that I knew."

But what about the hospital? Why couldn't I restore myself then? Why did I have to suffer through all of the casts, and cuts, and contusions? Why couldn't I just—regenerate, like I did in the canyon? I think, folding my arms across my chest, not fully buying it.

"Only love heals. Anger, guilt, and fear can only destroy and separate you from your true capabilities." He nods, his eyes grazing over me.

"And that's another thing." I glare at him. "Your ability to read my mind, when I can't read yours. It's not fair."

He laughs. "Do you really want to read my mind? I thought my air of mystery was one of the things you liked about me?"

I gaze down at my knees, my cheeks burning as I think of all the embarrassing thoughts he's been privy to.

"There are ways to shield yourself, you know. Maybe you should go see Ava."

"You know Ava?" I gape, feeling suddenly ganged up on.

He shakes his head. "My only connection to Ava is through you, your thoughts about Ava."

I look away, watching a family of bunnies hop by, then back at him. "So the racetrack?"

"Premonition, you did it too."

"What about the race you lost?"

He laughs. "I have to lose a few, otherwise people tend to get suspicious. But I certainly made up for it, don't you think?"

"And the tulips?"

He smiles. "Manifesting. Same way you made the elephant, and this beach. It's simple quantum physics. Consciousness brings matter into being where there was once merely energy. Not nearly as difficult as people choose to think."

I squint, not really getting it. No mater how *simple* he thinks it is.

"We create our own reality. And yes you can do it at home," he says, anticipating my next question, the one that just formed in my head. "In fact, you already do, you're just not aware of it because it takes so much longer."

"It doesn't take longer for you."

He laughs. "I've been around awhile, plenty of time to learn a few tricks."

"How long?" I ask, gazing at him, remembering that room in his house and wondering exactly what I'm dealing with.

He sighs and looks away. "Very long."

"And now I'll live forever too?"

"That's up to you." He shrugs. "You don't have to do any of this. You can simply put the whole thing out of your mind and go on with your life. Choosing to *let go* when the time is right. I only provided the ability, but the choice is still yours."

I stare out at the ocean, its sparkling waters so brilliant, so beautiful, I can hardly believe it exists because of me. And even though it's fun to play with such powerful magic, my thoughts soon turn to darker things. "I need to know what happened with Haven. That day I caught you . . ." I grimace at the memory. "And what about Drina? She's immortal too, right? Did you make her that way? And how did this even begin? How did you become immortal in the first place? How does such a thing even happen? Did you know she killed Evangeline, and almost killed Haven too? And what's up with your creepy room?"

"Can you repeat the question?" He laughs.

"Oh, and another thing, what the heck did Drina mean when she said she's killed me over and over again?"

"Drina said that?" His eyes go wide as his face drains of color.

"Yeah." I nod, remembering her smug and haughty face as she broke the news. "She was all, *'Here we go again, stupid mortal, you always fall for this game, blah blah blah.'* I thought you were watching, I thought you saw the whole thing?"

He shakes his head, mumbling. "I didn't see the *whole* thing, I tuned in late. Oh God, Ever, it's all my fault, all of it. I should've known, I should've never gotten you involved, I should've left you alone—"

"She also said she saw you in New York. Or at least she told Haven that."

"She lied," he mumbles. "I didn't go to New York." And when he looks at me his eyes are etched with such pain, I reach for his hand and hold it in mine. Shaken by how sad and vulnerable he looks and wanting only to erase it. I press my lips against his warm waiting mouth, hoping to convey that whatever it is, there's a pretty good chance I'll forgive him.

"The kiss gets sweeter with every incarnation." He sighs, pulling away and brushing my hair off my face. "Though we never seem to make it further than that. And now I know why." He presses his forehead to mine, infusing me with such joy, such all-consuming love, then sighing deeply before pulling away. "Aw, yes, your questions," he says, reading my mind. "Where to begin?"

"How about the beginning?"

He nods, his gaze drifting away, all the way back to the beginning, as I cross my legs and settle in. "My father was a dreamer, an artist, a dabbler in sciences and alchemy, a popular idea at the time—"

"Which time?" I ask, hungry for places, dates, things that can be nailed down and researched, not some philosophical litany of abstract ideas.

"A *long* time ago." He laughs. "I *am* a tad bit older than you."

"Yes, but how old exactly? I mean, what kind of age difference am I dealing with here?" I ask, watching incredulously as he shakes his head.

"All you need to know is that my father, along with his fellow alchemists, believed that everything could be reduced down to one single element, and that if you could isolate that one element, then you could create anything from it. He worked on that theory for years, creating formulas, abandoning formulas, and then when he and my mother both . . . died, I continued the search, until I finally perfected it."

"And how old were you?" I ask, trying again.

"Young." He shrugs. "Quite young."

"So you can still age?"

He laughs. "Yes, I got to a certain point, and then I just stopped. I know you prefer the *frozen in time* vampire theory, but this is real life, Ever, not fantasy."

"Okay, so . . ." I urge, anxious for more.

"*So,* my parents died, I was orphaned. You know, in Italy, where I'm from, last names often depicted a person's origins or profession. *Esposito* means *orphan,* or *exposed*. The name was given to me, though I dropped it a century or two ago, since it no longer fit."

"Why didn't you just use your real last name?"

"It's complicated. My father was . . . hunted. So I thought it better to distance myself."

"And Drina?" I ask, my throat constricting at the mere mention of her name.

He nods. "Poverina—or, *little poor one*. We were wards of the church; that's where we met. And when she grew ill, I couldn't bear to lose her, so I had her drink too."

"She said you were married." I press my lips together, my throat feeling hot and constricted, knowing she didn't actually *say* that, though it was definitely implied when she stated her name, *her full name*.

He squints and looks away, shaking his head and mumbling under his breath.

"Is it true?" I ask, my stomach in knots, my heart pressing hard against my chest.

He nods. "But it's hardly what you think, it happened so long ago it hardly matters anymore."

"So why didn't you get divorced? I mean, if it *hardly matters,*" I say, my cheeks hot, my eyes stinging.

"So you're proposing I show up in court with a wedding certificate dating back *several centuries,* and ask for a divorce?"

I press my lips and look away, knowing he's right, but *still.*

"Ever, please. You've got to cut me some slack. I'm not like you. You've only been around, well in this life anyway, seventeen years, while I've lived hundreds! More than enough time to make a few mistakes. And while there are certainly plenty of things to judge me on, I hardly think my relationship with Drina is one of them. Things were different back then. *I* was different. I was vain, superficial, and extremely materialistic. I was out for myself, taking all that I could. But the moment I met you everything changed, and when I lost you, well, I never knew such agonizing pain. But then later, when you reappeared—" He stops, his gaze far away. "Well, no sooner had I found you, than I lost you again. And so it went, over and over. An endless cycle of love and loss—until now."

"So, we . . . *reincarnate?*" I say, the word sounding strange on my tongue.

"You do—not me." He shrugs. "I'm always here, always the same."

"So, who was I?" I ask, not sure if I really believe it, yet fascinated with the concept. "And why can't I remember?"

He smiles, happy to change the subject. "The journey back involves a trip down the River of Forgetfulness. You're not meant to remember, you're here to learn, to evolve, to pay off your karmic debts. Each time starting fresh, forced to find your own way. Because, Ever, life is not meant to be an open book test."

"Then aren't you cheating, by staying here?" I say, smirking at *Mr. Let Me Tell You How the World Works.*

He cringes. "Some might say."

"And how can you possibly know all of this if you've never done it yourself?"

"I've had plenty of years to study life's greatest mysteries. And I've met some amazing teachers along the way. All you need to know about your other selves is that you were always female." He smiles, tucking my hair behind my ear. "Always very beautiful. And always important to me."

I stare at the sea, manifest a few waves just for the heck of it, then make it all go away. Everything. All of it. Returning us to our outdoor living room.

"Change of scenery?" He smiles.

"Yes, but only the scenery, not the subject."

He sighs. "So after years of searching I found you again—and you know the rest."

I take a deep breath and stare at the lamp, clicking it off and on, on and off with my mind, trying to get a grip on all this.

"I broke off with Drina a long time ago, but she has this awful habit of *reappearing*. And the night at the St. Regis? When you saw us together? I was trying to convince her to move on, once and for all. Though obviously, it didn't quite work. And yes, I know she killed Evangeline, because that day at the beach, when you woke up alone?"

I narrow my eyes, thinking: *I knew it! I knew he wasn't surfing!*

"I'd just found her body, but it was too late to save her. And yes, I know about Haven too, though luckily, I was able to save her."

"So that's where you were that night—when you said you were getting a drink of water . . ."

He nods.

"So what else have you lied about?" I ask, folding my arms across my chest. "And where'd you go Halloween night, after you left my party?"

"I went home," he says, gazing at me intently. "When I saw the way Drina looked at you, well, I though it better to distance myself. Only I couldn't. I tried. I've been trying all along. But I just couldn't do it. I can't stay away from you." He shakes his head. "And now you know everything. Though I think it's obvious why I couldn't be quite so forthcoming at the time."

I shrug and look away, not willing to give in so easily, even if it's true.

"Oh, and my 'creepy room' as you call it? Well, it just so happens to be *my* happy place. Not unlike the memory you hold of those last blissful moments in the car with your family." And when he looks at me, I avert my gaze, ashamed for having said it. "Though I have to admit, I had a good laugh when I realized you thought I was a bloodsucker." He smiles.

"Oh, well excuse me. I mean since there are immortals running around, I figure we may as well bring on the faeries, wizards, werewolves, and—" I shake my head. "I mean jeez, you talk about all this like it's normal!"

He closes his eyes and sighs. And when he opens them again he says, "For me it is normal. This is my life. And now it's your life too, if you choose it. It's not as bad as you think, Ever, really." He looks at me for a long time, and even though part of me still wants to hate him for making me this way, I just can't. And when I feel that overwhelmingly warm, tingly pull, I gaze down at the hand that he's holding and say, "Stop it."

"Stop what?" He looks at me, his eyes tired, the skin surrounding them tense and pale.

"Stop making that warm, tingly, *you know*. Just stop it!" I say, my mind torn between love and hate.

"I'm not making that, Ever." His eyes are on mine.

"Of course you are! You're making it happen with your . . .

whatever." I roll my eyes and fold my arms across my chest, wondering where we possibly go from here.

"I'm not manifesting that. I swear. I'd never use trickery to seduce you."

"Oh, yeah, like the tulips?"

He smiles. "You have no idea what they mean, do you?"

I press my lips and look away.

"Flowers have meaning. There's nothing random about it."

I take a deep breath and rearrange the table with my mind, wishing I could rearrange my mind instead.

"There's so much to teach you," he says. "Though it's not all fun and games. You need to take caution, proceed with care." He pauses and looks at me, making sure that I'm listening. "You have to guard against the misuse of power; Drina's a good example of that. And you must be discreet—which means you can't share this with *anyone,* and I mean *no one,* understand?"

I just shrug, thinking: *Whatever.* Knowing he's read my thoughts when he shakes his head and leans toward me.

"Ever, I'm serious, you cannot tell a soul. Promise me."

I look at him.

He raises his brow, his hand squeezing mine.

"Scout's honor," I mumble, looking away.

He lets go of my hand and relaxes, leaning back against the cushions when he says, "But in the interest of full disclosure you need to know that there's still a way out. You can still *cross over.* In fact, you could've died right there in the canyon, but instead, you chose to stay."

"But I was prepared to die, I wanted to die."

"You empowered yourself with your memories. You empowered yourself with love. It's like I said earlier—*thoughts create.* And in your case, they created healing and strength. If you really wanted to die you would've simply given up. On some deeper level you must've known this."

And just when I'm about to ask him why he was sneaking into my room while I slept, he says, "It's not what you think."

"Then what was it?" I ask, wondering if I really want to know.

"I was there to . . . observe. I was surprised you could see me, I was *transmuted,* so to speak."

I wrap my arms around my knees and bring them close to my chest. Everything he just said went right over my head, but I get just enough of the gist to be suitably creeped out.

He shrugs. "Ever, I feel responsible for you, and—"

"And you wanted to check out the goods?" I look at him, eyebrows raised.

But he just laughs. "May I remind you of your penchant for flannel pajamas?"

I roll my eyes. "So you feel responsible for me, like—*like a dad?*" I say, laughing as he cringes.

"No, not like a dad. But Ever, I was only in your room that one time, the night we saw each other at the St. Regis, if there were other times—"

"Drina." I cringe, picturing her creeping around my room, spying on me. "Are you sure she can't come here?" I ask, glancing around.

He takes my hand and squeezes, wanting to reassure me when he says, "She doesn't even know it exists. Doesn't know how to get here. As far as she's concerned, you simply vanished into thin air."

"But how'd *you* get here? Did you die once, like me?"

He shakes his head. "There are two types of alchemy— physical, which I stumbled upon because of my father, and spiritual, which I stumbled upon when I sensed something more, something bigger, something grander than me. I studied and practiced and worked hard to get here, even learned TM." He stops and looks at me. "Transcendental Meditation from Maharishi Mahesh Yogi." He smiles.

"Um, if you're trying to impress me, it's not really working, I have no idea what any of that means."

He shrugs. "Let's just say it took hundreds of years for me to translate it from the mental to the physical. But you—from the moment you wandered into the field, you were granted a sort of backstage pass, your visions and telepathy are by-products of that."

"God, no wonder you hate high school," I say, wanting to change the subject to something concrete, something I can actually understand. "I mean, you must've finished like, a gazillion, bazillion years ago, right?" And when he winces, I realize his age is a serious sore spot, which is actually pretty funny, considering how he *chose* to live forever. "I mean, why bother? Why even enroll?"

"That's where you come in." He smiles.

"Oh, so you see some chick in baggy jeans and a hoodie, and you just have to have her so bad, you decide to repeat high school, just to get to her?"

"Sounds about right." He laughs.

"Couldn't you have found another way to ingratiate yourself into my life? It just doesn't make any sense." I shake my head and roll my eyes, getting worked up all over again, until he trails his fingers down the side of cheek and gazes into my eyes.

"Love never does."

I swallow hard, feeling shy, euphoric, and unsure all at once. Then I clear my throat and say, "I thought you said you suck at love." I narrow my eyes on his, my stomach like a cold bitter marble, wondering why I can't just be happy when the most gorgeous guy on the planet professes his love. Why do I insist on going all negative?

"I was hoping this time would be different," he whispers.

I turn away, my breath coming in short, shallow gasps as I say, "I don't know if I'm up for all this. I don't know what to do."

He pulls me tight against his chest, his arms wrapped around me, as he says, "There's no rush to decide." And when I turn, he has this faraway look in his eyes.

"What's the matter?" I ask. "Why are you looking at me like that?"

"Because I suck at good-byes," he says, attempting a smile that never gets past his mouth. "See, now there's two things I suck at—love and good-byes."

"Maybe they're related." I press my lips together, warning myself not to cry. "So where you going?" I fight to keep my voice calm and neutral, even though my heart doesn't want to beat, and my breath doesn't want to come, and I feel like I'm dying inside.

He shrugs and looks away.

"Are you coming back?"

"Up to you." Then he looks at me and says, "Ever, do you still hate me?"

I shake my head, but hold his gaze.

"Do you love me?"

I turn my head and look away. Knowing I do, knowing I love him with every strand of hair, with every skin cell, with every drop of blood, that I'm bursting with love, boiling over, but I just can't bring myself to say it. But then again, if he can truly read my mind, then I shouldn't have to say it. He should just *know*.

"It's always nicer when it's spoken," he says, tucking my hair behind my ear, and pressing his lips to my cheek. "When you do decide, about me, about being immortal, just say the word and I'll be there. I have all of eternity laid out before me; you'll find I'm quite patient." He smiles, then reaches into his pocket, retrieving the silver, crystal-encrusted, horse-bit bracelet he bought me at the track. The one I *returned* when I threw it at him that day in the parking lot. "May I?" he gestures.

I nod, my throat too constricted to speak, as he closes the clasp, then cradles my face between the palms of his hands. Brushing my bangs to the side, and pressing his lips to my scar, infusing me with all of the love and forgiveness I know I don't deserve. But when I try to pull away, he holds me that much tighter and says, "You have to forgive yourself, Ever. You're not responsible for any of it."

"What do you know?" I bite down on my lip.

"I know you blame yourself for something that's not your fault. I know you love your little sister with all of your heart and you ask yourself every day if you're doing the right thing by encouraging her visits. I know *you*, Ever. I know everything about you."

I turn away, my face wet with tears I don't want him to see. "None of that's true. You've got it all wrong. I'm a freak, and bad things happen to everyone I come near, even though I'm the one who deserves it." I shake my head, knowing I don't deserve to be happy, don't deserve this kind of love.

He pulls me into his arms, his touch calm and soothing, but unable to erase the truth. "I have to go," he finally whispers. "But Ever, if you want to love me, if you truly want to be with me, then you'll have to accept what we are. I'll understand if you can't."

And then I kiss him, pressing into him, needing the feel of his lips against mine, basking in the wonderful, warm glow of his love, the moment growing and swelling and expanding until it fills every space, every nook, every cranny.

And when I open my eyes and pull away, I'm back in my room, all alone.

thirty-two

"So what happened? We looked everywhere and never found you. I thought you were on your way?"

I roll over, turning my back to the window and chiding myself for failing to craft an excuse, which puts me in the awkward position of winging it. "I was, but then—well, I kind of got cramps, and—"

"Stop right there," Miles says. "Seriously, say no more."

"Did I miss anything?" I ask, closing my eyes against the thoughts in his head, the words scrolling before me like a late-breaking news ribbon on CNN: *Ew! Disgusting! Why do they insist on talking about that stuff?*

"Other than the fact that Drina never showed? Nope, not a thing. I spent the first part of the night helping Haven look for her, and the second part, trying to convince her she's better off without her. I swear, you'd think they were dating. Creepiest friendship ever, Ever! Ha! Get it?" He loves making pun of my name.

I clutch my head and crawl out of bed, realizing it's the first morning in over a week that I've woken without a hangover. And even though I know that qualifies as *a very good thing*, that doesn't change the fact that I feel worse than ever.

"So what's going on? Care to indulge in a little Fashion Island Christmas shopping?"

"Can't. I'm still grounded," I say, pilfering through a pile of sweatshirts and pausing when I get to the one Damen bought me on our Disneyland date, before everything changed, before my life went from very weird to extraordinarily weird.

"How much longer?"

"No say." I drop the phone on my dresser and pull a lime green hoodie over my head, knowing it doesn't really matter how long Sabine grounds me, if I want to go out, I'll go out, I'll just make sure to return before she gets home. I mean, it's hard to contain a psychic. Though it does provide the perfect excuse to stay home, lay low, and avoid all that random energy, which is the only reason I'm going along with it.

I pick up the phone just in time to hear Miles say, "Okay, well, call me when you're released."

I step into some jeans, then sit down at my desk. And even though my head's pounding, my eyes are burning, and my hands are shaking, I'm determined to get through the day without the aid of alcohol, Damen, or illicit trips to the astral planes. Wishing I'd been more insistent—demanded that Damen show me how to shield myself. I mean, why does the solution always seem to flow back to Ava?

Sabine tentatively knocks on my door and I turn as she steps into my room. Her face is pale and pinched, her eyes rimmed with red, and her aura has gone all spotty and gray. And I cringe when I realize it's all because of Jeff, and the fact that she finally uncovered his mountain of lies. Lies I could've unveiled from the very beginning, sparing her all of this heartache, if only I hadn't put my needs before hers.

"Ever," she says, pausing by my bed. "I've been thinking.

Since I'm not really comfortable with this whole grounding business, and since you're almost an adult, I figure I may as well treat you like one so—"

So you're no longer grounded, I think, finishing the sentence in my head. But when I realize she still thinks my troubles are due to my grief, my face burns with shame.

"—you're no longer grounded." She smiles, a gesture of peace I do not deserve. "Though I was wondering if you changed your mind about talking to someone, because I know this therapist who—"

I shake my head before she can finish, knowing she means well, though refusing any part of it. And when she turns to leave, I surprise myself by saying, "Hey, you want to go out for dinner tonight?"

She hesitates in the doorway, clearly surprised by the offer.

"My treat." I smile encouragingly, having no idea how I'll possiby get through a night in a big, crowded restaurant, but figuring I can use some of my racetrack money to cover the bill.

"That would be great," she says, tapping the wall with her knuckles before heading into the hall. "I'll be home by seven."

The second I hear the front door close and the dead bolt click into place, Riley taps on my shoulder and shouts, "Ever! Ever! Can you see me?"

And I nearly jump out of my skin.

"Jeez, Riley, you scared the *hell* out of me! And why are you yelling?" I say, wondering why I'm acting so crabby, when the truth is, I'm overjoyed just to see her again.

She shakes her head and plops onto my bed. "For your information, I've been trying to get through to you for *days*. I thought you lost your ability to see me and I was totally starting to freak!"

"I *did* lose my ability. But only because I started drinking—heavily. And then I got expelled." I shake my head. "It was a mess."

"I know." She nods, brows knit with concern. "I was watching the whole time, jumping up and down in front of you, yelling and screaming and clapping my hands, anything to try to get through to you, but you were too whacked to see me. Remember that one time, when the bottle flew out of your hand?" She smiles and curtsies before me. "That was me. And you're lucky I didn't conk you over the head with it instead. So, what the heck happened?"

I shrug and gaze down at the ground, knowing I owe her an answer, a valid explanation to ease her concern, but not sure where to begin. "Well, it's like, all that random energy just became so overwhelming, I couldn't take it anymore. And when I realized how alcohol shielded me from it, I guess I just wanted to keep that good feeling going, I didn't want to go back to the way I was before."

"And now?"

"And now—" I hesitate, looking at her. "And now I'm right back where I started. Sober and miserable." I laugh.

"Ever—" She pauses, averting her gaze before looking at me. "Please don't get mad, but I think you should go see Ava." And when I start to balk, she raises her hand and says, "Just hear me out, okay? I really think she can help you. In fact I *know* she can help you. She's been *trying* to help you but you won't let her. But now, well, it's pretty clear that you're running out of options. I mean, you can either start drinking again, hide in your room for the rest of your life, or go see Ava. Pretty much a no-brainer, don't you think?"

I shake my head despite all the pounding, then I look at her and say, "Listen, I know you're all enamored with her, and fine, whatever, that's your choice. But she's got nothing for me, so please just—just give it a rest already, would you?"

Riley shakes her head. "You're wrong. Ava can help you. Besides, what could it hurt for you to give her a call?"

I sit there, kicking my bed frame and staring at the ground, thinking the only thing Ava's ever done for me is make my life even worse than it is. And when I finally look at Riley again, I notice how she's ditched the Halloween costumes for the jeans, T-shirt, and Converse sneakers of a normal twelve-year-old kid, but she's also turned filmy, translucent, and practically see-through.

"What happened with Damen? That day you went to his house? Are you still together?" she asks.

But I don't want to talk about Damen, I wouldn't even know where to begin. Besides, I know she's just trying to shift the attention from herself and her lucent appearance. "What's going on?" I ask, my voice rising, frantic. "Why are you fading like that?"

But she just looks at me and shakes her head. "I don't have much time."

"What do you mean—*you don't have much time?* You're coming back, *right?*" I shout, panicking as she waves good-bye and disappears from sight, leaving Ava's crumpled-up card in her place.

thirty-three

Before I can even shift into *park*, she's at the front door, waiting.

Either she really is psychic, or she's been standing there since we hung up.

But when I see the concern on her face, I feel guilty for thinking it.

"Ever, welcome," she says, smiling as she ushers me up the front steps and into a nicely decorated living room.

I gaze all around, taking in the framed photos, the elaborate coffee table books, the matching sofa and chairs, amazed by how normal it is.

"You were expecting purple walls and crystal balls?" She laughs, motioning for me to follow her into a bright sunny kitchen with beige stone floors, stainless steel appliances, and a sunlit skylight overhead. "I'll make us some tea," she says, setting the water to boil and offering me a seat at the table.

I watch as she busies herself, placing cookies onto a plate, and steeping our tea, and when she takes the seat across from mine, I look at her and say. "Um, sorry for acting so—rude—and—everything." I shrug, cringing at how awkward and inadequate I sound.

But Ava just smiles, and places her hand over mine, and the moment she makes contact, I can't help but feel better. "I'm just glad you came, I've been so worried about you."

I gaze down at the table, my eyes fixed on the lime green placemat, not knowing where to begin.

But since she's in charge, she handles it for me. "Have you seen Riley?" she asks, her eyes on mine.

And I can't believe she chose to start there. "Yes," I finally say. "And for your information, she's not looking so good." I press my lips together and avert my gaze, convinced that she's some-how responsible.

But Ava just laughs—*laughs!* "Trust me, she's fine." She nods, taking a sip of her tea.

"Trust *you?*" I gape, shaking my head. Watching her sip her tea and nibble at her cookie in that serene calm way that really sets me on edge. "Why should I? You're the one who brain-washed her! You're the one who convinced her to stay away!" I shout, wishing I hadn't even come here. What a huge colossal mistake!

"Ever, I know you're upset, and I know how much you miss her, but do you have any idea what she's sacrificed in order to be with you?"

I gaze out her window, my eyes grazing over the fountain, the plants, the small statue of Buddha, bracing myself for a re-ally stupid answer.

"Eternity."

I roll my eyes. "Please, all she's got is time."

"I'm referring to something *more*."

"Yeah, like what?" I ask, thinking I should just set the cookie down and get the hell out of there. Ava's a nut bag, a phony, and she talks with such authority about the most outrageous things.

"Riley's being here with you means she can't be with them."

"*Them?*"

"Your parents and Buttercup." She nods, tracing her finger along the rim of her cup while looking at me.

"How'd you know about—"

"Please, I thought we were past this?" she says, her eyes right on mine.

"This is ridiculous," I mumble, averting my gaze, wondering what Riley could ever see in such a person.

"Is it?" She brushes her auburn hair from her face, revealing a forehead that's unlined and smooth, free of all worry.

"Fine. I'll bite. If you know so much, then tell me, just where do you think Riley is when she's not with me?" I ask, my eyes meeting hers. Thinking: *This ought to be good.*

"Wandering." She lifts her cup to her lips and takes another sip.

"Wandering? Oh, okay." I laugh. "Like you would know."

"She has no other choice now that she's chosen to be with you."

I gaze out the window, my breath feeling hot, abbreviated, telling myself there's no way this is true.

"Riley didn't cross the bridge."

"You're wrong. I saw her." I glare. "She waved good-bye and everything, they all waved good-bye. I should know. *I was there.*"

"Ever, I've no doubt what you saw, but what I meant to say was, Riley didn't make it to the *other side.* She stopped halfway and ran back to find you."

"Sorry, but you're wrong," I tell her. "That's not at all true." My heart pounding in my chest as I remember that very last moment, the smiles, the waves, and then—and then nothing—they disappeared, while I fought and begged and pleaded to stay.

They were taken, while I remained. And it's entirely my fault. It should've been me. Every bad thing can be traced back to me.

"Riley turned back at the very last second," she continues. "When no one was looking, and your parents and Buttercup had already crossed. She told me, Ever, we've been through it many times. Your parents moved on, you came back to life, and Riley got stuck, left behind. And now she spends her time wandering between visits to you, me, old neighbors and friends, and a few naughty celebrities." She smiles.

"You know about that?" I look at her, eyes wide.

She nods. "It's only natural, though most earthbound entities bore of it pretty quickly."

"Earthbound what?"

"Entities, spirits, ghosts, it's all the same. Though it's quite different from those who've crossed over."

"So you're saying Riley is stuck?"

She nods. "You have to convince her to go."

I shake my head, thinking: *It's hardly up to me.* "She's already gone. She barely comes around anymore," I mumble, glaring at her like she's responsible, but that's only because she is.

"You have to give her your blessing. You have to let her know it's okay."

"Listen," I say, tired of this discussion, of Ava butting into my business, telling me how to run my life. "I came here for help, not to listen to this. If Riley wants to stick around, then fine, that's her business. Just because she's twelve doesn't mean I can tell her what to do. She's pretty stubborn you know?"

"Hmmm, wonder where she gets it?" Ava says, sipping her tea and gazing at me.

But even though she smiles, tries to make like it's a joke, I just look at her and say, "If you've changed your mind about helping me, then just say so." I rise from my seat, my eyes teary, my body panicky, my head pounding, yet fully prepared to leave if I have to. Remembering what my dad taught me about the key to negotiating—that you have to be willing to walk away—no matter what.

She looks at me for a moment, then motions for me to sit. "As you wish." She sighs. "Here's how you do it."

By the time Ava walks me outside, I'm surprised to see that it's already dark. I guess I spent more time in there than I realized, going through a step-by-step meditation, learning how to ground myself and create my own psychic shield. But even though things didn't start off so well, especially all that stuff about Riley, I'm still glad I came. It's the first time I've felt completely normal, without the crutch of alcohol or Damen, in a very long time.

I thank her again, and head for my car, and just as I'm about to climb in, Ava looks at me and says, "Ever?"

I gaze at her, seeing her framed only by the soft yellow light of her porch now that her aura is no longer visible.

"I really wish you'd let me show you how to undo the shield. You might be surprised and find that you miss it," she coaxes.

But we've already been through this, more than once. Besides, I've made my decision and there's no going back. I'm saying hello to a normal life, and good-bye to immortality, Damen, Summerland, psychic phenomenon, and everything else that goes with it. Ever since the accident, all I wanted was to be normal again. And now that I am, I plan to embrace it.

I shake my head and stick my key in the ignition, looking up again when she says, "Ever, please think about what I said. You've got it all wrong. You've said good-bye to the wrong person."

"What're you talking about?" I ask, just wanting to get home, so I can start enjoying my life once again.

But she just smiles. "I think you know what I mean."

thirty-four

No longer grounded and released of all that psychic baggage, I spend the next few days hanging with Miles and Haven, meeting for coffee, going shopping, seeing movies, trolling around downtown, watching his rehearsals, thrilled to have my life back to normal again. And on Christmas morning, when Riley appears, I'm relieved I can still see her.

"Hey, wait up!" she says, blocking the door just as I'm about to head down the stairs. "No way are you opening your presents without me!" And when she smiles, she's so radiant and clear she appears almost solid, nothing flimsy, filmy, or translucent about her. "I know what you're getting!" She grins. "Want a hint?"

I shake my head and laugh. "Absolutely not! I love not knowing for a change," I say, smiling as she walks over to the middle of my room and executes a perfect series of cartwheels.

"Speaking of surprises." She giggles. "Jeff bought Sabine a ring! Can you believe it? He moved out of his mom's house, got his own place, and is begging her to come back and start over!"

"Serious?" I say, taking in her faded jeans and layered tees, glad to see she's done with the costumes and no longer copying me.

She nods. "But Sabine will send it right back. I mean, at least from what I can tell. It's not like she's actually received the ring yet, so I guess we'll wait and see. Still, people rarely surprise you, you know?"

"Still spying on celebrities?" I ask, wondering if she has any dish.

She makes a face and rolls her eyes. "God no. I was being seriously corrupted. Besides, it's always the same old thing, shopping binges, food binges, drug binges, followed by rehab. Wash, rinse, and repeat—yawn."

I laugh, wishing I could reach out and hug her instead. I was so afraid I'd lost her.

"What're you looking at?" she asks, peering at me.

"You." I smile.

"*And?*"

"*And*, I'm so glad you're here. And that I can still see you. I was afraid I'd lost that ability when Ava showed me how to make that shield."

She smiles. "To be honest, you did. I really had to ramp up my energy so you could see me. In fact, I'm using some of yours. Do you feel tired?"

I shrug. "A little, but then again, I just woke up."

She shakes her head. "Doesn't matter. It's still me."

"Hey Riley." I look at her. "Are you still . . . *visiting Ava?*" I ask, holding my breath as I wait for the answer.

She shakes her head. "Nah. I'm over that too. Now come on, I cannot wait to see your face when you unwrap your new iPhone! Oops!" She laughs, placing her hand over her mouth as she backs right through the closed bedroom door.

"You're really staying?" I whisper, making my exit the traditional way. "You don't have to leave, or be somewhere else?"

She climbs on top of the banister and slides her way down, looking back at me and smiling when she says, "Nope, not anymore."

Sabine returned the ring, I had a new iPhone, Riley was back to visiting every day, sometimes even accompanying me to school, Miles started dating one of the *Hairspray* backup dancers, Haven dyed her hair dark brown, swore off everything goth, began the painful process of lasering off her tattoo, burned all of her Drina-dresses, and replaced them with emo. New Year's came and went, marked by a small gathering at my house that included sparkling cider for me (I was officially off the sauce), contraband champagne for my friends, and a midnight dip in the Jacuzzi, which was pretty tame as far as New Year's parties go, but not at all boring. Stacia and Honor still glared at me, pretty much the same as before, even worse on the days when I wore something cute, Mr. Robins got a life (one without his daughter or his wife), Ms. Machado still cringed when she looked at my art, and between it all was Damen.

Like caulk around a tile, like binding in a book, he filled all of my blank empty spaces and held everything together, kept it all contained. Through every pop quiz, every shampoo, every meal, every movie, every song, every dip in the Jacuzzi, I held him in my mind, comforted just by knowing he was out there—somewhere—even though I'd decided against him.

By Valentine's Day, Miles and Haven are in love—though not with each other. And even though we sit together at lunch, I may as well have been on my own. They were too busy hovering over their Sidekicks to notice my existence, while my iPhone sat beside me, silent and ignored.

"Omigod, this is *hilarious!* You can't *believe* how brilliant he is!" Miles says, for the gazillionth time, gazing up from his text, his face flushed with laughter, as he thinks of the perfect reply.

"Omigod, Josh just gifted me like, *a ton of songs!* I am so not worthy," Haven mumbles, thumbs tapping a response.

And even though I'm happy for them, happy that they're happy and all that, my mind is on sixth-period art, and I'm wondering if I should ditch. Because here at Bay View High, today is not only Valentine's Day, it's also Secret Heart Day. Which means that those big, red, heart-shaped lollipops, the ones with the little pink love notes they've been pushing all week, are finally distributed. And while Miles and Haven are fully expecting to receive theirs even though their boyfriends don't go here, I'm just hoping to get through the day, somewhat sane, and mostly unscathed.

And even though I fully admit that ditching the iPod/ hoodie/dark sunglasses combo has allowed for a considerable amount of renewed male interest, it's not like I'm interested in any of them. Because the truth is, there's not one guy in this school (on this planet!), who could ever compare to Damen. No one. Nada. Just not possible. And it's not like I'm in a hurry to lower my standards.

But by the time the sixth-period bell rings, I know I can't ditch. My ditching days, like my drinking days, are pretty much over. So I suck it up and head to class, immersed in my latest, ill-fated assignment—to mimic one of the *isms*. And I happened to choose cubism—making the mistake of thinking it would be easy. But it's not. In fact, it's far from it.

And when I sense someone standing behind me, I turn and

say, "Yeah?" Peering at the lollipop he holds in his hand, then focusing back on my work, assuming it's a case of mistaken identity. But when he taps me again, this time I don't bother looking, I just shake my head and say, "Sorry, wrong girl."

He mumbles something under his breath, then clears his throat and says, "You're that Ever chick, right?"

I nod.

"Then take it already." He shakes his head. "I gotta get through this entire box before the bell rings."

He tosses me the lollipop and makes for the door, and I set down my charcoal, flip the card open, and read:

> *Thinking of you*
> *Always.*
> *Damen*

thirty-five

I race through the door, anxious to get upstairs so I can show Riley my lollipop valentine, the one that made the sun shine, the birds sing, and turned my whole day around, even though I refuse to have anything to do with the sender.

But when I see her sitting alone on the couch, seconds before she turns and sees me, something about the way she looks, so small and alone, reminds me of what Ava said—that I've said good-bye to the wrong person. And the air rushes right out of me.

"Hey," she says, grinning at me. "You can't *believe* what I just saw on *Oprah*. There's this dog who's missing his two front legs, and yet he can still—"

I drop my bag on the floor and sit down beside her, grabbing the remote and pushing *mute*.

"What's up?" she says, scowling at me for silencing *Oprah*.

"What are you doing here?" I ask.

"Um, hanging on the couch, waiting for you to come home . . ." She crosses her eyes and sticks out her tongue. "Duh."

"No, I mean, why are you *here*? Why aren't you—*someplace else*?"

She twists her mouth to the side and turns back to the TV, her body stiff, face immobile, preferring a silent *Oprah* to me.

"Why aren't you with Mom and Dad and Buttercup?" I ask, watching as her bottom lip starts to quiver, at first only slightly, but soon, a full-blown tremble, making me feel so awful, I have to force the words to continue. "Riley." I pause, swallowing hard. "Riley, I don't think you should come here anymore."

"You're *evicting* me?" She springs to her feet, eyes wide with outrage.

"No, It's nothing like that, I just—"

"You can't stop me from visiting, Ever! I can do anything I want! *Anything!* And there's *nothing* you can do about it!" she says, shaking her head and pacing the room.

"I'm aware of that." I nod. "But I don't think I should encourage you either."

She crosses her arms and mashes her lips together, then plops back down on the couch, kicking her leg back and forth like she does when she's mad, upset, frustrated, or all three.

"It's just, well, for a while there it seemed like you were busy with something else, somewhere else, and you seemed perfectly happy and okay with it. But now it's like you're here all the time again and I'm wondering if it's because of me. Because even though I can't bear the thought of not having you around, it's more important for you to be happy. And spying on neighbors and celebrities, watching *Oprah*, and waiting for me, well, I don't think it's the best way to go." I stop, taking a deep breath, wishing I didn't have to continue, but knowing I do. "Because even though seeing you is the undisputed best part of my day, I can't help but think there's another—better—place for you to be."

She stares at the TV as I stare at her, sitting in silence until she finally breaks it. "For your information, I *am* happy. I'm perfectly fine and happy, *so there.*" She shakes her head and rolls her eyes, then crosses her arms against her chest. "Sometimes I live here, and sometimes I live somewhere else. In this place called Summerland, which is pretty dang awesome, in case you don't remember it." She sneaks a peek at me.

I nod. Oh, I definitely remember it.

She leans back against the cushions and crosses her legs. "So, best of both worlds, right? What's the problem?"

I press my lips and look at her, refusing to be swayed by her arguments, trusting that I'm doing the right thing, the only thing. "The *problem* is, I think there's someplace *even better.* Someplace where Mom and Dad and Buttercup are waiting for you—"

"Listen, Ever." She cuts me off. "I know you think I'm here because I wanted to be thirteen and since that didn't happen I'm living vicariously through you. And yeah, maybe that's partly true, but did you ever stop and think that maybe I'm here because I can't bear to leave you either?" She looks at me, her eyes blinking rapidly, but when I start to speak, she holds up her hand and continues. "At first I was following them, because, well, they're the parents and I thought I was supposed to, but then I saw how you stayed back, and I went to find you, but by the time I got there, you were already gone, I couldn't find the bridge again, and then, well, I got stuck. But then I met some people who've been there for years, well, the earth version of years, and they showed me around and—"

"Riley—" I start, but she cuts me right off.

"And just so you know, I *have* seen Mom and Dad and Buttercup, and they're fine. Actually, they're more than fine, they're *happy.* They just wish you'd stop feeling so guilty all the time.

They can see you. You know that, right? You just can't see them. You can't see the ones who crossed the bridge, you can only see the ones like me."

But I don't care about the details of who I can and can't see. I'm still stuck on that part about them wanting me to stop feeling so guilty, even though I know they're just being all nice and parental, trying to ease my guilt. Because the truth is, the crash is my fault. If I hadn't made my dad turn back so I could go get that stupid Pinecone Lake Cheerleading Camp sweatshirt I'd forgotten, we never would've been in that spot, on that road, at the exact same time that some stupid confused deer ran right in front of our car, forcing my dad to swerve, fly down the ravine, crash into the tree, and kill everyone but me.

My fault.

All of it.

Entirely mine.

But Riley just shakes her head and says, "If it's anyone's fault, then it's Dad's fault, because everyone knows you're not supposed to swerve when an animal darts in front of your car. You're supposed to just hit it and keep going. But you and I both know he couldn't bear to do that, so he tried to save us all but ended up sparing the deer. But then again, maybe it's the deer's fault. I mean, he had no business being on the road when he has a perfectly good forest to live in. Or perhaps it's the guardrail's fault for not being stronger, firmer, made of tougher stuff. Or maybe it's the car company's fault for faulty steering and crappy brakes. Or maybe—" She stops and looks at me. "The point is, it's *nobody's* fault. That's just the way it happened. That's just the way it was supposed to *be*."

I choke back a sob, wishing I could believe that, but I can't. I know better. I know the truth.

"We all know it, and accept it. So now it's time for you to know it and accept it too. Apparently it just wasn't your time."

But it was my time. Damen cheated, and I went along for the ride!

I swallow hard and stare at the TV. *Oprah* is over and *Dr. Phil* has taken her place—one shiny baldhead and a very large mouth that never stops moving.

"Remember when I was looking so filmy? That's because I was getting ready to cross over. Every day I crept closer and closer to the other side of the bridge. But just when I decided to go all the way, well, that's when it seemed like you needed me most. And I just couldn't bear to leave you—I still can't bear to leave you," she says.

But even though I really want her to stay, I've already robbed her of one life. I won't rob her of the afterlife too. "Riley, it's time for you to go," I say, whispering so softly part of me is hoping she didn't actually hear it. But once it's out, I know it's the right thing to do, so I say it again, louder this time, the words ringing with resonance, conviction. "I think you should go," I repeat, hardly believing my own ears.

She gets up from the couch, her eyes wide and sad, her cheeks shining with crystalline tears.

And I swallow hard as I say, "You have no idea how much you've helped me. I don't know what I would've done without you. You're the only reason I got up each day and put one foot in front of the other. But I'm better now, and it's time for you—" I stop, choking on my own words, unable to continue.

"Mom said you'd send me back eventually." She smiles.

I look at her, wondering what that means.

"She said, *'someday your sister will finally grow up and do the right thing.'*"

And the moment she says it, we both burst out laughing.

Laughing at the absurdity of the situation. Laughing at our mom's penchant for saying, *"Someday you'll grow up and—fill in the blank."* Laughing to relieve some of the tension and pain of saying good-bye. Laughing because it feels so damn good to do so.

And when the laughter dies down, I look at her and say, "You'll still check in and say hi, right?"

She shakes her head and looks away. "I doubt you'll be able to see me, since you can't see Mom and Dad."

"What about Summerland? Can I see you there?" I ask, thinking I can go back to Ava, have her show me how to remove the shield, but only to visit Riley in Summerland, not for anything else.

She shrugs. "I'm not sure. But I'll do my best to send some kind of sign, something so you'll know I'm okay, something specifically from me."

"Like what?" I ask, panicked to see her already fading. I didn't expect it to happen so quickly. "And how will I know? How can I be sure it's from you?"

"Trust me, you'll know." She smiles, waving good-bye as she fades.

thirty-six

The moment Riley is gone, I break down and cry, knowing I did the right thing, but still wishing it didn't have to hurt so damn much. I stay like that for a while, curled up on the couch, my body folded into a small tight ball, remembering everything she said about the accident, and how it wasn't really my fault. But even though I wish I could believe it, I know it's not true. Four lives were ended that day, and it's all because of me.

All because of a stupid, powder blue, cheerleading camp sweatshirt.

"I'll get you another one," my dad said, gazing into the rearview mirror, his eyes meeting mine, two matching sets of identical blues. "If I turn around now, we'll hit traffic."

"But it's my favorite," I whined. "The one I got at cheer camp. You can't buy it in a store." I pouted, knowing I was mere seconds from getting my way.

"You really want it that bad?"

I nodded, smiling as he shook his head, took a deep breath, and turned the car around, meeting my gaze in the rearview mirror the same moment the deer ran onto the road.

I wanted to believe Riley, to retrain my brain to this new way of thinking. But knowing the truth pretty much guaranteed I never would.

And as I wipe the tears from my face, I remember Ava's words. Thinking if Riley was the right person to say good-bye to, then Damen must be the wrong one.

I reach for the lollipop I'd placed on the table and gasp when I see it's morphed into a tulip.

A big, huge, shiny, red tulip.

Then I race for my room, pull my laptop onto my bed, and run a search on flower meanings, skimming down the page until I read:

> In the eighteen hundreds, people often communicated their intentions through the flowers they sent, as specific flowers held specific meanings. Here are a few of the more traditional ones:

I scroll down the alphabetical list, my eyes scanning for *tulips* and holding my breath as I read:

> Red tulips—Undying love.

Then, just for fun, I look up white rosebuds and laugh out loud when I read:

> White rosebuds—The heart that knows no love; heart ignorant of love.

And I know he was testing me. The whole entire time. Holding this huge life-changing secret with absolutely no idea how to tell me, not knowing if I'd accept it, reject it, or turn him away.

Flirting with Stacia just to get a reaction, so he could eavesdrop on my thoughts and see if I cared. And I'd become so adept at lying to myself, denying my feelings about practically everything, I ended up confusing us both.

And while I certainly don't condone what he did, I have to admit that it worked. And now, all I have to do to see him again is just say the words out loud and he'll manifest right here before me. Because the truth is, I do love him. I've loved him without ceasing. I've loved him since that very first day. I loved him even when I swore that I didn't. I can't help it, I just do. And even though I'm not so sure about this whole *immortal* business, Summerland *was* pretty cool. Besides, if Riley is right, if there is such a thing as fate and destiny, then maybe it applies to this too?

I shut my eyes and imagine the feel of Damen's warm wonderful body curled around mine, the whisper of his soft sweet lips on my ear, my neck, my cheek, the way his mouth feels when it parts against mine—I hold onto that image, the feel of our perfect love, our perfect kiss, as I whisper the words I've held all this time, the ones I was too scared to speak, the ones that will bring him back to me.

I say them over and over again, my voice gaining strength as they fill up the room.

But when I open my eyes, I'm alone.

And I know I waited too long.

thirty-seven

I head downstairs, in search of some ice cream, knowing a rich and creamy Häagen-Dazs Band-Aid can't possibly heal my broken heart, though it just might help soothe it. And after retrieving a quart from the freezer, I cradle it in my arms and reach for a spoon, then the whole thing crashes to the ground when I hear a voice say:

"So touching, Ever. So very, very touching."

I bend over, squeezing the toes that got nailed by a quart of Vanilla Swiss Almond, as I gape at a perfectly turned-out Drina— legs crossed, hands folded, a prim and proper lady, seated right there at my breakfast bar.

"So cute how you called out for Damen after conjuring that chaste little love scene in your head." She laughs, her eyes grazing over me. "Ah, yes, I can still see inside your head. Your little psychic shield? Thinner than the Shroud of Turin, I'm afraid. Anyway, as far as you and Damen and your happily ever after, and after, and after?" She shakes her head. "Well, you know I can't let that happen. As it turns out, my life's work has been destroying you, and little do you know, I still can."

I gaze at her, concentrating on my breath, keeping it slow

and steady, while I try to clear my mind of all incriminating thought, knowing she'll only use it against me. But the thing is, *trying* to clear your mind is about as effective as telling someone to *not* think about elephants—from that moment on that's *all* they'll think about.

"Elephants? Really?" She groans, a low evil sound that vibrates the room. "My God, what *does* he see in you?" Her eyes rake over me, filled with disdain. "Certainly not your intellect or wit, since we've yet to see any evidence it exists. And your idea of a love scene? So Disney, so Family Channel, so *dreadfully boring*. Really, Ever, may I remind you that Damen's been around for *hundreds* of years, including the free-love sixties?" She shakes her head at me.

"If you're looking for Damen, he's not here," I finally say, my voice scratchy, hoarse, like it hasn't been used for days.

She lifts her brow. "Trust me, I *know* where Damen is. I *always* know where Damen is. It's what I do."

"So you're a stalker." I press my lips together, knowing I shouldn't antagonize her, but hey, I have nothing to lose. Either way, she's here to kill me.

She twists her lips and holds up her hand, inspecting her perfectly manicured nails. "Hardly," she mumbles.

"Well, if that's how you've chosen to spend the last three hundred years, then some might say—"

"More like six hundred, you dreadful little troll, six hundred years." She looks me over and scowls.

Six hundred years? Is she serious?

She rolls her eyes and stands. "You mortals, so dull, so stupid, so predictable, so *ordinary*. And yet, despite all your obvious defects, you always seem to inspire Damen to feed the hungry, serve mankind, fight poverty, save the whales, stop littering, recycle, meditate for peace, just say no to drugs, alcohol, big spending, and just about everything else that's worthwhile—one horribly boring altruistic pursuit after another. And for what? Do you ever learn? *Hello! Global warming!* Apparently not. And yet, *and yet,* somehow Damen and I always seem to get through it, though it can take far too long to deprogram him, return him to the lusty, hedonistic, greedy, indulgent Damen I know and love. Though believe me, this is just another little detour, and before you know it, we'll be back on top of the world again."

She moves toward me, her smile growing wider with each approaching step, slinking around the large granite counter like a Siamese cat. "Quite frankly, Ever, I can't imagine what it is that you see in him. And I don't mean what every other female, and let's face it, most males, see in him. No, I mean, it's because of Damen that you always seem to suffer. It's because of Damen that you're going through all of this now. If only you hadn't lived through that damn accident." She shakes her head. "I mean, just when I thought it was safe to leave, just when I was sure you were dead, the next thing I know Damen's moved to California because, *surprise,* he brought you back!" She shakes her head again. "You'd think after all of these hundreds of years, I'd have a little more patience. But then, you really do bore me, and clearly that's not *my* fault."

She looks at me but I refuse to respond, I'm still deciphering her words—*Drina caused the accident?*

She looks at me and rolls her eyes. "*Yes,* I caused the accident. Why must everything be so spelled out for you?" She shakes her head. "It was *I* who spooked the deer that ran in front of your car. It was *I* who knew your father was a sappy, kindhearted fool who'd gladly risk his family's life to save a deer. Mortals are always so predictable. Especially the earnest ones who try to do good." She laughs. "Though, in the end, it was almost too easy to be any fun. But make no mistake, Ever, this time Damen's not here to save you, and I *will* stick around to get the job done."

I scan the room, searching for some sort of protection, eyeing the knife rack on the other side of the room, but knowing I'll never get to it in time. I'm not fast like Damen and Drina. At least I don't think I am. And there's no time to find out.

She sighs. "By all means, please, get the knife, see if I care." She shakes her head and checks her diamond-encrusted watch. "I'd really like to get started though, if you don't mind. Normally I like to take my time, have a little fun, but, today being Valentine's Day and all, well, I have plans to dine with my sweetie, just as soon as I've eliminated you." Her eyes are dark and her mouth is twisted, and for the briefest moment, all the evil inside springs right to the surface. But then just as quickly it's gone again, replaced by a beauty so breathtaking, it's hard not to stare.

"You know, before you came along, in one of your . . . earlier incarnations, I was his one true love. But then you showed up and tried to steal him away, and it's been the same old cycle ever since." She slinks forward, each step silent, quick, until she's standing directly before me, and I've had no time to react. "But now I'm taking him back. And he always comes back, Ever, be clear about that."

I reach for the bamboo cutting board, thinking I can slam it over her head, but she lunges for me so fast she knocks me off balance and slams my body into the fridge, the blow to my back stealing my breath as I gasp and fumble and fall to the ground. Hearing the *thwonk* of my head cracking open when it slams against the floor as a trail of warm blood seeps from my skull to my mouth.

And before I can move or do anything to fight back, she's on top of me, slashing at my clothing, my hair, my face, whispering into my ear, "Just give up, Ever. Just relax and let go. Go join your happy family, they're all waiting to see you. You're not cut out for this life. You have nothing left to live for. And now's your chance to leave it."

thirty-eight

I must've blacked out, but only for a moment, because when I open my eyes, she's still right there on top of me, her face and hands stained with my blood as she croons and coaxes and whispers, trying to convince me to let go, to just let myself go, once and for all, to just slip away and be done with it all.

But even though that might've been tempting before, it's not anymore. This bitch killed my family, and now she's gonna pay.

I shut my eyes, determined to get back to that place—all of us in the car, laughing, happy, so full of love, seeing it clearer now than ever before, now that it's no longer clouded by guilt, now that I'm no longer to blame.

And when I feel my strength surging inside me I lift her right off me and throw her across the room, watching as she flies right into the wall, her arm jutting out at an unnatural angle as her body tilts to the floor.

She looks at me, eyes wide with shock, but soon she's up and laughing as she dusts herself off. And when she lunges at me, I throw her off again, watching as she soars across the kitchen and all the way into the den, crashing through the closed french doors and sending an explosion of broken shards through the room.

"Quite the crime scene you're creating," she says, plucking glass daggers from her arms, her legs, her face, the wounds closing up as soon as they're cleared. "Very impressive. Can't wait to read all about it in tomorrow's paper." She smiles, and just like that, she's on me again, fully restored, determined to win. "You're in over your head," she whispers. "And frankly, your pathetic show of strength is getting a little redundant. Seriously, Ever, you're one lousy hostess. No wonder you don't have any friends; is this how you treat all your guests?"

I push her off, ready to toss her through a thousand windows if I have to. But I've barely completed the thought when I'm side-swiped by a horrible, sharp, squeezing pain. Watching as Drina steps toward me, face pulled into a grin, paralyzing me so that I can't even stop her.

"That would be the old *head in a vise with serrated jaws* trick." She laughs. "Works every time. Though, in all fairness, I did try to warn you. You just wouldn't listen. But really, Ever, it's your choice. I can ratchet up the pain—" She narrows her eyes as my body folds in agony, slumping toward the floor as my stomach swirls with nausea. "Or, you can just—let—yourself—go. Nice and easy. Your choice."

I try to focus on her, watching as she moves toward me, but my vision is distorted, and my limbs so rubbery and weak, she's like a fast-moving blur I know I can't beat.

So I close my eyes and think: *I can't let her win. I can't let her win. Not this time. Not after what she did to my family.*

And when I swing my fist toward her, my body so feeble, clumsy, and defeated, I'm surprised when it lands square in her chest, grazing the front of her, before falling away. And I stagger back, devoid of all breath, knowing it wasn't nearly enough, didn't do any good.

I shut my eyes and cringe, waiting for the end, and now that it's inevitable, I hope it comes soon. But when my head clears and my stomach calms, I open them again to find Drina staggering back toward the wall, clutching her chest, and staring accusingly.

"Damen!" she wails, looking right past me. "Don't let her do this to me, *to us*—"

I turn, to see him standing beside me, gazing at Drina and shaking his head. "It's too late," he says, taking my hand, entwining his fingers with mine. "It's time for you to go, Poverina."

"Don't call me that!" she wails, her once amazing green eyes now blurred by red. "You know how I *hate* that!"

"I know," he says, squeezing my fingers as she shrivels and ages then fades from our sight, a black silk dress and designer shoes the only evidence she ever existed.

"How—" I turn to Damen, searching for answers.

But he just smiles and says, "It's over. Absolutely, completely, eternally over." He pulls me into his arms, covering my face in a trail of warm wonderful kisses, promising, "She'll never bother us again."

"Did I—*kill her*?" I ask, not quite sure how I feel about that, despite what she did to my family, and all the times she claimed to have killed me.

He nods.

"But—*how*? I mean, if she's immortal, then wasn't I supposed to cut off her head?"

He shakes his head and laughs. "What kind of books are you reading?" Then his face becomes very serious when he says, "It doesn't work like that. There's no beheading, no wooden stakes, no silver bullets, it all comes down to the simple fact that revenge weakens and love strengthens. Somehow you managed to hit Drina right in her most vulnerable spot."

I squint, not quite understanding. "I hardly touched her," I say, remembering how my fist met her chest, but just barely.

"The fourth chakra was your target. And you hit the bull's-eye."

Huh?

"The body has seven chakras. The fourth chakra, or heart chakra as it's sometimes called, is the center of unconditional love, compassion, the higher self, all of the things Drina was lacking. And that left her defenseless, weakened. Ever, her *lack of love* is what killed her."

"But if she was so vulnerable, why didn't she guard it, protect it?"

"She was unaware, deluded, led by her ego. Drina never realized how dark she'd become, how resentful, how hateful, how possessive—"

"And if you knew all that, why didn't you tell me before?"

He shrugs. "It was just a theory I had. I've never killed an immortal, so I wasn't sure if it would work. Until now."

"You mean there are others? Drina's not the only one?"

He opens his mouth as if to say something, but then closes it firmly. And when I look in his eyes I see a flash of—regret, remorse? But just as quickly, it's gone.

"She said some things about you, and your past—"

"Ever," he says. "Ever, look at me." He tilts my chin until I finally do. "I've been around a long time—"

"I'll say, *six hundred years!*"

He cringes. "Give or take. The point is, I've seen a few things, done a few things, and my life hasn't always been so good or so pure. In fact, most of it's been quite the opposite." I start to pull away, not sure if I'm ready to hear this, but he pulls me back to him and says, "Trust me, you're ready to hear this, because the truth is I'm not a murderer, I'm also not evil. I just—" He pauses.

"I just enjoyed a taste for the good life. And yet, every time I met you, I was willing to throw it all away, just to be near you."

I yank free, this time successfully. Thinking: *Oh jeez! Oh no! Classic case of boy losing girl, only this time it's over and over again, spanning the centuries, each time ending before they can do the deed. No wonder he's interested, I'm the one who keeps getting away! I'm like a living, breathing, forbidden fruit! Does this mean I have to remain a virgin for eternity? Disappear every few years just to keep his interest? I mean, now that we're stuck with each other for all of eternity, the moment the deed is done it's just a matter of time before this particular train arrives in Boring Town U.S.A. and he'll be looking to enjoy the "good life" again.*

"*Stuck with me?* That's how you see it? As though you'll be *stuck with me,* for all of eternity?" And the way he looks at me I can't tell if he's amused or offended.

My cheeks burn, having temporarily forgotten that my thoughts are not at all private where he's concerned. "No, I—I was afraid you'd feel that way about *me*. I mean, it's classic love story fodder—the one who got away—*again and again and again!* No wonder you've remained so entranced! It had nothing to do with me! You've spent six hundred years trying to get in my pants!"

"Petticoats, pantaloons, trust me, pants didn't come into fashion until much, much later." But when I don't laugh, he pulls me to him and says, "Ever, it has *everything* to do with you. And if you don't mind my saying, it's been my experience that the best way to deal with eternity is by living it one day at a time."

He kisses me, but only briefly, before he shifts his body and starts to pull away, but I grab hold of his hand, and pull him back to me. "Don't go," I say, gazing at him. "Please don't ever leave me again."

"Not even to get you some water?" He smiles.

"Not even for water," I tell him, my hands exploring his face, his incredibly beautiful face. "I—" The words halt in my throat.

"Yes?" He smiles.

"I missed you," I finally manage.

"And so you did." He leans in, pressing his lips to my forehead, then quickly pulling away.

"What?" I say, seeing the way he's looking at me, his grin spread wide and warming his face. Then I slide my fingers under my bangs, and gasp when I realize my scar's disappeared.

"Forgiveness is healing." He smiles. "Especially forgiving yourself."

I gaze at him, looking right into his eyes, knowing there's something more to say, but not sure I can go through with it. So I close my eyes instead, thinking that if he can read my mind then I shouldn't have to say the words out loud.

But he just laughs. "It's always better when it's spoken."

"But I've already said it, that's why you came back, right? I thought you would've come sooner. I mean it would've been nice to have had some help."

"I heard you. And I would've come even sooner, but I needed to know you were truly ready, and not just lonely after saying good-bye to Riley."

"You know about that?"

He nods. "You did the right thing."

"So, you almost let me die in there, because you wanted to be sure?"

He shakes his head. "I never would've let you die. Not this time."

"And Drina?"

"I underestimated her, I had no idea."

"You can't read each other's thoughts?"

He gazes at me, smoothing his thumb against my cheek. "We learned how to cloak them from each other long ago."

"Will you show me how to cloak mine?"

He smiles. "In time I'll teach you everything, I promise. But Ever, you need to know what all of this really means. You'll never be with your family again. You'll never cross that bridge. You need to know what you're getting yourself into." He holds my chin and looks in my eyes.

"But I can always, sort of, just—*drop out*—right? You know, give up? Like you said?"

He shakes his head. "It becomes much harder once you're ingrained."

I look at him, knowing it's a lot to give up, but figuring there's got to be some way around it. Riley promised me a sign, and I'll take it from there. But in the meantime, if eternity starts today, then that's the way I'm going to live it. For this day, and this day only. Knowing that Damen will always be by my side. *I mean, always, right?*

He looks at me, waiting.

"I love you," I whisper.

"And I love you." He smiles, his lips seeking mine. "*Always* have. *Always* will."

"Close your eyes and picture it. Can you see it?"

I nod, eyes closed.

"Imagine it right there before you. *See* its texture, shape, and color—got it?"

I smile, holding the image in my head.

"Good. Now reach out and touch it. *Feel* its contours with the tips of your fingers, *cradle* its weight in the palms of your hands, then combine all of your senses—sight, touch, smell, taste—can you taste it?"

I bite my lip and suppress a giggle.

"Perfect. Now combine that with feeling. *Believe* it exists right before you. Feel it, see it, touch it, taste it, accept it, *manifest it!*" he says.

So I do. I do all of those things. And when he groans, I open my eyes to see for myself.

"Ever." He shakes his head. "You were supposed to think of an *orange*. This isn't even close."

"Nope, nothing fruity about him." I laugh, smiling at each of my Damens—the replica I manifested before me, and the flesh-and-blood version beside me. Both of them equally tall, dark, and so devastatingly handsome they hardly seem real.

"What am I going to do with you?" the real Damen asks, attempting a disapproving gaze but failing miserably. His eyes always betray him, showing nothing but love.

"Hmmm . . ." I glance between my two boyfriends—one real, one conjured. "I guess you could just go ahead and kiss me. Or, if you're too busy, I'll ask him to stand in. I don't think he'd mind." I motion toward the manifest Damen, laughing when he smiles and winks at me even though his edges are fading and soon he'll be gone.

But the real Damen doesn't laugh. He just shakes his head again and says, "Ever, please. You need to be serious. There's so much to teach you."

"What's the rush?" I shrug, fluffing my pillow and patting the space right beside me, hoping he'll move away from my desk and come join me. "I thought we had nothing *but* time?" I smile. And when he looks at me, my whole body grows warm and my breath halts in my throat. And I can't help but wonder if I'll ever get used to his amazing beauty—his smooth olive skin, brown shiny hair, perfect face, and lean sculpted body—the perfect dark yin to my pale blond yang. "I think you'll find me a very eager student," I say, my eyes meeting his—two dark wells of unfathomable depths.

"You're insatiable," he whispers, shaking his head and moving beside me, as drawn to me as I am to him.

"Just trying to make up for lost time," I murmur, always so eager for these moments, the times when it's just us, and I don't have to share him with anyone else. Even knowing we have all of eternity laid out before us doesn't make me any less greedy.

He leans in to kiss me, clearly forgetting about our lesson. All thoughts of manifesting, remote viewing, telepathy—all of that psychic business replaced by something far more immediate, as he pushes me back against a pile of pillows and covers my body with his, the two of us merging like two vines basking in the warmth of the sun.

His fingers snake under my top, then slide along my stomach to the edge of my bra as I close my eyes and whisper, "I love you." Words I once kept to myself. But after saying it the first time, I've barely said anything else.

Hearing his soft muffled groan as he releases the clasp on my bra, so effortlessly, so perfectly, nothing awkward or fumbling about it.

Every move he makes is so graceful, so perfect, so—

Maybe too perfect.

"What's wrong?" he asks, as I push him away. His breath coming in short, shallow gasps as his eyes seek mine, the area around his eyes tense and constricted in the way I've grown used to.

"Nothing's wrong." I turn my back to him and adjust my top, glad I completed the lesson on shielding my thoughts, since it's the only thing that allows me to lie.

He sighs and gets up from the bed, denying me the tingle of his touch and the heat of his gaze as he paces before me. And when he finally stops and faces me, I press my lips together, knowing what's next. We've been here before.

"Ever, I'm not trying to rush you or anything. Really, I'm not," he says, his face creased with concern. "But at some point you're going to have to get over this and accept who I am. I can manifest anything you desire, send telepathic thoughts and images whenever we're apart, whisk you away to Summerland at a moment's notice. But the one thing I can't ever do is change the past. It just *is*."

I stare at the floor, feeling small, needy, and completely ashamed. Hating that I'm so incapable of hiding my jealousies and insecurities, hating that they're so transparent and clearly displayed. Because no matter what sort of psychic shield I create, it's no use. He's had six hundred years to study human behavior—to study *my* behavior—versus my seventeen.

"Just—just give me a little more time to get used to all this," I say, picking at a frayed seam on my pillowcase. "It's only been a few weeks." I shrug, remembering how I killed his ex-wife, told him I loved him, and sealed my immortal fate, less than three weeks ago.

He looks at me, his lips pressed together, his eyes tinged with doubt. And even though we're merely a few feet apart, the space that divides us is so heavy and fraught, it feels like an ocean.

"I'm referring to *this* lifetime," I say, my voice quickening, rising, hoping to fill the void and lighten the mood. "And since I can't recall any of the others, it's all I have to go on. I just need a little more *time*, okay?" I smile nervously, my lips feeling clumsy and loose as I hold them still, exhaling in relief when he sits down beside me, lifting his fingers to my forehead and seeking the space where my scar used to be.

"Well, that's one thing we'll never run out of." He sighs, trailing his fingers down along the curve of my jaw as he leans in to kiss me, his lips making a series of pauses, from my forehead, to my nose, to my mouth.

And just when I think he's about to kiss me again, he squeezes my hand and moves away, heading straight for the door and leaving behind a beautiful red tulip in his place.

Visit **stmartins.com/AlysonNoel**
and sign up to receive more previews of *Blue Moon*